This fifth volume in the *Chrysalis* series of all-original science fiction stories once again presents the very best writing by recognized masters of the art, established professionals and brilliant newcomers. You can trust *Chrysalis 5* to tell you fourteen *good* stories by...

ORSON SCOTT CARD

SUSAN JANICE ANDERSON

CHARLES L. GRANT

HILBERT SCHENCK

ALAN RYAN

TIMOTHY ROBERT SULLIVAN

KARL HANSEN

PAT MURPHY

SOMTOW SUCHARITKUL

DAVID F. BISCHOFF

GLENN CHANG

BARRY MALZBERG

BILL PRONZINI

CHERRY WILDER

JAY A. PARRY

HAVE YOU READ THESE BEST-SELLING SCIENCE FICTION/SCIENCE FANTASY ANTHOLOGIES?

CHRYSALIS (287, $1.95)
edited by Roy Torgeson
The greatest anthology of original stories from the pens of the most talented sci-fi writers of this generation: Harlan Ellison, Theodore Sturgeon, Nebula Award winner Charles L. Grant, and other top storytellers.

SCIENCE AND SORCERY (345, $1.95)
compiled by Garrett Ford
Zoom to Mars to learn how an Earthman can become a Martian or take a train ride with a man who steals people for a new kingdom. Anything and everything is possible in this unique collection by top authors Ray Bradbury, Isaac Asimov, Frederik Pohl and Cordwainer Smith, plus many others.

SWORDS AGAINST DARKNESS (239, $1.95)
edited by Andrew J. Offutt
All-original tales of menace, high adventure and derring do make up this anthology of heroic fantasy, featuring novelets and stories by the great Robert E. Howard, Manly Wade Wellman, Poul Anderson, Ramsey Campbell, and many more . . . with a cover by the unsurpassable fantasy artist, Frank Frazetta.

SWORDS AGAINST DARKNESS II (293, $1.95)
edited by Andrew J. Offutt
Continuing the same outstanding success of the first, Volume II includes never-before-published novelets and stories by best-selling authors Andre Norton, Andrew J. Offutt, Manly Wade Wellman, and many others.

SWORDS AGAINST DARKNESS III (339, $1.95)
edited by Andrew J. Offutt
Here is Volume III in the highly successful SWORDS AGAINST DARKNESS anthologies, including first-time published short stories and novellas by best-selling writers Ramsey Campbell, Manly Wade Wellman, Richard L. Tierney, Poul Anderson, plus 9 others!

Available wherever paperbacks are sold, or order direct from the Publisher. Send cover price plus 35¢ per copy for mailing and handling, to Zebra Books, 21 East 40th Street, New York, N.Y. 10016. DO NOT SEND CASH!

CHRYSALIS 5

EDITED BY ROY TORGESON

ZEBRA BOOKS
KENSINGTON PUBLISHING CORP.

ZEBRA BOOKS

are published by

KENSINGTON PUBLISHING CORP.
21 East 40th Street
New York, N.Y. 10016

Copyright © 1979 by Roy Torgeson

INTRODUCTION copyright © 1979 by Roy Torgeson
ADAGIO AND BENEDICTION copyright © 1979 by Orson Scott Card
RETURNING TO CENTER copyright © 1979 by Susan Janice Anderson
AND WEARY OF THE SUN copyright © 1979 by Charles L. Grant
WAVE RIDER copyright © 1979 by Hilbert Schenck
SHEETS copyright © 1979 by Alan Ryan
MY FATHER'S HEAD copyright © 1979 by Timothy Robert Sullivan
PORTRAIT FOR A BLIND MAN copyright © 1979 by Karl Hansen
NIGHTBIRD AT THE WINDOW copyright © 1979 by Pat Murphy
COMETS AND KINGS copyright © 1979 by Somtow Sucharitkul
ALL THE STAGE, A WORLD copyright © 1979 by David F. Bischoff
THE FACES OF MEN copyright © 1979 by Glenn Chang
READING DAY copyright © 1979 by Barry Malzberg and Bill Pronzini
A LONG, BRIGHT DAY BY THE SEA OF UTNER copyright © 1979 by Cherry Wilder
GODS IN THE FIRE, GODS IN THE RAIN copyright © 1979 by Jay A. Parry

Cover art copyright © 1979 by Carl Kochich

All rights reserved. No part of this book may be reproduced in any form or by any means without the prior written consent of the Publisher, excepting brief quotes used in reviews.

First Printing: September, 1979

Printed in the United States of America

For Margot
 who wore a diaphanous white Halston
 and for Real Fantasy
 which, alas, is all too rare
 which is all too rare

CONTENTS

INTRODUCTION 9
Roy Torgeson

ADAGIO AND BENEDICTION 17
Orson Scott Card

RETURNING TO CENTER 29
Susan Janice Anderson

AND WEARY OF THE SUN 49
Charles L. Grant

WAVE RIDER 70
Hilbert Schenck

SHEETS 89
Alan Ryan

MY FATHER'S HEAD 104
Timothy Robert Sullivan

PORTRAIT FOR A BLIND MAN 142
Karl Hansen

NIGHTBIRD AT THE WINDOW 159
Pat Murphy

COMETS AND KINGS 171
Somtow Sucharitkul

ALL THE STAGE, A WORLD 191
  David F. Bischoff

THE FACES OF MEN.....................202
  Glenn Chang

READING DAY 245
  Barry Malzberg and Bill Pronzini

A LONG, BRIGHT DAY BY THE SEA
  OF UTNER 250
  Cherry Wilder

GODS IN THE FIRE, GODS IN
  THE RAIN 261
  Jay A. Parry

INTRODUCTION

by

Roy Torgeson

A renaissance is taking place in the science fiction field; the rebirth of the original anthology. When *Chrysalis 1* was published two years ago, "people who knew" said that there would never be a *Chrysalis 2* because the original anthology was dead and no one was writing short fiction anyway. They were wrong. This is the fifth volume in the *Chrysalis* series, two more are in the works and other publishers are starting their own series. The original anthology market is very much alive and, partially as a result of this, authors are writing dynamite short fiction. I think that the success of the *Chrysalis* series had a lot to do with reviving this endangered species.

Whenever a renaissance takes place, the people involved have the freedom to experiment. My publisher has placed no restrictions upon me and I have imposed no limitations upon writers. On the contrary, I have encouraged them to write whatever was in their heads, however unusual it might be. My only criteria for selecting stories for inclusion in the *Chrysalis* series is that the authors involved must tell me good stories, dynamite stories. They have and that is why the *Chrysalis* series is the most varied and, in my opinion, the best original science fiction anthology.

Now for a few words about the authors and their stories:

Since Orson Scott Card's first sale in 1976, he has sold thirty-seven stories. Also, a collection and two novels, *Capitol, Hot Sleep* and *A Planet Called Treason* have been published this year while another collection and novel, *Monkey Sonatas* and *Mikal's Songbird* are already scheduled for publication in 1980. Along the way, he won the 1978 John W. Campbell Award and earned nominations for both the 1979 Nebula and Hugo Awards. *Adagio and Benediction* is a philosophical story dealing with the roles of intellect and feeling. The story of Delot Bramwi's search for wisdom and the "reward" fate grants him will make you feel both proud and humble to be a human being.

Returning to Center by Susan Janice Anderson is a story. That is, it has a beginning, a middle and an end. However, like *The Fossil* in *Chrysalis 3*, it is more than a good story. In it, Susan has captured a mood or feeling which lingers with the reader well after completing the story.

And Weary of the Sun by Charles L. Grant is a contemporary urban fantasy dealing with the everyday frustrations and fears which all of us experience. Charlie is a master of this fantasy form and his writing is an excellent example of the way in which good fantasy literature can capture the emotions of the real world fare more efficiently and powerfully than so-called realistic fiction.

Hilbert Schenck is Head of the Oceanographic Department at Rhode Island University and the author of many books on oceanography and scuba diving. Fortunately, for the past year he has also been using his expert knowledge of the sea to write science fiction. *Wave Rider* contains much fascinating scientific information and it probably could be classified as "hard" science fiction. However, the story itself is a deeply moving tale of a man and his ship joined in a final attempt to master the seas. Later this year, a collection of Schenck's stories about the sea will be published under the title, *Wave Rider*.

Formerly an English teacher and now a full-time writer and book reviewer, Alan Ryan once sold sheets at Macy's. It was only a brief interlude between careers, but the memory lingered on. *Sheets* is the literary exorcism of this memory. It is a chilling horror story about the utter madness involved with working at a soul-destroying job. After reading it, you might want to check out the kind of sheets you have on your bed, just in case.

Timothy Robert Sullivan's first two sales were to that marvelous magazine of science fiction discoveries, *Unearth* and his third was to *New Dimensions 9*. *My*

Father's Head is Tim's fourth sale and it is truly phantasmagoric. He draws the reader into the horrifying alien world he has created, even to the point of accepting, as a given, the terrible moral imperative of the human society inhabiting it and feeling a deep personal involvement with the hero in his ghoulish quest. Talk about suspension of disbelief!

A medical doctor who planned to turn full-time writer this July, Karl Hansen has been called back to active duty with the Indian Health Service, to serve as a Medicine Man for the Mountain Ute Nation in the foothills of the San Juan Mountains in Colorado. I hope that he is soon released from involuntary servitude because he can write like a demon. (If you have read Karl's previous stories in the *Chrysalis* series, I'm sure that you will appreciate my choice of the word, "demon.") *Portrait for a Blind Man* is an analogy to the Viet Nam fiasco, showing what could happen if war lasted indefinitely. The problem with prolonged warfare is mental, so if minds can be hardened, war can go on forever. But a price will be paid.

When not writing fiction, Pat Murphy writes and edits scientific articles on sundry subjects. Her latest article includes the astonishing fact that if a chicken had the same growth potential as a tuna, a single chicken could provide enough meat to feed 100,000 people. *Nightbird at the Window* is Pat's third sale. Her fourth sale was to Charlie Grant for *Shadows 3* and, I'm happy to say, her fifth sale will appear in *Imaginary Worlds*, my new original fantasy anthology. *Nightbird at the Window* is an eerie fantasy concerning twin brothers, one who dreams hideous nightmares and the other who sleeps dreamlessly . . . until one night the roles are reversed.

At the age of twenty-six, Somtow Sucharitkul has already gained a considerable reputation as a composer, conductor and scholar in the contemporary music field. A native Thai, Somtow has lived in England, Japan, Holland, France and the U.S., and at the moment he commutes between Bangkok and Washington, D.C. How he finds time to write science fiction and fantasy I do not know, but I'm glad that he does. He possesses a remarkably keen "sense of story" and a classical sense of imagery. *Comets and Kings* is a truly beautiful story in which Somtow portrays Alexander the Great with compassion and understanding. It captures the soul of this man who would conquer the world.

David F. Bischoff is a young writer who is going places. Two of his novels, *Nightworld* and *Tin Woodman* (with Dennis Bailey), have been published this year and a third, *Star Fall*, is scheduled for 1980. *All the Stage, A World* stems from Dave's interest in literature as a philosophical tool and Shakespeare's *Hamlet* as a political essay. In part, it is a most unusual explication of the play while, at the same time, metaphorically reflecting a stark vision of a frightening future.

The Faces of Men by Glenn Chang is a beautifully written anthropological story. In addition, it goes much deeper than the stereotypical variety which Chad Oliver, in particular, pretty much took to its limits in the fifties and early sixties. It explores the notion that we are all aliens to someone, even ourselves at times.

Barry N. Malzberg and Bill Pronzini have collaborated on three suspense novels, most recently *Night*

Screams, three science fiction anthologies, including *Shared Tomorrows*, and twenty-five short stories, which have appeared in leading science fiction and mystery magazines. On their own, both are writers of considerable talent. Barry has published a long list of science fiction stories and novels, and he was the recipient of the first John W. Campbell Award for his novel, *Beyond Apollo*. Bill has published more than a dozen mystery novels and is a two-time winner of the Mystery Writers of America Award, the Edgar. *Reading Day* is a very short, short story, but it conveys a potent message to all of us who love to read.

Cherry Wilder's *A Long, Bright Day by the Sea of Utner* is a science fiction fairy tale, told from the perspective of a "magical creature." Written with great tenderness, it is a finely polished little gem. I am happy to say that it is just the first in a series of stories concerning a castaway civilization of humans on a strange planet of landlocked seas and curious life forms.

Jay A. Parry is an associate editor of *Ensign*, a slick monthly magazine primarily serving the members of the Mormon Church. His first science fiction sale was a collaboration with Orson Scott Card, but *Gods in the Fire, Gods in the Rain* is his first solo sale. The setting is a small Midwestern town. The time is the not-so-distant future after the total economic collapse of the country. The mood and feeling conveyed is reminiscent of Ray Bradbury's best work.

Again I thank the authors for letting me share in their creativity, and my special thanks to Carl Kochich, whose cover painting captures the essence of this anthology: a combination of science fiction and fantasy.

>Roy Torgeson
>New York City
>July, 1979

ADAGIO AND BENEDICTION

by

Orson Scott Card

Delot Bramwi is dead. To me, the loss is more personal than to most people whose lives he touched; but I do not plan to write of my grief. He would have called my grief trivial; or else he would have said it was far too important to entrust to mere words.

I write by way of a preface to Delot Bramwi's last work. He knew of his coming death months before, and he conceived a project of breathtaking scope—and he failed. But in the failure he also created this small testimony, which is perhaps a more fitting capstone to the monument to himself that his life already was. It is a small work, as, in the end, we saw that Father Delot was a small man; not small among men, of course, for mankind is not noted for high concentrations of greatness among the general population, but rather he was small as all of us are small, when pitted against such powers as death and decay and sorrow. But he hoped.

The hagiography is already begun. Stories of his remarkable feats of mind when he was four or five years old already circulate among the people who already say *Delot* as if the name were not a common one. Intellectuals prefer higher folklore; historians have the true tales, which are no less remarkable than the invented ones, because all tell a kind of truth of the man.

I will tell only two stories in my preface, hoping I do not write more to introduce his last words than he wrote himself.

My father was one of the first merit prefects; and after Delot's descension from power, my father brought me, at age eleven, to Father Delot's school.

"It is my daughter, Lovina," he said, and Delot nodded. But Delot's assistant, a grim young man named Soren Tuk, shook his head.

"I have her tests," he said coldly, "and they do not merit consideration for this school."

I understood enough to know that he was saying I was not bright enough to enter. My father was distressed. Soren seemed ready for an argument. Only Delot was calm.

"I will not try to change your mind then," my father said, knowing that Father Delot was incorruptible, even by friendship.

"Wait," said Father Delot.

"You can't," said Soren, "be thinking of making an exception for such an unremarkable child."

"Lovina," said Delot to me, and I came forward. He put his left hand on my cheek and his right hand on the back of my neck, cradling my head and making me feel both confident and excited, though I was rather young to realize the implications of who he was. "Young girl," he said, "do you see my dilemma? I love your father very much—there is nothing I would deny him that is in my power to give. Yet when I set up this school, it was to be for remarkable children—children like Soren— who have the potential in their minds for solving the world's problems. How can I violate my standards? Do you understand?"

I nodded.

"Then tell me what I should do," he said, "and I will abide by your decision, if I can."

And so I thought. And at eleven I was a keen-witted child in a way—but not so keen-witted that solutions sprang full-blown into my mind. So I spoke staggeringly. I remember the ideas, and I will set them down clearly here, but at the time I did not speak half so well.

"My father knows that he has your love, so that if you deny him his request, he will know that you did not do it to hurt him, and so he will not be hurt.

"Your school has a purpose, and taking me in would not fulfill that purpose, but would instead distract from it. Therefore, to be kind to me would be cruelty to the other children you have taken in, and the greater good would be to refuse me.

"And as for me, I know I am not brilliant or exceptional. I did not ask to be brought to this school. I came because I love my father, and he wants me to be the kind of girl who can enter a school like this. But it isn't my fault or your fault if I am not."

Although I spoke haltingly, Father Delot smiled when I was through and turned to Soren. "There are kinds of wisdom your tests don't uncover, Child Soren," he said. And he smiled at my father and told him he would gladly take me into his school.

Since that time Soren's tests have proved correct. Intellectually I am far from being the equal of even the least bright of Father Delot's students. But despite this, Father Delot left me in joint control of the school with Soren. Why? There are obvious speculations, but this one fact is certain: Father Delot does not judge people as others do.

And another anecdote:

A famous artist from Selway came to Father Delot once when he reigned as Lycurgus from Talloman Hartwith. The artist demanded that the national-level prefectures be abolished. "They have too much power over the day-to-day lives of the people," declared the artist.

"There is no power," answered Delot, "except over the day-to-day lives of the people—unless you find a race that lives year to year. Power is only over people's acts, and they act day to day."

"The NLPs have too broad a discretionary power," insisted the artist. "There is nothing to stop them from declaring a particular person a threat to the society and banning him, without any reason at all. They have the potential for tyranny. They have nearly absolute power, and absolute power corrupts absolutely."

Then Delot answered with an answer that I believe is typical of the way he dealt with all such questions:

"The fact that a saying is ancient does not make it true. The truth is that the absolutely corrupt must also corrupt all their powerful acts. In ancient times, power went to those who sought it; the seeking of power itself is corrupt; hence that saying had the appearance of wisdom, just as some people thought the crowing of the cock brought the sunrise.

"The national-level prefects are chosen against their will. They despise power and have better things to do with their time than to govern. Because of this, I am aware of no case where a prefect has even approached the limits of his power. Do you have any examples of abuse?"

"It is the potential for abuse," said the artist, "that frightens me."

At this Delot laughed, and finally said, "My friend, you are an artist. Do you believe that art has an effect on people?"

"Yes."

"Does it change their nature or their behavior?"

"It does, but it is not *political*."

"True. It is much stronger than mere political power. For where governments can only affect the way their citizens act, artists change the ways in which people think and feel. Furthermore, artists can do this with their audience being scarcely aware that any such change is happening."

"You overestimate our ability."

"You underestimate my power of observation. Those who hunger after power used to go into politics. But those who lust after power so much that they are unwilling to compromise and therefore cannot succeed in politics, those become artists. They are far more dangerous than any politician.

"And yet. There is not enough beauty in the universe. So we tolerate your power because of the gifts you give us. If we removed or limited your power, we would lose your gifts, wouldn't we?"

"If you grant that we have such power, yes."

"The gift of government is domestic peace and international security, without making it excessively difficult for people to enjoy life. Your prefect must have power to give that gift. His is an art, too. You are only jealous because he is able to succeed more often than you are. A society in which the artists control the public is as dangerous as a society in which the government controls the artists."

And the interview ended.

Why I chose these two incidents I do not know; but both stories I know to be true, and to me they express the essence of Delot Bramwi. The disease that killed him also took his mind. But the brief testimony that follows is, perhaps, his clearest statement. Though the subtleties of philosophy were already beyond him, his human emotions were, I believe, never clearer. Perhaps in losing his mind he found his heart; but that implies that it was at one time unfound. And that I know was never the case. He always hoped.

His words:

The disease is such that the man who has it does not know that his mental powers are failing. He does not feel his brain deteriorate. He does not see the foolishness of his ideas. In short, he blissfully loses his mind without mourning, and only those around him see, and understand, and weep the loss.

Most men, therefore, are not told when they contract the illness. I, however, am Delot Bramwi; the legend has it that I will not eschew truth whatever the pain it costs. Therefore the timid physicians collectively screwed up their courage and informed me that within the next year my mind would deteriorate and I would become a mental three-year-old, happily sucking my thumb as I died.

It was not cheerful news, but I am able to bear many things well. I took it, not as a condemnation, but rather as a reprieve. Instead of death and madness taking me by surprise, I would have the jump on them. I had time to do a Work.

Not a monument to make sure my name would stand forever. My name shall already stand forever. From the time the Council of Worlds petitioned me, sued me, pleaded with me to take the mantle of Lycurgus and build the human universe again into an edifice that would both endure forever and make life worth living for as many individuals as possible, it was plain that in the success or failure of my work, the very audacity of the project would guarantee my fame.

And after thirty-one years as dictator of mankind, I had constructed on the wreckage of the sleepy old empire a new order. When I saw that the machine was capable of running itself, I voluntarily left the seat of power and returned to my home, to my small school, to the disciples who thought I had something left to teach them, to my friends who wisely knew that I had much love left to take and give.

So the Work I resolved to do was not one to build my name. Rather I resolved that I would write what no other human being could write: the treatise on the ultimate truth of the human condition. If this is hubris, tell me who had a better training.

I have met every possible problem that can come before a magistrate, and I have solved it, not just for my time, but for future generations.

I have tasted and used absolute power, and I have surrendered it and felt the helplessness of the king shorn of royalty.

I have been hated, loved, feared, resented, despised, and worshipped, and I am not, or at least was not, insane.

For these reasons, I thought I understood something of the truth, and so I began to write. I confided my project in only a few disciples, and for days and hours and weeks and months I spoke within the confines of my office the words that would be assembled into the perfect masterpiece of wisdom.

I wax ironic.

What gives a man reputation for wisdom? I claimed none at first, just operated my little school. And yet, somehow, when those encumbered with the burden of government reached their most desperate hour, realizing that the worlds of men were ungovernable by mutual consent, my reputation for wisdom was such that they decided, without interview, without study, without even much thought, that I would be the god in the machine, that I would come to them and hold the Furies at bay until, at last, the peace of the eternities could come to them.

Whether that reputation for wisdom was deserved or not at the start, when my thirty-one years of government ended I felt that I had, after all, found wisdom as a result of carrying out the work for which wisdom had been thought to be prerequisite.

That was what I tried to write. And as the words flowed from my lips, I marveled at the wisdom of them. Thought led to thought, idea to word, sound to song, mood to vivid passion, until the whole of me, and all the contents of my mind, were set into the tapes, ready for editing.

And then I called to me my two most devoted disciples: Soren Tuk, a man of keen wit and cruel insight, who could slay a lie almost before it had been uttered, and Lovina N, a woman of compelling kindness, who could comfort the dead and bring peace to the madman's heart.

They had been hearing my words almost as I uttered them for all the months of my Work, and I planned to charge them with its preparation for publication.

"You will put commas where the commas ought to be; you will take my thoughts and order them where order demands they fit." And they nodded, and were ready to agree.

But I have respect for their minds, and so I also asked a question.

"Child Soren," I asked, "what do you think of what I have written?"

He did not answer.

And in his silence I heard a terrible roar. I heard again all the frivolity of my life. I remembered, oddly, that I had fathered eleven children in eleven of the most intelligent women I could find, and had called it my own private program of eugenics. Where were these children? Why was I unable to find them and cling to them and force them to keep at bay the terrible truth that waited in Child Soren's silence?

"You keep silence," I said, "and therefore it is doubly important that you speak."

Lovina shook her head and stared intently at Child Soren, and so I demanded that Soren tell me, and he told me:

"Father Delot, you were too late. The disease has outstripped you. Your clarity is gone. There is neither logic nor progression in your final work. There is no insight that has not been worn out long ago by thin minds and easy speakers. Your final wisdom is only the foolishness of an old man about to die."

"It isn't true," cried Lovina, to protect me.

But Child Soren said to her, and his voice was fervent, exalted: "All his life Father Delot has lived for truth. Do I betray him this near his death with a lie?"

And so we stayed in silence, and at last I found what I truly wanted to do, and I said, "Fix the commas, then, Child Soren, and place the manuscript before the scholars. It will have value as a lesson in decay, and it may be compared with my works in days when my mind was clear and my creation was great."

And then they left me alone, and I sat in darkness in the office that existed only to capture all my words and preserve them forever. And now it is morning, and I have sat through the night, and I realize that where I thought to leave a testament, I can only leave a testimony; I am a witness without the wit to add to the sum of human knowledge. Will even these words, then, be valueless?

It doesn't matter. I will say them:

Truth is a search, not a finding, and in the last of my life I am losing all that I had found. That is the bitterest truth of my life. Child Soren cut me to the heart with truth; my blood is on the floor and I haven't the courage to taste it, to swallow it, to make it part of me again. I am beaten. I have failed.

All my life I hated flattery; yet now I realize that it is not the lie that is cruel, but the discovery of the lie. Because my mind's death is so near, there would have been no discovery and hence no cruelty had Child Soren lied to me; I would never have felt the agony of trust broken. The lie would have been my comfort as I lost all that had made my life worth living; and comfort, however arrived at, is beauty, which transcends mere accuracy of detail. The truth of a thing is higher than its facts.

I would have wished to die happily; now I will die with failure overriding all my accomplishments.

And yet.

And yet I now wonder if we did not find the highest truth of all, yesterday: that my writing was indeed my testament, that the vague and confused and contradictory and hackneyed ideas in it were in fact the compost which gave fertility to all my acts. What if my reputation for wisdom was unearned, and the foolishness of my final Work was all I ever had within me?

Does my former work then topple? Do nations divide away, does oppression recommence, is despair once more the order of the worlds of men? Does the unworthiness of the builder undermine the beauty of that which he built?

That would be foolishness.

The only wisdom I had was to believe that I could do the work I was asked to do; what I did could have been done, therefore, by any equally foolish man. I acted, and my act will have its effects long after my words have been forgotten.

And so I say to Child Soren: Revere the living acts of undespairing men. These are the only truth that is inviolable.

I say good to the universe; I laugh and cry and clap as the music goes adagio through its inconsistent songs; selah to my life; amen to all lives; and if this, too, is foolishness, then treasure it for love of my own wizened beauty, for that will remain even after my thought is, finally, gone.

I am three years old at last, and I will play.

RETURNING TO CENTER

by

Susan Janice Anderson

To Bob and Erland

By twilight, the Senior Educator and I had nearly reached the tide pools. But I was unable to share in Jonathan's enthusiasm, my mind still on the co-opers.

"Wonder if I'll understand them any better after my next Wandering," I said, half to myself.

"Don't think it gets any easier as you get older," said Jonathan, shaking his head. "We've grown too far from our origins."

I wanted to ask more but the subject seemed to

bother him. Senior Educators rarely liked to talk about the origin of Center.

"We're almost at the tide pools now," said Jonathan, his face brightening.

I watched his weathered features—the intricate lines a map of his long travels and introspection—and I wondered how I would look several Wanderings hence. We had arrived at the tide pools now, and, for the moment, all conversation about the co-opers was forgotten. More like a child than a Senior Educator, Jonathan rushed from the van, his arms waving wildly. I groaned inwardly, knowing we wouldn't leave for hours. Right now I longed for nothing more than a good night's sleep.

"Crazy biologists," I grumbled, "they're insatiable. We mythmakers need a chance to rest now and then."

"Rosanna, Rosanna of the Wind," Jonathan yelled, "come out here. So many fascinating organisms."

By the time I started out over the slippery rock, Jon was almost out of sight.

"Only one last co-op," I told myself, yawning, "then back to Center."

The thought of the blue-green forests momentarily revived me. Once I had rested up I could begin work on my myth, the creative expression of all I had experienced on my Wanderings. But like a dark dissonant note, the image of the co-opers entered my mind, clouding and confusing my imaginings.

I followed my reflection in the water, watching the brownish tints of my skin blend into the reddish orange of the setting sun. Orange starfish floated in geometric dance past prickly sea urchins. I walked as lightly as I could, aware that under my feet sea grasses breathed and limpets and mussels awaited the coming tide. A careless step could crush a snail's translucent shell or rip algae from their precarious rootings. And as some people gather seashells, I gathered images that I could weave into my myth.

"Hurry up, old sea crab," I yelled affectionately at Jonathan but the waves drowned out my words.

Shells glistened in the tide pools, almost all fragments. I caught sight of mother-of-pearl, tinted faint green by sea moss. My hand reached through myriad strands of interwoven life, stirring up clouds of sand and sending small organisms scurrying. I held the shell briefly up to the reddish light, then let it slip through my fingers, a tiny meteor rushing toward a watery sky.

No telling yet what form my myth would take. I never knew in advance which language the images would choose. Sometimes they flowed forth as dance or song, sometimes in words and pictures. But only in the calm introspective environment of Center could my myth begin to emerge. How many images from the natural world I had gathered in our months of Wandering, always punctuated by the long dark silences of the co-opers.

"Rosanna, look what I've found," called Jonathan.

I hurried over slippery rocks, trying not to lose my footing. Now Jonathan was becoming a tiny shadow fading into twilight. He was holding something in his hand, his eyes wide with excitement. At first, I could see nothing. Then I made out the outlines of a shell, so thin it was almost transparent. And I saw small gesticulating claws.

"A ghost shrimp," said Jon, "and these are its swimmerets."

I watched the tiny limbs open and close, helpless in a sea of air. For a moment, I wearied of our endless Wanderings and wanted nothing more than to return to the blue-green forests of Center, where most journeys are inner ones. The ghost shrimp was calmer now, its feelers inquisitively exploring the surface of Jon's hand.

Yet who's to say, I thought, what images the next few days may bring?

Gently, Jonathan placed the ghost shrimp on a rock and it scurried away into the darkening water.

Mist covered the coast as we drove onward the next morning. Finally the sun emerged, revealing wet mossy cliffs and dark trees. Beyond, the ocean stretched silver into the distance.

"The last co-op," said Jon as we turned off the main road.

The familiar feeling of frustration hit me, coupled with a desire to find out as much as I could on this last visit. We headed up a dirt road that seemed to wind endlessly into the mountains. For several miles, we saw no signs of animal life except for an occasional black-tailed deer or a rabbit. For awhile, I forgot about the co-op and was a little startled when we reached a gate.

"No more Wanderings for another six months," said Jon, his voice tinged with regret.

And though this was only my first Wandering, I understood some of his ambivalence. I would miss the freedom of continual movement, unhindered by fixed place or possessions, the ever-changing stream of images. Yet, more and more frequently now, Center filled my dreams. And when I would eventually grow weary of the deep meditative calm, a new Wandering would begin. But if only I could go a little farther before this first Wandering ended.

Jumping out of the van, I flung open the gate, mentally preparing myself for yet another encounter with the polite but distant co-opers. A woman was walking toward me. Though she was hardly older than myself, her hands and forearms looked weathered and toughened from long hours of outdoor work.

"New here, aren't you?" she said with a directness that surprised me.

I nodded. "My first Wandering."

We walked toward a building made of roughly hewn wood, almost totally devoid of ornamentation except for a few carvings and an occasional pane of stained glass. And as I had noticed in the other co-ops, even the architecture reflected the sparse lives of the co-opers. How different from the intricately carved walls of Center, the tapestries and the gardens. Jon joined us and we headed into the main building.

"Can't take much time off," the woman said as she poured tea. "We've got a lot of work left on the garden and we're hoping there won't be an early frost this year."

"Don't let us interfere with your work, Tanya," said Jonathan.

"That's okay," she said, "I needed a break." Turning to me she asked, "So how does Wandering suit you?"

"Not bad," I answered. Emboldened by Tanya's openness and curiosity, I began to say more than usual. "There's a lot that still puzzles me about your way of life. As a mythmaker, I keep feeling I know almost nothing about . . ."

33

A warning look from Jonathan stopped me. Noticing his discomfort, Tanya pretended not to have heard me and began talking about the crops. Eventually she rose to return to the garden.

"Better give the two of you a chance to rest up and prepare for this evening," she said.

When she had left, I turned to Jonathan. "Why did you stop me? She seemed willing to talk about their mythology."

He looked at me for a long time. "We've come to educate, not to reopen old wounds. Delving deeper can only cause pain."

And just as when I questioned him about the origins of Center, I sensed that the pain he spoke of was his own.

"Come, Rosanna," he said gently, "help me arrange the specimens."

And as I touched iridescent shells and traced the structure of branching seaweed, for awhile I again became absorbed in the world of images.

"So," Jonathan was saying, "our own life cycle is closely interwoven with the life cycles of all other organisms and therefore . . ."

As Jon spoke, I watched the campfire light flicker over the faces of the co-opers. How distant they all seemed as though my travels over the past months had taught me almost nothing about their inner thoughts and feelings, their dreams and mythologies. Politely, they listened to Jonathan, their weathered features rarely betraying their reactions. Only Tanya seemed unafraid to show her emotions. Her eyes intent, sometimes she would nod enthusiastically, sometimes shake her head.

"Walk lightly as you explore the tide pools, for even on the rocks beneath your feet, myriad life forms await the coming tide, dependent on the subtle interaction between temperature and . . ."

As my turn approached, I began to experience my habitual nervousness. Would the images flow forth freely? How would my audience receive them? I looked over at Tanya who smiled and winked. Thankful for at least one sympathetic face, I took my place by the campfire.

"There are many ways to perceive the natural world and integrate ourselves into the larger cycle of life," I began, my voice thin and trembling. "My way is through images."

As words and song rushed forth, gradually the circle of faces around me faded and I began to flow with the tides and the sun. I sang of geological ages of molten rock and inland seas, of mountains lifting up and glaciers sculpting U-shaped valleys. Seas evaporated and reformed and, like branches on a tree, myriad organisms stretched forth. I danced over tide pools and onto the new earth. Glaciers melted in cascading streams of blue-white water and mosses grew on the wet rock. In rain forests and deserts, animal and plant life proliferated in endless modulations. And our planet moved, a glittering dot of light, through a sea of alien worlds. Cosmic tides brought forth new stars and carried others into darkness.

I sang of Center and the alternating cycles of studying and Wandering, of the harmonious union of the natural world and the human consciousness. And I sang of the co-ops we had visited, of the different ways of life we had observed. Usually I stopped at this point, but then I caught sight of Tanya's face. There was a curious intensity to it that reminded me of our conversation that afternoon, of the question she had pretended not to hear. And seeing that Jonathan was absorbed in his own thoughts, I asked that question again, but this time indirectly, through images.

I sang of the mythmaker's work, of gathering images and piecing them together. And very lightly I touched on the areas of darkness, the parts of the myth that still remained incomplete. Almost imperceptibly, I saw Tanya nod. Then our presentations were over and co-opers gathered around, their reserve finally broken. Eagerly they examined specimens, asked questions, and told us of their own experiences. Simultaneously drained and revived, we finally rose. Just as we were leaving, Tanya drew me aside.

"To meet our mythmakers," she whispered, "you must travel into the shadow of the mountain."

I wanted to ask more but saw Jonathan watching me, his eyes both curious and troubled.

That night I dreamed I was back at Center, beginning work on my myth. Soft grasses surrounded me, their feathery heads bending in the wind. Beyond stretched the blue-green forests and the buildings of Center, their walls covered with the carvings of countless mythmakers. Putting my instrument to my lips, I began to play. Clear notes flowed forth, tracing an endless multiplicity of images. Like clouds they moved across a rapidly changing sky. Sunset blended into sunrise, forest into ocean, each co-op into a larger whole, all bound together by the course of our

Wanderings. But as my tone poem reached the last co-op, the notes stopped and I could play no further. Like a wall of solid rock, the barrier stretched in front of me, silencing my myth.

Putting my instrument aside, I spread pieces of fabric over the grass, fitting colors and shapes to the images of my myth. But one space remained blank, and the absence of form and color began to dominate the larger whole. Again, like the impenetrable surface of a mountain, the barrier stopped me. But this time, instead of turning away, I stared even more intensely into the emptiness. As I looked more closely, I could make out tiny pinpoints of light in the darkness. Then the clearing and Center began to vanish. I was standing under a nighttime sky, distant stars dimly illuminating a barren landscape.

Beneath my bare feet, I felt pulverized earth. Above me stretched a mountain and I stood cloaked in its shadow. I began to dance, translating the images of my myth into movement. Shadows whirled around me, tracing alien patterns over my arms and legs. Wordlessly I leaped, my body reaching toward the mountain. And when I again touched earth, I saw I had been dancing on the edge of a precipice.

Trembling, I bent over and looked into the abyss. At first I saw only darkness, then the faint glimmer of water, like the entrance to a subterranean lake.

"To meet our mythmakers," came Tanya's voice, "you must travel into the shadow of the mountain."

"Our work here's done," said Jonathan. "It's time to return to Center. Forget about the co-oper mythmakers."

"But I have to see them to complete my myth," I argued.

Seeing I wasn't to be dissuaded, he shook his head sadly. "They dwell on things that are better forgotten."

"What kinds of things?"

"You'd only be inflicting needless suffering on yourself."

"What kinds of things?" I insisted.

He didn't answer. "It's time to go back, our Wandering's over."

"I don't want to return with fragments," I said angrily.

"Sometimes fragments are better than..." he began.

"What are you so afraid of?" I blurted out.

When I saw the pain my words caused him, I instantly regretted the question. Suddenly the lines in Jonathan's face made him look old and tired. He turned and looked at me with great sadness.

"Strange," he said, almost to himself, "how our origins never seem to let go of us no matter how hard we try to run from them."

I watched Jonathan struggle inwardly. Frightened, I wanted to say something that would alleviate his pain. But the process that I had inadvertently set into motion now proceeded to conclusion. For a long time Jon sat very still, head bowed. When he finally looked up, I could see that his eyes were moist.

"We thought only of replanting," he said, "of covering the scars and hiding the ugliness."

"Please," I said quickly, "I don't have to go. Let's forget it."

"No," he said, so softly I could hardly hear him.

"Both of us will go."

My throat tightened and I shook my head. "It isn't necessary," I said, "Tanya's agreed to show me the way."

"I'm going for my sake as much as yours," he said. "It's time I uncovered the roots again."

Questions raced through my mind as we started out with Tanya the next morning. But remembering Jonathan's pain, I was silent. We drove in the co-op van, a rusty affair that bounced every time we hit a rough spot in the road. At first we passed through thick forests that reminded me of Center but as we began to climb, the vegetation grew sparser and solid cliffs of granite emerged. Occasionally we saw a grove of bleached trees, their lifeless branches twisted into grotesque configurations.

"Turnoff's not far from here," said Tanya. "It's not a very well-traveled road."

"Don't the mythmakers ever visit the co-op?"

She looked at me strangely. "They never leave the mountain," she said. "It's a place where they feel closest to the source of their powers."

I wondered silently how one could ever grow close to granite cliffs that seemed almost totally devoid of life except for a few straggling pines.

Reaching the trail head, we shouldered our packs. We crossed a meadow of subalpine vegetation, pale yellow flowers, clusters of purple blossoms, tight bunches of grasses.

"Glacier and avalanche lilies," said Jonathan excitedly. "We're very fortunate to have hit their brief flowering season."

I winked at Tanya. Now absorbed in the myriad wildflowers, for a moment, at least, Jonathan seemed to have forgotten his pain. Soon, however, I began to pay more attention to my aching muscles and labored breathing than to Jon.

We left the meadow and began climbing over crumbly yellowish soil toward a ridge. Almost no vegetation was visible now, and I remembered what Jonathan had said about the short and precarious growing season of the subalpine. Even the slightest variation in temperature or moisture could destroy the delicate plants. For a moment, I felt uneasy. Then we reached the top of the ridge where we stopped for awhile to rest. Tiny purple flowers and Indian paintbrush clung tenaciously to the small bits of soil between the boulders.

"There's a way station on the other side where we can have lunch," said Tanya.

At the mention of the way station, Jonathan's face grew tense.

"Yes," he said, "I spent many hours at that station."

We continued to wind around the ridge. The path turned abruptly, ending in large lichenous boulders. For several feet, we made our way over jagged rock. Then suddenly the trail reemerged. Now we encountered patches of snow, some tinted pink. Tanya scooped up a cupful.

"You have to avoid the red stuff," she explained. "It's a sort of bacteria that lives in the meltwater."

Then ahead of us loomed a house on stilts built on the very edge of the mountain. As we climbed the stairs, I remembered my dream of the precipice. Though the shelter was neatly stocked with bedding and food supplies, there was no one in sight. Jon entered first, opening cabinets and drawers with a familiar hand.

"We would spend hours watching clouds come over the mountain," he said softly. "Toward afternoon, the goats would come out, then the marmots. So quiet and peaceful until . . ." He broke off and I could see his eyes were moist.

"Until what?" I asked softly.

He pointed into the ravine. "The story lies there," he said, "down there with the mythmakers."

Looking down I could see the distant gleam of water flowing past shadowy rocks.

"I can only take you as far as the river," Tanya said. "Beyond that, you must find your own way."

"Why?" I asked, suddenly apprehensive.

"My time has not yet come to meet the mythmakers," she said and something in her words made me shiver.

"But why are we allowed to go?"

"You come from the outside and you too are a mythmaker. He," she gestured at Jonathan, "has already been once before."

The shale crumbled and slipped as we headed down the mountain and we had to grasp hold of roots and boulders. Half running, half sliding, we reached the bottom, raising great clouds of dust. We sat down on moss-covered rocks and splashed cool water over our hands and faces.

As I listened to the music of the river, I noticed a series of evenly placed stones and logs forming a sort of natural bridge. A light mist rose from the water, partially obscuring the opposite bank.

"How much further?" I asked Tanya.

She shrugged. "That depends."

"On what?"

"The mythmakers choose their own time to appear. All you can do is follow the trail."

Silently we watched water flow over rocks toward an unknown destination. Then Tanya rose and headed back up the mountain. We watched her sturdy frame climb over boulders until she disappeared over the ridge.

"Come," said Jonathan, without hesitation.

We headed toward the natural bridge. Stepping from stone to stone, we made our way over to the opposite bank. Ducking our heads under low branches, we moved onto the shadow side of the mountain.

We followed the river for several miles, seeing no one. Then the path turned abruptly and we descended toward a deep ravine that wound its way into the mountain. I began to hear water, far more powerful than the sound of the river. Then I caught sight of an enormous waterfall and behind the rushing water, I could make out a cave.

The trail led directly behind the waterfall into the mouth of the cave. As my eyes became accustomed to the dark, I looked up. Water over geological ages had worn away rock into intricate and complex patterns, the facets of some gigantic jewel. Distant rays of light filtered down through the chimneys of the cave. Sitting down on a rocky ledge, I could feel moss and stone reverberate with the noise of the waterfall. The sound began to resonate through my own body. And again, I felt something like the calm of Center but now mingled with the awareness of new and alien powers.

* * *

We sat motionless, listening to the sound of the water. Beneath the falls stretched a row of leafless trees, their bleached branches deprived of sunlight. I stared at the twisted shapes that somehow managed to survive in semidarkness. Through my peripheral vision, I thought I saw something flicker, but when I turned, all I could see were the dark walls of the cave, stretching endlessly into the mountain.

"The mythmakers will choose their own time to appear."

Tanya's words echoed through my mind as I fought a growing impatience. On the other side of the waterfall, I could see where the trail emerged, serpentining its way down the mountain. But the path into the cave remained invisible. A light wind blew through the cave, raising powdery soil. Suddenly Jonathan leaned forward, as though straining to hear something. Rising, he beckoned me to follow.

We headed deeper into the cave. What had first seemed to be solid rock now turned out to be a twisting passageway. Water ripples flickered over the walls, continually revealing new recesses and tunnels. The noise of the waterfall grew muffled, and below I could hear the trickle of an underground river. Then the passageway turned, descended, and opened out into a large subterranean cave.

Like pieces in an intricate ivory chess set, stalagmites stretched upward. Above them, polished and gleaming, grew stalactites, their mirror images. Here the underground river emerged, feeding its strange and convoluted creations. His eyes alert, Jonathan stood very still, waiting. Then I heard a rustling sound. At first I thought it was coming from the river, but it grew continuously louder. Jonathan beckoned me to join him.

"Soon, Rosanna," he whispered.

And not long after he had spoken, I saw someone emerge from the recesses of the cave. From a distance, I judged the man to be far older than Jonathan, so deeply were the wrinkles etched into his face. But as he drew nearer, I realized the two must be around the same age. Like rock that has undergone much weathering, his thin body seemed to have been shaped by severe and violent forces. There was an uncomfortable few moments while the two stared at each other, neither speaking. At last, both made tentative moves forward, then embraced.

"You've finally chosen to return," said the man, his voice echoing strangely through the cave.

Jonathan shook his head. "Rosanna of the Wind wanted to speak with you."

The man looked at me with gentle eyes, so different from the harsh contours of his face, and I almost had the feeling he could see into the very depths of my mind.

"Few from Center ever visit anymore. Why did you seek us out?"

"I needed to complete my myth," I began, my voice trembling.

When I had finished, the mythmaker was silent, as though carefully considering his words.

"I can show you what has remained hidden," he said, "but I must warn you: the more you learn about our mythology, the more you'll understand about your own origins. For we are rivers from the same source."

I watched the muscles in Jon's face tighten but he said nothing, determined to let me make my own choice.

"Please share your knowledge with me," I said.

The mythmaker gestured, and from the depths of the cave other mythmakers appeared, their robes fluttering like unearthly leaves. Faces weathered, eyes calm, they gathered around the mythmaker.

"The branches have spread wide, but the roots return to the same source," he intoned.

Then turning, he motioned us to follow. We traced the course of the river, past stalagmites and rocky shelves. With practiced ease, the mythmakers darted in and out of the outcroppings, but several times I bruised myself. Then we left the cave and entered a long subterranean passage. The mythmakers began to sing in a sonorous chant whose notes echoed against the damp walls. Something in the music made me shiver, and I thought of spirits long dormant being awakened. The chant grew more turbulent and dissonant as we proceeded. The passageway was entirely dark now, and I crept along slowly, never losing hold of the wall. Suddenly, the procession stopped and the mythmaker spoke.

"The way ahead is narrow," he said. "Each must pass through one at a time."

I heard the rustle of the mythmakers' robes and felt the pressure of Jonathan's hand as his turn came. But when I tried to move forward, I encountered solid rock. Running my hands over the walls, I called out, but the only answer was the distant echo of the mythmakers' footsteps. With my palms, I covered every inch of the wall but could find no opening. Behind lay darkness, ahead, a barrier separating me from my myth and Center. Again I cried out, but my voice echoed hollowly against stone. Finally I sat down and touched water. On an impulse, I moved my hand along the stream bottom. This time when I touched the wall, I could feel a narrow passageway leading out of the cave.

Crouching over, I passed through. Now dim rays of light filtered toward me. Running up an incline, I emerged into brilliant sunlight. Motionless, the group stood at the edge of a sheer drop, their faces filled with pain. Joining them, I looked out. All I could see was something resembling an enormous mudfall.

Dead snags of trees, violently uprooted, had been strewn in every direction, their lifeless trunks bleaching under harsh sun. Deep scars ran down the side of the mountain, marking the erosion that had carried away even granite boulders. Nowhere could I detect any signs of plant or animal life. Not even the tough subalpine grasses grew here.

The mythmaker moved toward me, his eyes strangely innocent in his gnarled face.

"Here is where Center began," he said.

But all I could see was the desolate landscape.

"I don't understand," I said. "What does a natural cataclysm have to do with . . ."

I felt Jonathan's hand on my shoulder and his face looked deeply troubled.

"Rosanna," he said with difficulty, "no natural forces destroyed this mountain."

I tried to make some sense out of his words. An idea began to form, but it was so alien to anything I had ever learned that I almost rejected it immediately. All our lives we had been taught that human beings must live in harmony with the natural world, and this was the lesson we transmitted in our Wanderings. But suppose this hadn't always been so?

I waited for Jon to say something, to contradict my suspicions. But he and the mythmakers remained silent. Feeling dizzy, I leaned against the rock shelf.

"Was it people?" I asked weakly.

Jonathan nodded.

Now, as I looked at the mountain, I began to feel physically ill. Chaotic images swirled through my brain. I could see the mountain as it once had been, populated by myriad species of plants and animals. Then one by one their voices grew silent. Dry soil crumbled and washed away. I saw people trample wild flowers, tear down trees, kill animals.

"No!" I screamed but the images refused to leave my mind. I could hardly hold on to the rock shelf. Then all went dark.

Jonathan and the mythmaker were bending over me, their eyes filled with concern.

"But why do you stay here?" I asked the mythmaker weakly. "How can you stand it?"

He looked at me with great calm. "All forms of life are united," he said. "We bear a kinship even with those who were responsible for the darkness. Only if we admit we have that potential can we choose not to use it."

The images of destruction still circled through my mind, but now other images began to emerge, experiences from my Wanderings and from Center. And I could sense the two sets of images fitting together into a larger pattern. Both Jonathan and the mythmaker had been right—replanting was necessary but the roots must not be forgotten. And just as I had shared Center's knowledge with the co-opers, so would I transmit the co-opers' teachings back to Center.

"Come," I said to Jonathan. "I'm beginning to see the form my myth will take."

AND WEARY OF THE SUN

by

Charles L. Grant

They called me Mr. Sunshine.
And it seems so long ago.
But sooner or later I'll have to go in. It's not a matter of making up my mind; that's already been done. Nor is it a matter of nerve, courage, or the stoking of an adrenalin furnace to fire me past the barrier. Rather, it comes down as all things do to a question of resignation: how many times can I continue to pass by the gates and still feel as though I am accomplishing something.
Like defiance.
Or rejection.

I keep telling myself that it's only a park, that it's only my sensitized imagination that turns the rust on the iron gates to long-dried blood.

I keep telling myself that.

But sooner or later I'll have to go in.

There's no place else . . . no place at all.

My undistinquished but perfectly competent position in the firm's legal department was officially eliminated in April. Though the firm's and the country's economy had dictated this some months before, I'd quite naturally refused to believe it would happen to me. The other guy, sure, but not to me. But when the time came, I had sense enough, at least, to leave without burning bridges. There was always a chance things could turn around.

The self-pity came afterward, when I was alone, watching television and wishing I didn't have the chance to sleep late the next morning. And, characteristically, that pity turned to anger, a helpless and frustrating rage that had no power at all to penetrate the walls of my bedroom.

And even then it wouldn't have been so bad if the little things in my life had kept their places. Like the whittling knife I couldn't find to finish the dragon I was carving for my nephew. Or the damned church key that somehow managed to vanish when I wanted to open a can of juice. Or the black sash that contrived to evaporate when I wanted to tie closed the brushed-satin smoking jacket I wore when I cast myself as Ronald Coleman and dreamed marvelous dreams of enticing, hungry women.

It was then that I decided I needed someone to tell

me what a great guy I was. Since Angela was on the West Coast, I called Jerry Lennox and arranged to meet him in our favorite misery hole.

I waited an hour before he finally appeared, cursing the electronics experts of the world who couldn't devise a simple razor that would dip into the cleft of his chin without gouging half of it away. "I'll tell you, Hank," he said without preamble, hunkering down in a corner of the booth, "there is a conspiracy against good-looking guys like me. I'd bet my life on it."

He toasted me silently with draft Guinness, and stared—waiting for me to plunge into my self-pitying bath. But suddenly I refused to indulge in his penchant for dispensing comfort or my own verbal suicide. I revived my anger instead and spent a full hour coating the System with impotent venom, blaming myself as much as anyone for the loss of my job.

"The problem is," I said, "I should have been more forceful. I should have looked for a way to build me a power base, you know what I mean? Made myself indispensable or something."

"You didn't, though," he said quietly.

I snapped my fingers for another drink. "I didn't, you're right. So there's no sense, then, in kicking myself around, is there? Barn doors and horses, right?"

"See?" Jerry said, spreading his arms. "That's what I do for you, pal. Bring out the old school spirit, the pick-up-the-ball-and-run-whether-you-have-it-or-not attitude that's made this country of ours so great. You ain't called Mr. Sunshine for nothing, old son."

"Nicely put," I said, fishing in my sour for the cherry. "Now what do you say you invite me to your place so I can see how badly you're treating my poor sister?" I reached into my jacket for my billfold, and froze ... moved to the other side ... patted my trousers and scratched my forehead.

"Perfect way to end such a day. You forgot it."

I shook my head slowly. "I could have sworn I had it when I left the apartment."

He laughed and slid a bill under the ashtray. "Don't worry about it. Let's go on and see if Mary has something in the fridge."

We moved slowly through the gathering crowd toward the exit, had reached the sidewalk before I recalled sliding the billfold into my pocket as I preened in front of the foyer mirror. Immediately, I begged off riding home with him. There were credit cards, a great deal of money, and if someone picked my pocket I'd have to make a trip to the local precinct.

"Such an understanding little citizen," he said as I walked with him to the corner parking lot. "There should be more of you, you know that, Sunshine?"

"Knock it off, Jer."

"Whatever you say, Sunshine. I'll go ahead and tell Mary to put on the coffee."

I nodded, not really listening, already moving down the street, my eyes trying to cover as much of the sidewalk as they could. All I saw for my diligence were shoes, wrappers, broken bottles, discarded paper bags, and a flash or two of unexciting legs.

By the time I reached my building, my neck was sore, I was sore, and I took it all out on the stoic black doorman who thought I was probably celebrating another one of my legal coups. As it was, when I reached my apartment and checked the small foyer on my hands and knees, the wallet had, as I feared, vanished indeed.

"This," I said then to the thin-faced, dark-eyed reflection in the mirror, "calls for a clear-headed drink."

I flung open the doors to the cabinet that separated the television from the fish tank, clapped my hands in anticipation, and discovered that the bottle of my favorite Irish whiskey was empty. When I couldn't recall the time I'd last dipped into it, I became so depressed that I went straight to bed without calling Jerry and Mary to apologize.

I dreamed I was drowning, and all the episodes, well-intentioned, passed before me, giggling;

I dreamed I was a target in a midway dart game, and there was a sign that labeled me as distinctive but without impact;

I dreamed my parents were still alive, proud of my profession and wondering why;

I dreamed a strange thing that faded to the edge of perception, made me think to myself how odd, how curious, that dream had been . . . without understanding why.

The following morning at breakfast I scribbled on a pad the names of men and firms I'd been in contact with over the past ten years, checking those who might be interested in adding me to their corporate rosters. Then I shaved, dressed, draped my overcoat over my arm, and left whistling for the hunt.

All day.

All week.

And when Angela finally returned from her trip, I was at her door before she'd unpacked. When we had kissed, touched, sipped a glass of wine, and touched again, I told her what had happened to her hero while she'd been gone. Surprisingly, her tears came without apology, her commiserations without preface, and she asked what I intended to do about it.

"Do? What do you think I'm doing? I'm wearing mile-wide grooves in goddamned sidewalks, using up more telephone time than I know I can pay for, and thinking seriously about swallowing my miserable pride and checking in on unemployment with the rest of the herd."

She pushed impatiently at the sagging wings of black hair that refused to stay away from her eyes, and took another glass of wine. "Maybe you should write a letter to the *Times,*" she said.

"Big deal," I muttered, and blinked stupidly when she slammed her glass onto the table and reached out as though to slap me. She thought better of it, however, and attacked her hair instead.

Curious, and somewhat frightening.

I tried to cover the awkward moment by rising and moving to the living-room window. The city was waking up for the night, and the suns trapped in window frames and fluid marquees made me think of the day Angela and I had watched it all from the roof late one summer evening. We had pretended we were on Mars, and the lights were meteorites our magicians had captured just for us. We stayed there until dawn, to watch the Earth rise in fire.

"Look, Angela," I said without turning around, "there's no sense fighting it. I mean, I got the sack and there's nothing I can do about it but hunt up another job. I accept it. With no family to worry about, that part's easy. What's a letter to the editor going to accomplish?"

"Well, for one thing it might get you mad," she said. "Maybe then you'll stop being such a goddamned nice guy and learn to live in the real world for a change."

I felt the words as though they were a blow. I turned, then, and leaned against the sill, my arms folded loosely across my chest. "Change my spots, is that it?"

"Ha! You put yourself in pretty tough company, pussycat. Change your clothes, anyway."

It was uncanny the way she sounded like Jerry sometimes; and when, for no reason at all, I said so, she suddenly looked as though I'd caught her pulling the wings off a fly—guilty, frightened, and arrogantly defensive. It passed, but not swiftly enough.

Then: "Hank, have you talked with Jerry recently?"

"Sure. Well, a couple of days ago. Why?"

She poured herself another drink, emptied it, and poured another. "Just . . . well, just before I left I had lunch with him. He wanted me to photograph some buildings for him on the coast. He . . . he wanted to know how strong I thought you were."

There was nothing I could say. I hadn't the vaguest idea what she was talking about, and she changed the subject quickly to the state of the state of California. She was getting herself drunk, more talking than drinking herself into it, and when I realized that I wasn't going to get anything more out of her I kissed her as she sprawled on the couch, promised to call when I was more sure of what I would be doing with the rest of my life, and left.

On the way down in the elevator, I felt my arms. Strong? What the hell for?

* * *

Two days later I went over to see my sister and her husband. Mary was out, however, and when I walked in unannounced Jerry swept some papers he'd been working on into a desk drawer and hustled me into the kitchen where, after several beers and worldly epigrams on the stupidity of a world that could not recognize my latent genius, he suddenly leaned back in his chair and stared at me.

"Tell me something, Hank—have you ever thought of getting away for awhile?"

"You mean a vacation?" I rubbed a finger in one burning eye. "Get away from it all, back to Nature and commune with the unspoiled spirits of the wilderness? That sort of thing?"

"No. I mean ... getting away. Literally, getting away."

Despite the beer my throat went dry. "You don't mean permanently, do you?"

"Oh, for Christ's sake, Hank!" He snatched up an empty can and crushed it, flung it hard toward a garbage bag alongside the sink.

"What the hell are you so mad about? I can't read your mind, you know."

His silent debate was a visible thing, and I felt as if I should have left the room.

"Have you spoken with Angela lately?"

"All right," I said, finally fed up. "All right, what in God's name are you two up to? No," I decided abruptly, with one hand raised to forestall him. "No, forget it. Whatever you told her, it's scared her to death. And I don't think I want to know it. In fact, I know I don't want to know."

"Hank," he said as Mary and Stevie came laughing into the room, "where's your tie? The one I gave you for Christmas."

My hand went automatically to my throat. The shirt I was wearing wasn't meant to be closed at the neck, but as he turned up a cheek to be kissed by his wife I saw the sidelong glance he gave me, the knowing... the *knowing* I hadn't been able to find it for days.

Two weeks later Mary called me.

Jerry was gone.

He was more than an hour late in coming home from work, and for Jerry that was the cardinal sin. He already had too little time to spend with his son, and every moment he was able to take in playing with him was a moment to be cherished, not one to be thrown away without the grace of an explanatory call.

I swallowed any mention of police and hospitals for the moment, and tried to learn instead if Jerry had made any hints at all about working late. Then I tried to make her laugh, but her silences were well deep, her quick breaths dangerously close to sobs. And my jokes were so feeble I nearly gagged as I heard them.

"All right, Sis, I'll try to scare him up."

"Hank, would you? God, you're a doll. I'd go myself but... well, I don't want to leave Stevie by himself."

I understood and I told her so, rang off, and made my first call—to Jerry's office. He wasn't there, of course. And he hadn't been for quite some time. He had been fired, and he hadn't had the nerve to tell anyone about it.

Swearing did my mood some good, but not the search. I made sure Angela would call the police stations and hospitals for me, then I went to the streets, furious that my best friend had so little confidence in me that he couldn't bring himself to take a dose of my sympathy. And what he was doing to his wife and son was, in my view, virtually unforgivable. The first man I saw I nearly punched. The impulse rose, but it faded immediately, and I was, under the circumstances, remarkably calm.

By eleven, then, I had run out of bars, restaurants, and the half-dozen nightclubs we'd frequented on birthdays and holidays. I called Angela from one of the latter, and she reported failure, hung up before I could question her further.

Between one and three I called my sister twice, the second time she said she would contact the police. I tried to talk her out of it, but she was being Irish stubborn and I backed down quickly.

It was nearly dawn when I sagged into a corner telephone booth to let Mary know I was going home to bed. And as I fished a dime from my pocket, I saw Jerry across the street. He was alone, suited as though for work, leaning forward as he walked as if it were an effort to keep from breaking into a run.

I dropped the dime and slapped open the door, called out but he'd already turned into a side street. Idiot, I thought, and played matador with several cabs who refused me the courtesy of a right-of-way across their corrida. I ran, grabbed the edge of the last building and catapulted myself around the corner.

The street was deserted, and I stopped as suddenly as if someone had yanked me from behind.

As athletic as Jerry had been during our mutual college careers, there was absolutely no way he could have made it to the next block that fast. I turned to stare in the direction of the booth, looked back and began walking slowly, examining each of the narrow doorways for clues to his exit.

The street was narrow, with no neon glare to create flickering shadows; there were only two curtains of white at either end, and the faint reflection of a single lamp post in the rainbows of oil trembling in the gutters. Sounds, too, were muffled: traffic passing behind me like dim conversations from a room you couldn't get into, my shoes scraping on the sidewalk until I lifted up onto my toes.

It was June, and I was shivering.

Then I had visions: of a gang of desperate highwaymen leaping down from the rooftops to snatch me off to some hidden camp in the untamed mountains, of a hunchbacked servant dragging his clubbed foot like a serpent's tail as he led me into the depths of a Balkan laboratory. More realistically, my skin tightened and my shoulders hunched. This was like tethering a goat for a tiger, I thought glumly; the first mugger who looks down here is going to think he's died and gone to heaven.

I almost passed the gates without seeing them.

The brick wall was high, and topped with jagged slate and glinting glass teeth. The gates themselves were open wide enough to admit a single person moving sideways, but the attitude of their facade kept me from doing much more than grabbing the twists-of-iron bars and peering into the black. There was a park back there in the darkness, but how far it penetrated I had no idea. There were no lights within, only the deeper black of full-leaved trees, and the streetlight penetrated not at all.

I called out once. There were no echoes.

I swallowed to moisten my throat, and called again. I cursed. I pleaded. I invoked Mary and their son.

I turned away and went to Angela's. She wouldn't let me in. She wouldn't even answer the door.

I slept for the best part of twenty-four hours, finally rousing myself enough to head for Mary's. Steven was asleep, and we waited for the police to come, to call, to send us a message that Jerry had been found—alive, dead, lying in a coma in some remote hospital ward. I told her about the park, but she dismissed it with the saddest of smiles that told me it was a nice idea, Hank, but typical of me. I would have argued, but I was too confused.

"He lost his job, you know." My relief must have been comical, because she patted my hand and laughed. "I called his boss yesterday, while you were sleeping. He told me. I didn't believe it."

"Neither did I, Mary. But that's the way he is, you—"

She shook her head quickly, and I was startled. "No," she said sharply. "That's exactly *not* how he is. Never. He always shared things with me. We spent an hour trying to figure out how to get you a job before you called me. When he had that tumor, he called right from the office."

Jerry's tumor—on the side of his neck—had been exorcized (I will always believe, and the hell with science) in record time, almost as though it'd been a mistake in the first place. Jer must have felt that way too because he joked about it constantly—not an easy thing to bring off since both our fathers died that way.

"No, Hank Seyton," she said again, more loudly, "he's not the way you think he is. There was ... is something else, and I have to find out what it is."

At this point Mary became too much like my mother for comfort. She flared when she should have melted, exploded when she should have swooned. Should have. That's what our father had taught me all the years he tried to force my mother into doing what he thought she should have done. Mary, however, had learned her lesson well. And I decided then it wasn't the time to mention Jerry's "getting away" nonsense. I still needed proof I wasn't being a idiot.

"Well," I said, "what do we do now?"

"Wait," she answered without hesitation, grinning at my astonishment. "We tried, Hank, and we failed. We're not professionals, the police are. We wait until they have something to tell us. Meanwhile, maybe we should think of something to help them find him. His dinner's getting cold." She looked at me suddenly, and that's when she cried. Without a sound, without movement—only the tears, and the constant whisper of the refrigerator.

I reached out a hand and watched it grow cold in the air over the table.

I felt for a handkerchief to sponge her sorrow, and there was none.

I heard Jerry talking about getting away, and I was cold again because I understood then that he was talking about something I might never understand.

I stood helplessly, wandered through the apartment and stopped in the bathroom to check his toilet articles, stopped in the bedroom to stare at the clutter atop his chest of drawers.

His hairbrush was gone, the one I had given him some faint and forgotten Christmas. And there were other spaces where things should have been, and weren't. In the closet several of his favorite ties were gone, and his one checked suit. When I'd seen him on the street the suit had been brown—and tweed.

"His keys, too."

I dropped the tie I was holding and spun around, one hand pressed to my chest. "Damn, Mary, don't you know better than to scare a man like that? I could have dropped dead!"

She wandered to the bed and tugged at the quilted spread. "A couple of weeks ago he complained about losing the keys. There was only one to the front door and the safe-deposit box, but he liked to have them in his pocket."

That much I already knew. Jerry without those keys bouncing in his hand wouldn't be Jerry. He claimed they kept him from smoking.

"He's not coming back, you know."

"Nonsense, Mary. He'll be found, don't you worry."

"You believe that?"

It was an uncomfortable question. The truth was, I thought him dead and was fighting to keep the grief from expanding out of its leaden nest in my stomach. I tried a disclaimer, but she brushed past me into the living room, swept a pile of magazines to the floor from the glass coffee table and patted the cushion beside her. I sat. She reached into an end-table drawer and pulled out a Manila folder, creased and smudged, torn at one corner. She shoved it into my hands.

"What is it?"

"Open it," she said, pushing nervously at her hair

while I set it on the table and flipped back the cover.

There were papers inside, sketches of buildings Jerry had been working on—the hive for a communications center in Denver, the one I once called a pillbox with a grin, an insurance building in Santa Fe. Four or five more I did not recognize, all of them signed with his peculiar scrawl in the lower left-hand corner. And none of them were completed. Frowning puzzlement, I turned over each page looking for the preliminary specifications he ordinarily scribbled there; the papers were blank.

"Okay," I said slowly, trying to think, "so he was working on a few things in his spare time. He never could keep his work in the office, you know that."

"Look again," as I knew she would insist, so I groped for my pen to gnaw on while I thought further. It was gone, and I rolled my eyes to the ceiling. "I'll tell you, Sis, I'm getting plain senile these days."

She laughed shortly and handed me a pencil.

And without that pencil I might have missed it—but in tracing each line as an aid to thought I noticed that few of them were complete but rather a series of long dashes. And in each succeeding sketch the dashes were shorter. Something new, I guessed, maybe a way to force himself to slow down while he focused on the building's next step. But Mary would have none of it. Jerry never worked that way; his preliminary conceptions were paintings in themselves, complete to the last leaf on whatever shrubbery there was.

I studied the last drawing again, held it close to my face and saw the missing window on the third floor, the corner on the seventh, an absent tree in an oval garden where symmetry demanded one. It was sloppy . . . or it was speaking a language neither of us yet knew.

I didn't like them.

They whispered to me.

"Interesting," I said inanely.

"Take them home, Hank," she said, handing me the folder. "Maybe they'll help."

"But don't you and Stevie—"

"We have to get used to it, Hank."

"You're being stupid, Mary. Jer is not dead. He'll be back, I promise you."

She agreed, much too hastily, and bustled me through the door, waiting in the hallway until I'd stepped into the elevator.

When I arrived home, the doorman asked me for my identification.

It was short. A note pinned to the door of Angela's apartment. I was not to worry, she told me, not about her and not about Jerry. She was running back to the coast to think some things over. She also said she was very, very frightened, and Jerry was very brave.

And me? "Be brave, Mr. Sunshine. He says it's all for the best."

He says.

Good God, was I really so damned sappy that no one could trust me?

July, and no job. Someone stole my car from the building's garage. The police told me to wait it out, but not to hold out hope. If it were found, which they doubted, there might not be anything left to drive.

Jerry was still gone.

I walked the streets again, less jaunty, less assured,

and one Saturday afternoon I found the park again, the one the police said simply did not exist.

It was hot and humid; a dose of August to come.

But it was remarkably cool under the trees, so much so that I had to redon my jacket. And, in not knowing where to look or even why I was there in the first place, I wandered.

Parks, I'd always thought, were for kids and lovers, but this one was different; there was no one here. No field for games, no birds, no insects, nobody making love in the shadows to the droning of bees. I stopped at a marble fountain for an unsatisfactory drink, stepped around the bulk of a massive weeping elm, and saw the theater.

It was, to be specific, a low stage with neither ceiling nor walls, a theater in the round, and there were several dozen folding chairs rippling back from the apron.

I stood quietly for a time, then walked down one of the aisles and leaned against the stage. Dreams of dreams made me smile with a hint of melancholy, wondering why I hadn't run away to the theatrical circus as once I'd hoped—and I had not because I hadn't then or now the nerve, or the confidence. I pushed away, then, and blew out what might have been a sigh, then stopped when I saw a glint of metal toward the center of the nearly black wood. I stared, rubbed my eyes, and hoisted myself puffing onto the stage.

Keys. Two of them.

A cough, and I spun around in a half-crouch, straightening then and nodding as if I weren't nervous at all.

"I'm glad you could come."

She was tall, auburn, dressed in a lightweight gray

suit. No makeup that I could detect, nor a recognizable accent. She carried a clipboard in her left hand, in her right a pen—and though there must have been a thousand like it in the world, I would have sworn then it was mine.

"I'm sorry," I said, walking unsteadily to the apron, "but you said . . . I didn't know I was expected. In fact, I don't even know you. Not very suave of me, but I've never been very good at names, especially lately."

She returned my smile, dutifully only, then frowned as I jumped lightly to the ground. "Are you leaving?"

"Why, is there a performance or something?"

She checked what seemed to be a schedule, or a list, and glanced up at me without raising her head. "There's always something here, Mr. Seyton."

The afternoon was warm, the stage bare but for the keys, and the sound of her voice like a mother to a child who had to know there were no giants. There was nothing threatening at all, nothing lurking or stalking . . . but I was terrified.

Stage . . . woman . . . keys . . . woman . . .

I twisted around and bolted, stumbling over chairs and flinging them out of the way. There was no *reason*, I kept telling myself as I raced toward the gates, no reason at all that I should want to scream.

I should have, I think. When I returned to the apartment, my telephone was disconnected and a notice slid under the door marking my eviction: A European conglomerate had purchased land and building and would clear it all in precisely ninety days.

And Mary was dead, evidently deciding that life without Jerry was neither inviting nor coveted. Steven was at her in-laws where, the note said, he'd be properly taken care of.

Time compressed, as did the images imprinted thereon, and my next conscious act was leaning against a lamppost and staring at the folder I'd taken from my apartment. There was something there, something I'd missed that he didn't want me to; but I couldn't find it. I stared and glared until my eyes watered, looked away to see the sunset, looked back and saw it. The last sketch. Two men standing near the spot where the tree should have been—Jerry looking at me, and taking off my jacket with one hand.

In the other was a mask...of me...looking angry.

My own face, the face on the body, was a blank.

A light drizzle began to fall, steaming off the streets. I held the folder tightly and spent several long blocks weeping for my sister, for my nephew who could have been my son. And when the tears passed into the rain that drenched me, chilled me in spite of the midsummer darkness, I braced myself against a phone booth I had known a hundred centuries ago and thought of the stage in the park, and another stage I'd seen in London. Where a man played a king and railed against God and denied him as a tale told by an idiot. It had affected me then, and it moved me now. Not that I believed it. Idiots can do better than this, I thought; and I refused to succumb to the notion that I were merely a minor character in some foolish cosmic melodrama.

That was the easy way out.

Jerry, however, had discovered another. He had told Angela about it, and she'd run away. He tried to tell me, and all I could do was make weak sport. And then...then he'd tried to break through the walls of my ego by showing me how, just how it was done: the sloughing off of the tumor had been the first step.

And when I still didn't understand, from wherever he was, he began to take parts of me against my will.

The bars of the gate are cold in my hands, and I no longer feel the clothes sodden upon my back. Staring into the rain-wavering blackness, I see visions of myself as I was, disintegrating by bits and lonely pieces. A car passes behind me, its headlights making slashes of the rain, and as the glow drifts away I can see that I have left no shadow on the *walk at my* feet.

A Welsh poet once said that at least once in each life a man's *eyes cry out for the* balm of fleeting night and are oh *so weary of the sun that marks their days.*

And it's true.

But this escape, if escape is what it is, is not necessarily permanent, not if you don't wish it. A *transitory limbo, a restructuring perhaps, and an enhancing of one's emotional foundation. Jerry will be back,* then, more light filled than ever, and he'll give to the world its most magnificent soaring structures. He'll be *back because he left his keys to console me, and in my ignorance, all they had done was teach me how to* hate.

And hate I did at my dear Mary's death. Steven's loss. Angela's flight.

She called me Mr. Sunshine.

But it's raining now, you see.

That's *why I'm afraid to go in there now, to meet the woman with auburn hair, who's been patiently waiting, knowing I'll return; I'm afraid to take my position on that stage and go . . . wherever one has to go to gather strength to do what has to be done . . . to learn new lines . . . to nurture new power.*

I am afraid . . . because after all that has been done and all that has been said and all that has been seen . . . I know now that I will be back. And when I come back, when I return to the world outside the park . . .

I am going to be angrier still than I ever thought I could . . .

My smile has been taken from me . . .

And this time someone is going to pay.

WAVE RIDER

by

Hilbert Schenck

When Arthur Piver, the salesman turned marine architect, was run down and lost at night off the Southern California coast in one of his own yachts, his dream of a twenty-four-hour, sailing speed record died, for the time, with him. Piver was a designer of trimarans, three-hulled sailing vessels of high speed and immense stability; and he believed that if one of these boats could be driven onto the crest of a great wave, one of the monsters that occasionally sweep across the South Pacific in the 'Roaring Forties,' he could ride it for an entire day and totally eclipse the old, clipper-ship runs. The extreme clipper, *James Baines* of Boston, had apparently achieved a twenty-four hour average of twenty-one knots, if one believes the navigation and the log book. Piver estimated that a forty-foot Tri, on a thousand-foot-long wave, could easily double this speed if she could be sailed continuously on the downward slope and if the wave stayed together.

Trimarans had their problems. Their stability and stiffness resulted in dismastings when gusts caught them and sheet-release mechanisms failed to act quickly enough. Running down the face of a great sea they tended to dig in one or the other outer hull and pitchpole forward. But because they rode in the upper two feet of water, being light and keelless, they could surf: run in the continuously downward-moving water on the front face of large waves. Under these conditions the only limitation on boat speed was the wave's forward-speed itself, and the larger the wave, the faster this became.

Arthur Piver's dream stayed in the heads of people to whom such matters are of interest, but there were many problems to overcome before Tri's could practically attempt such feats. The Americas Cup developments in the seventies and eighties brought in the boron alloys and internally-stressed mast structures strong enough to withstand both the shocks to which multihulled sailboats are prone and the wind gusts before which they refuse to lean over. Microprocessors and servo-systems were developed that sensed changes in wind, sea, attitude, and accelerations and provided the helmsman with continuous steering corrections. But Americas Cup Rules Committees continued to resist any mechanical intervention in the steering of a Twelve

Meter or in the movement of its sheets, so by the turn of the century interactive programmers had achieved a final development, the talking yacht. Twelve Meters spoke continuously to their helmsman and sheet captains of tiny adjustment and wheel shifts. This was entirely within the rules, for any instrument that can sense and report has been acceptable throughout the Twelve-Meter phase of the Americas Cup.

The problems in the pursuit of Arthur Piver's dream were different. A computer could not steer the big Tri's on a wave-face as well as a skilled helmsman; this had been proven by some deadly experiments along the South Forties. The feedback from the rudder and hull to the man simply could not be duplicated by any multiply-linked servos. But what the Tri captain needed was data assimilation. He had to find and vector his wave, and this took days of computation and projection, plus absolute judgement in the interception and face-riding. The talking Tri's gave helm advice to their skippers as on the Twelves, but they also assimilated satellite and oceanographic weather data and projected local conditions in time.

The best of these unusual sailboats was *Wave Rider*, a forty-two-foot, titanium-hulled Tri with outer hulls as sharp as knife edges. *Wave Rider's* structure consisted of braced tension members designed to present a minimum of area to seas breaking up between the hulls, yet to resist the worst of the torsional shocks that tend to tear Tri's apart. She was sloop-rigged with a fully-battened main and a variety of jibs and spinnakers that were set forward by *Wave Rider* herself, that is, by the computer and servos.

Wave Rider made two attempts on the twenty-four-hour sail record. In the first of these she was sailed by Joseph Spanos and his wife, Beth, herself a talented interactive programmer. Fourteen hours into the run, moving over sixty knots on a one-hundred-and-ten footer, *Wave Rider* was suddenly caught by a local side gust and rolled upward past her stability limit. The wave crest caught the tip of the sail, the yacht inverted and the mast snapped. Beth Spanos was killed instantly by a whipping stay. Her husband was saved from the inverted Tri nine hours later by a long-distance rescue copter.

One year later, in January when the easterlies really blow in the South Forties, high and steady, Spanos and *Wave Rider* made a second attempt. This is their story.

The mother ship for the effort was a chartered freighter, *Osaka Merchant*, which had the feature of a telescoping crane that could set *Wave Rider* into the water next to the ship even in considerable sea states. Funding came mainly from the TV people; they had two crews aboard, but project management was handled by the patrician sailmaker, Hillary Brent of Marblehead, whose "Brent-cut" sails appeared in the Americas Cup and other important sailing races.

But until *Wave Rider* went in, the most important, and expensive, member of the team was the project's oceanographic consultant, Professor Bob Richart, a single-handed ocean sailor himself and the best in the world in wave-state prediction.

Richart worked day and night in the *Osaka Merchant's* small chart room, now crammed with extra electronics. The project had a direct link with the South Pacific oceanography satellite, SEASAT IV, hanging in synchronous orbit roughly over Macquarie Island.

SEASAT, using interferometric instruments, provided detailed wave maps of the whole southern ocean as well as adequate wind-field data obtained from cloud motion.

Osaka Merchant had rolled and pitched south in excellent, calm weather, much to everyone's disgust, but as January arrived the Trades finally began to blow south of latitude forty-five, steady at about Beaufort six, and SEASAT began to show interesting wave growths.

Joe Spanos, a short, stocky man in his early thirties, grim and withdrawn with everyone, spent almost as much time in the chart room as the oceanographer. Now he was there continuously as the bearded Richart searched and focused the SEASAT images and made his predictive calculations.

"This is a good wind, Joe," said Richart on the third night.

"See," he pointed to bright dots on the big screen, "that's a group of sixty-footers heading about due west. They're going to overrun these smaller ones and grab their energy." He pointed. "Furthermore, the way they're bunching now means they'll soon be eating each other. And when two sixty-footers add, you get big stuff. And the bigger it gets, if the wind holds, the faster they grow. I don't believe waves over a hundred feet follow the one-third-power law; the energy transfer from the wind goes up much faster. You've got that tremendous boundary-layer suppression."

Spanos peered in his expressionless way at the oceanographer, whose face and beard were lit weirdly green from the screens. "You think it's go, Doc?"

Professor Richart nodded. "If you run at your best

speed about sou'west, you'll come into their zone ahead of the big ones. Of course, *Wave Rider* will be getting her SEASAT input so she can put you in a big set."

"Those guys'll have run a ways before I get there," said Spanos, "You think any might be breaking?"

Richart shook his head. "I can't see why. The wind is steady and the sea deep. Once they eat each other and get really big, they tend to be stable for long periods. I mean, what local anomaly bothers a hundred footer at fifty . . . sixty knots? Anyway, you can always climb up on the back of one and wait for the foam to die down." Richart turned and peered up at Spanos. "What you're trying may be impossible, you know," he said suddenly. "You got in fourteen good hours the last time and then a fluke. But statistically, those flukes *have to come*, Joe. It may just be impossible to get a whole day without something like that."

Spanos' thin eyes blinked once or twice. "*Wave Rider* won't roll up this time, Doc. She can dump sail now in three seconds, if a wing goes too high. That won't happen again."

Professor Richart rubbed his beard. "The same thing never happens again, my friend. It's always different."

Tall, silver-haired Hillary Brent poked his head in the room. "From this talk, I'd say you've found a wave?"

Both men nodded, and Brent turned to Spanos. "You set to go in the water, Joe?"

The short man nodded again, but somehow the three of them did not move or act, as though not quite wanting to start what they had come for. Hillary Brent, peering in the dim light at Spanos, put his hand on the shorter man's shoulder. "We've come a long way to this, Joe," he said in his quiet, Boston voice. "You most of all."

Joe Spanos looked at one man and then the other. He was a Greek-American from Baltimore, a yacht-club boy who won the World Dragon Championships at sixteen, in between teaching rich folk's kids to sail. He had been across all the great oceans in sailboats, dismasted, overturned, ridden on the fringes of hurricanes. "I miss Beth," he said to them in a soft voice. "Once this is done, complete, maybe that can end too."

Professor Richart sighed. "Is it really so important that we sail faster than some old, stiff-collared, Boston fart of a hundred-and-fifty years ago? Sometimes I feel like we're all here just to prove you're better than any of your ancestors, Hill."

"We're here, my friends, to provide the circuses, along with the bread, to the flaccid masses of the world. Those paunchy slobs and their fatso wives will live your adventure, Joe, in their overstuffed living rooms through the eyes of the Reuters U-2 cameras." Hillary Brent wrinkled his straight, pointed nose.

Joe Spanos suddenly smiled, his lips parting for the first time. "Those fatso slobs, Hill, happen to be my folks and friends. And don't blame them. The reason we're doing this is because we're hobby nuts so obsessed with a completely useless idea that in any other society we'd have been locked up long since."

Professor Richart reached his hand up and took Joe's arm. "Joe, I'll be in continual touch with *Wave Rider* so she'll have sizes, locations, and vectors from me to confirm her direct reception from SEASAT. Once you're on a wave, *Wave Rider* will be watching local conditions while I stay on the big picture so as to let you know about approaching wave trains, wind shifts, and any other junk. Okay?"

Spanos nodded and squeezed Richart's shoulder. "Suddenly I can't wait to be up on that face," he said to no one in particular.

Wave Rider, fully rigged with sails furled and waiting, sat in the well of *Osaka Merchant*. The loudspeakers called out into the dusk, "All crew and technical personnel. We are launching *Wave Rider*. Report to the well deck."

The floodlights went on with blinding force and the cameras started. Joe Spanos, in a waterproof jumpsuit of bright orange, the letters "Brent-Cut" across his back, climbed up the port hull and crawled over the wing structure to the main-hull cockpit. There he shrugged on his bouyancy suit and umbilical safety line. This line, which allowed him to roam from one end of the Tri to the other but always remain connected in case he went overboard, had at its core the wires connecting Joe Spanos with *Wave Rider's* interactive computer system. A throat mike and ear-bone speakers let Joe and *Wave Rider* speak to each other continuously without shutting out other sounds.

After he had adjusted the bone-conduction pads, Joe stared around, then up at the forward poop deck where the multieyed cameras pointed at him. "You ready, baby?"

"Systems are all go, Joe sweetie," said *Wave Rider*.

"This is a piece of cake, baby. Sea state three, if that." Spanos shoved his thumbs up, the deck crew cast off *Wave Rider's* traveling straps and the winch whined.

The big Tri, guided by three dozen hands, swung up

and off over the side. They waited for a calm spot and then dropped her rapidly down into the water with a thump of stressed, titanium panels.

"Oof!" said *Wave Rider*.

"Okay, baby?" said Joe Spanos quickly.

"Fine, Joe. I'm just not used to that kind of deceleration."

Spanos ran forward and cast-off the four-point sling which was then rapidly drawn up from the Tri. *Wave Rider*, now free of the freighter, drifted rapidly away downwind.

"Put up, baby, while I get these sails hoisted," said Joe Spanos. As soon as the wind caught an edge of sail, the Tri answered to her rudder and swung up to windward. In a minute the sails were tight and pulling, and *Wave Rider* was driving off in a good breeze southwest, as the men along the freighter's rail waved their caps and cheered after her.

"Baby," said Joe Spanos. "We've got a good eight hours before we hit the big stuff. "I'm going to sack in. As the saying goes, call me if the wind shifts."

"Aye, aye, Cap'n," said *Wave Rider* in his ear. "And I'll keep the bleedin' mate out of the blessed rum bar'l."

Joe Spanos grinned and slid below into the thin, tiny cabin. He swung up on the narrow bunk and wondered if he would sleep. He had not slept well for a year, even at sea. He lay on the stiff bunk, his body rolling idly back and forth as *Wave Rider* drove steadily over the long, low swells in a wind that blew like a wind tunnel, without variation. Joe Spanos felt his vessel move easily under him, heard its comfortable creak and groan as it adjusted continuously to ever-different water profiles. The last thing he remembered was *Wave*

Rider's "Nighty-night, Joe," whispered in his ear.

With the dawn came quite different conditions. The waves were much larger now, still long and swelly, but greatly swollen. The Tri climbed up and up on each large hill, then looked down from its eminence at the valley of considerable depth. She then coasted down the hill, scooting south across its face, turning a bit west at the bottom to run up the next large mound.

"Time for breakfast, Joe," said *Wave Rider* in a calm, but loud voice. Spanos woke with a start from a deep, heavy, resting sleep such as he could not remember. He felt the yacht skim down the face of a thirty-footer and grinned.

"That's more like it, baby," he said drowsily. "Time for me to steer?"

"I can manage these, Joe," said *Wave Rider*. "Get some food and coffee. Professor Richart figures that if we turn southeast at about eleven-hundred today, we'll run right into the northern edge of a set of monsters. We can turn south again once we get on one toward the area of maximum height. Then hang on there for the rest of the run."

"How big?" asked Joe Spanos, crouched over his swaying, gimballed stove and busily stirring eggs, bacon, sausage, and tomatoes together.

"Richart guarantees hundred-footers, Joe. But he says the wind is still picking up and they could go bigger."

"What do you think, baby?"

There was a pause. "I think we'll have the ride of our lives," said *Wave Rider*. "You scared, Joe?"

Spanos fed himself with the rapid, methodical relish of the long-distance sailor. "Tense. Light-headed. But not scared, Beth."

"Please, Joe. Don't call me that. I'm not your wife."

Spanos shrugged and gulped hot coffee. "You're what's left of her. You make her jokes, say her things. I miss you like hell, Beth."

The yacht sailed steadily, up and down, over the hills of water. "Joe, Beth made me, programmed me, designed me. But I'm not her. I can't give you what she did. I'm *Wave Rider*, Joe."

"You think I'm a nut?" muttered Spanos into his cup. "Who can make love to a Tri?" He briskly rubbed his hands together. "Okay, I won't say it, if it bothers you, *Wave Rider*. Or is it *Ms. Wave Rider?*"

"Don't be sore with me, Joe sweetie. I like 'baby' fine. We've got a big day coming, love."

Joe Spanos swung up through the narrow hatch and took the wheel. "I'm not sore, baby. I feel great! As the drunk mouse said, 'Bring on that damn cat!'" He peered southeast over the rim to where the giants scuffled and grew and began to run.

Before noon they hardened *Wave Rider's* tack and went southeast tight to windward. At fourteen-thirty *Wave Rider* spoke softly. "You should see the set to the east soon, Joe. SEASAT has us within two miles and they can see them now on the U-2 image."

Spanos put his binoculars to his eyes as the Tri topped an especially huge wave and breathed a whistle.

"Oh, wow, baby. It's the Rocky Mountains!"

The first wave of the set, even though a mile away, bulked all along the horizon and seemed to build and grow as it came at them.

"Take number three, Joe. That's Grandpa."

Wave Rider, now completely dwarfed by the

hundred-footer bearing down on them, began to drive up its great slope, higher and higher, slicing upward at an angle to the wave face, the east wind flowing down the slope with a steady scream. They zoomed up over the top and before them was the next and bigger wave in the set.

"If the third is bigger than that, it's a record, baby!" shouted Spanos, for this time they climbed and climbed a slope that steepened continuously ahead of them. The downwave hull of the trimaran dug sharply into the wave face and they ran along a contour, then worked higher and higher until they burst over the steaming wave top and faced number three.

"One-forty, Joe," said *Wave Rider*. "A damn big mother!"

"Yes sir! That's my baby!" said Spanos.

The wave completely dominated the view ahead. They could see it left and right out to the limit of vision, a huge rolling slope of grey-blue motion. It looked as hard as rock.

They approached it over the long hollow at an acute angle and began to run along the lower face.

"How far up, baby?"

"Wind steadier near the top, Joe, but it's trickier and steeper."

They worked higher, running south along the face. "We're on, baby. Tell them to start the clocks."

"I did, Joe, a minute ago. Our day has begun, love."

They sailed higher up the face, which still towered above them, now running directly south on the contour. The high wind poured from the east over the wave crest and flowed down the face, and *Wave Rider* took this on her port beam, still driving south across the wave, but moving far more rapidly west with the whole wave-set, its group velocity now at sixty-one knots.

Sometimes the peak was irregular and the wind would gust for a moment, up or down. When a lee came, Spanos turned the Tri more down the face to let gravity carry him to where the wind would be stronger on the lower, flatter water. When an upward wind gust caught them they turned up the wave front, heading for the curling, irregular top. The wind tended to be actually less on the crest since an eddy formed there as the high wind, partly entrained and driven by the waves themselves, blew up and over the sharpening wave top. This great curling eddy contained spume and spray, so the crest was constantly bathed in a smoky swirl of chill fog.

Joe Spanos steered silently, intently, feeling the Tri's motion and listening to her advice. "Port a bit, Joe. Steady. Wind gusting. We're leaning a bit far, baby. Hold her, Joe. Now run down. That's it. Watch that starboard tip, Joe . . . A bit west, love. Steady now . . ."

The wave grew steadily all that afternoon, the wind now a scream of cold air, the grey-blue face dotted here and there with foam and minor breaks. The monster was overrunning its consorts, its own velocity increasing steadily. As dusk came, *Wave Rider* spoke softly to Spanos, "It's over one-sixty, Joe. Bigger than the *Ramapo* wave."

The Tri was referring to the record wave-height measurement made years back by the *U.S.S. Ramapo*, a Navy oiler, in these same seas.

Spanos grunted. "Hell, baby. The satellites have looked at plenty bigger since."

"They're in the sky, Joe. Not in the water."

As night fell, Spanos could no longer see the entire wave, and he depended more and more on the Tri's special senses to tell him where they were on the face. The wave was now so large and moving so rapidly that the face wind was actually decreasing. The wave was running away from the gale that berthed it.

In the dark the phosphorescence glowed along the crest and inside the wave itself. Because the great sea was a static-electricity generator, *Wave Rider's* rig twinkled and glowed, and fingers of blue fire crackled off the crosstrees and mast. The stays lit up and the yacht hissed and sparked.

"Does that tickle, baby?" said Joe, trying to see the white crest above them.

"Just a little static, love."

The moon came up, and it seemed for a while as though they were not moving at all, just rolling and pitching on an endless hillside of stationary water. To starboard, far off, was another huge, dim hillside and between a shadowed, choppy, mysterious valley. Yet the whole was moving at almost seventy miles an hour.

The wind wave was so huge that it created its own weather. The slackening, easterly wind reversed in the early morning and a whole gale now blew up the face. *Wave Rider* went over to starboard tack to maintain her southerly course. But the face water and wind were now in direct opposition, and instability surges began to move up the face, like ripples in a snapped blanket. Sometimes these grew and broke, other times they tore off the upper ten feet of the wave in a huge spume of wet cloud, blowing in shreds off to the east. This continual stream of water and vapor blowing backward was accompanied by spectacular blue sheets of Saint Elmo's fire, some of them hundreds of feet long, pouring skyward through the ripping, torn cloud stream.

The sun rose behind the wave and for a while they were in deep shadow. But Joe Spanos could see that the wave ahead had shrunk and was now no more than a foothill running in front of its gigantic consort. "Grandpa's like the Walrus and the Carpenter," said Joe. "He's eaten every one."

"Over two hundred feet high and two-thirds mile in length, love. Seventy-four knots. The biggest ever, Joe."

That morning they rode, rearing and bucking, over a worsening, chopping face. The instabilities grew and ten- to twenty-foot breakers, on a thirty-degree running face, charged up at them continually. And then, near noon Joe heard *Wave Rider's* level voice stop in mid-advice. A moment later she spoke loudly.

"Joe! Richart says we're starting to run in over the South New Zealand Shelf. Grandpa's feeling bottom already! They can detect steepening north of us."

Spanos steered them around a steep breaker and grunted. "How long till the break, baby?"

"They want you off the wave now, Joe! Brent is on. He's ordering you off. It's going to steepen and we won't be able to climb back out of it, Joe!"

Spanos stared this way and that, driving them south on the face.

"Joe, please. They want to talk, sweetie."

"If you put them on, I'll pull these bone pads off and do this completely by myself," said Spanos evenly.

"I wouldn't do that Joe. I told them I'm talking

to you."

"Then tell me how long before the curl gets here, baby. You're hooked into SEASAT and all that stuff. I know Richart won't tell us."

"I'll tell you, Joe. We might just make twenty-four hours. The break will start a hundred miles north of us and I figure the advance won't be over fifty knots, so we should finish the run."

Joe Spanos grinned at the wild, white chop around him as the reefed main and storm jib snapped in stiff bluster.

By noon the instability rollers had degenerated into random, impossibly steep chop so the entire face was now white breakers, and *Wave Rider* pitched and rolled wildly, trying to hold her place on the wave. "The break's begun, Joe. We might still get out."

"What's the advance speed?"

"About fifty knots, Joe."

"And we only need ninety minutes, baby. We're going to prove that three million bucks and a few coo-coos can beat old Donny McKay any time, providing he gives us a hundred-and-fifty-year start."

"They're all after me, Joe! They want to talk so bad, sweetie! I've got to tell them something. Joe?"

"Tell them it's my heart's desire, Beth," said Joe in a whisper. "Oh, Beth, it's a long year, lover."

Grandpa was steepening above them and the crest was being torn more and more deeply by wind gusts. *Wave Rider* dropped lower on the face to gain some lee from the modest hill running ahead of them. Visibility was poor in the sudden sheets of spray and foam that whipped over them, and the cockpit ran with continuous gouts of water. The wave towered above them, mountainous, craggy, no longer smooth and rolling as the day before but now a true grandfather giant, swollen and pocked with erupting pustules of white broken water, ragged and ripped along the top where streamers of green water tore off, spreading a cloud-cover of hundreds of square miles behind the monster.

And in the midst of the screaming, pounding seas, Joe finally heard the Tri coolly say, "The twenty-four hours are up. Mean speed, sixty-six knots. Congratulations, Captain Spanos. It's been a privilege to make this run with you."

"Thank you, faithful *Wave Rider*," said Spanos in a formal voice, grinning. "And let's not forget Grandpa while we're handing out medals."

"Joe, sweetie, we'll meet him soon enough. Grandpa's crest is over seventy degrees steep now. We can't sail up over that."

"How soon, Beth?"

"Maybe twenty minutes, Joe."

Spanos stood and put the helm hard over. "Jibe ship! Why should Grandpa have to wait?"

Wave Rider spun counterclockwise as her rig slammed over and they went on port tack, scooting up the face of the wave now heading north.

Soon they could see in the far distance ahead of them the great cloud and confusion of the wave's collapse. The curl ran steadily south along the crest and, looking up the face, Joe could see the top beginning to roll up over them. The entire wave was forming a gigantic tunnel, a hole in the water, and the wind now blew south out of that tunnel as they drove close-hauled into it. Grandpa had utterly changed in an instant, metamorphosed into a leaping, continuous, arching roof of water high over them, turning the sunlight ever-darker green. And far ahead, way down along that narrowing, collapsing, yet vast structure, Joe saw the white ruin of the wave coming at him out of steam and cloud, filling all the great space within the curl.

Joe Spanos stood, steering *Wave Rider* and steadily watching the smashed wave-face grow as the flowing, vaulting water-roof thickened and fell implacably downward.

"Okay, Beth," he said quietly. "It's coming, lover. Oh . . . Beth. Oh God, I love you, Beth!"

"It's been beautiful," said *Wave Rider*. "I love you, Joe."

The collapse-face grew, blocking all else. Joe felt the curl-water catch *Wave Rider's* masthead and begin driving her port hull downward.

"You've been patient, Grandpa," said Joe at the end. "We three are one flesh."

The TV audience, estimated at between ten and fifteen percent of all the people in the world, got their raw, red meat then. They saw *Wave Rider*, a tiny, bold insect on the gigantic, ruined face, turn and confront the running break. They saw her drive into the cavern of the curl and, for a millisecond, saw her mast poke out of the white smash of the wave, then, the tumbling glitter of her hulls. And the networks replayed it all at various speeds for some days thereafter.

Yet the designers had worked a minor miracle with *Wave Rider*. They found her later, floating awash and upright, every deck projection: mast, rails, stays, helm, ripped away. Hillary Brent rigged her again and she was the center of all eyes at the next Americas Cup match, cutting sleekly through the spectator fleet with everyone pointing and photographing the shining yacht.

But *Wave Rider* was an expensive toy so Brent leased her to a classy, high-rise resort in the Bahamas where rich people would pay plenty for a day's outing on the fastest sailboat in the world. Eventually the Smithsonian, after prodding by some congressional yachtsmen, began to negotiate the purchase of the vessel with Brent Sails, Inc. But that next fall was a bad one for hurricanes and a violent one nicked that part of the Bahamas. Somehow, *Wave Rider* got loose. They watched her from the hotel through the rain squalls, driven hard onto the outer reef and teetering there for a while. Then the wind shifted and she blew off onto the ocean side; the coral heads had punctured her hulls and she swept off to the east to sink in five thousand feet of water.

With *Wave Rider* gone, people eventually forgot about the twenty-four hour sailing record. The Smithsonian directors had no idea where they would have put the yacht, anyway.

But always after that, among the small, specialized group who watch the big wave sets from satellites and the decks of vessels, the Spanos Wind Wave is invoked when one wishes to compare with the greatest of them all. And when Bob Richart now and then follows a big one with a high-resolution SEASAT camera, he finds it easy to imagine a tiny *Wave Rider*, stoutly and endlessly skimming across that distant, running face.

SHEETS

by

Alan Ryan

A few days after he started work in the menswear department, a woman approached him and asked where they had moved the bathrobes that had been right over *there*. He confessed that he was new in the department; in fact he was new to Macy's entirely, and in an excess of honesty, he told her that she undoubtedly knew the store better than he did. Oh my, yes, she said, she knew the store inside out; her day wouldn't be complete unless she ran into Macy's on her lunch hour.

George April thought about that woman often in the weeks that followed, and wondered about her sanity.

When he wasn't wondering about his own.

The menswear department wasn't really so bad, he told himself. After all, the job was only for Christmas and, small as they were, he was glad to see the paychecks. You can't be too picky, he reminded himself, when you've been out of work for six months. Not exactly what he'd had in mind when he quit his teaching job, but it certainly was the real world he'd been seeking. Only sometimes it was more real than he cared for.

Then he got lucky. Or so everyone said, when, two days after Christmas, all the temporary help was let go, and he and a few others were kept on as extra help for the January white sale.

George felt a little guilty at not being as pleased about it as all the others were. Hey, the others all said, they let fifteen hundred people go, but they kept the twenty of us. Fifteen hundred. Twenty out of fifteen hundred! Hey, you know, they'll probably keep us on and make us permanent after this. George did his best to smile and agree. It didn't help any to reflect that he was about ten years older, ten years devoted mostly to a costly education, than any of the others.

So he was transferred to the sheet department and found that the most frustrating part of the job was not the boredom itself. The boredom was crushing, a thick enveloping fog that settled around his head as soon as he arrived in the department every morning. But the frustration came from the knowledge that he alone of all of them was the only one who felt it.

How can they *not* be bored, he asked himself constantly. How can they stand it? What do they think about while they stare into space, waiting for a customer to interrupt the revery?

George alternately, and sometimes simultaneously, loved and hated the customers. They could be maddening, rude, demanding, contemptuous of the salesclerks. But they interrupted the boredom. They were something to *do*, something to deal with, something to think about. God, something to think about!

Oh yes, there was something to think about.

Patterns.

From the first day he worked in the department, George ranked the problem of the patterns at the top of his private and lengthy list of aggravations.

"Lou," he said, standing at his cash register on the first day, "this package isn't marked. Do you know what pattern it is?" Lou was one of the regulars, a man older than his years, collar rumpled, tie stained, who would look more at home shuffling his feet outside on OTB parlor than he did at a cash register in Macy's.

"That?" Lou said. "That's Summer Rose."

"Summer Rose," George repeated. "Is that how you look it up in the price list?"

"You look it up by the manufacturer first. Then you look it up by the name of the pattern."

"Oh, okay. But they're usually marked, right? They have the name of the pattern on them."

"Nah," Lou said sourly, "ya gotta learn 'em."

"They're not marked," George said, his voice flat and toneless.

"Yeah," Lou said, "ya gotta learn 'em. Don't worry about it, kid. When you're here as long as me, ya know all the names by heart."

The next customer presented Lou with a set of sheets

he didn't recognize, and he had to go out on the floor to the display to look up the name of the pattern on the price card.

And George hadn't been called, "Kid," in at least fifteen years. He spent more than an hour calculating it as closely as possible. That hour, at least, passed fairly painlessly.

"Hi, baby, it's me."

"Hi. Are you on your lunch hour already?"

"No, I ducked out for a few minutes. If they're looking for me, I'll say I went to the men's room. They can't can me for that, after all."

"Oh, okay. Is it busy?"

"Busy! Are you kidding? Of course, it's not busy."

"Oh. Honey, do you feel all right?"

"I feel okay."

"Is something wrong?"

"Listen, if you want me to hold on to this job, you better talk me out of quitting. Because it's really driving me up the wall. Honey, you can't imagine how boring it is. You can't imagine it. You spend all your time hoping the time will go by. You wait and wait and you figure it's about an hour or so, then you look at your watch and it's maybe seven minutes. Honey, it's driving me crazy. It really is."

"Poor baby. I know how it is. It was like that when I worked at the boutique. Try not to think about it."

"Honey, you don't understand. That's the whole problem. I can't help but think about it. There's nothing else to do in that goddamn sheet department."

"Okay, honey, listen, we'll talk about it tonight. I have to get back to work."

"Okay, but I feel like those goddamn sheets are smothering me."

"Honey, I really have to go. Mr. B. is looking at me funny."

"Okay, okay."

"I really have to go."

"I said okay."

"Good-bye."

"'Bye."

So he began learning the patterns and counting the days until the end of the white sale.

There were close to a hundred different patterns in the price list, but only half that many on display. If a customer asked for something she had seen in the catalogue or on display a month ago, the standard answer was that it was out of stock. At first he would go to one of the stockmen and ask if there were any in the stockroom. There never were. The stockmen were afflicted with the same mental and physical lassitude that deadened everyone and everything in the sheet department. The trick in dealing with disappointed or annoyed customers was to look distressed and genuinely concerned about the problem. In any case, they went away empty-handed.

Some days he was assigned to stand out on the floor, straightening the stock of sheets and pillowcases and assisting customers in finding what they wanted. Even on the days when he was assigned a cash register, he still wandered out onto the floor and listlessly moved some packages of sheets around on the display tables. Most of the other clerks stayed at their registers, glassy-eyed, unless a supervisor told them to go out and straighten the stock.

Something made him think one day of Richard Henry Dana and *Two Years Before the Mast* and the books of C. S. Forester. What was it? Then he realized. Straightening the stock was the department-store equivalent of picking oakum, in the old days of sailing vessels, wooden ships, voyages that lasted for endless months and months. Keep moving. Keep your body moving. Do something, anything, make the time go by, make it pass somehow. Just get through this hour for now, worry about the others after this.

By the end of the first week, he knew the names of most of the patterns. When he started at it, he thought he should be able to master them in an hour or so. After all, when he was a teacher, he used to learn the names of three dozen students in a few minutes of the first class. Sure, it was something of a parlor trick, meant to impress the kids, but he had been able to do it. Never missed.

It took him a week to learn the names of four dozen patterns. A mental block, he figured. I'm blocking them out because I hate them so much. My brain is getting soft. This place is driving me crazy. When I get home, I'm going into the bedroom and rip the sheets off the bed. I never want to sleep on sheets again. I never want to look at sheets ever again as long as I live. If I live. These goddamn sheets are smothering me.

There were times when he felt that his air was cut off, that he couldn't breathe. He shook off the feeling and put it down to the excess of heat on that floor of the store. Everyone, even the customers, said it was too warm. He still found his breathing labored.

At the beginning of his second week in the

department, he worked out a plan. He figured out the details of it as he rode to work on the subway, newspaper unopened in his hands.

There were four types of patterns. He called them Geometrics, Flowers, Sillies, and Butterflies. Nothing official in those names, God knows. They were his own names for the various types. All of the patterns fell into one or another of those four types. He ignored the solids—white, light blue, dark blue, pink, yellow, light green, dark green, light this, dark that, light, dark, light, dark—and the patterns designed for children. Those he tried not to think about at all. At best they would be a last resort. He would come to them at the end. If he had to. Only if he had to.

Geometrics. For the first week of the plan, this week, he would try to deal only with the Geometrics. He would have to handle what customers were buying, of course, but other than that, he would deal only with the Geometrics.

While he was out on the floor, straightening the stock, picking oakum, as he thought of it, he would straighten only the Geometrics. He would memorize the patterns, study them, learn them, feel them. Concentrate on them. Think about nothing else. Study the colors, name the colors, all those rich exciting names that colors can have. Aquamarine, cerise, puce, mustard, burnt orange, rust, lilac. Great. Great!

That was it. He was saved. He would spend the day, no, the week, looking for aquamarine, cerise, puce, mustard, burnt orange, rust, lilac.

The morning went quickly that day. He looked for colors, debated with himself at great length and with greater eloquence over the proper name for the exact color of that stripe. Orange? No. Closer to peach. Well, maybe, but not a ripe peach. A ripe peach would have a fuller, richer color than that. If this is a peach, it must have been hidden from the direct rays of the sun by a large leaf. The color was too pale, too thin, too lacking in intensity. Ah, but then could it properly be called peach at all, if that were the case?

And the morning passed.

In the afternoon, he grew a little tired of the colors. It took more mental effort than he had anticipated to keep up the search and the naming of the colors and the arguments over the correctness of the names. He hadn't thought at first that it would be so difficult to concentrate on them.

But it was. By the time he left the store that day, his head was swirling with huge blotches of nameless colors, shapeless monsters of refracted light, that blurred into each other and swam at him sullenly from somewhere behind his eyes.

The next morning he gritted his teeth, tightened his jaw, and resisted the impulse to drop the Geometrics and go on to the Flowers. No, the Flowers would have to wait until next week. This week was for Geometrics. He wasn't done with them yet. Yes, he was going to get the better of them. Yes, he was. He *was*.

As soon as he started that day, he headed directly for the Geometrics. Don't let yourself be enticed by the Flowers. They're for next week.

One of the patterns he had classified as a Geometric was called Pinafore Plaid. Yes, ma'am? No, sorry, only in blue and beige. No, ma'am. King-size pillowcases? In the blue? No, ma'am, sorry, out of stock.

Pinafore Plaid. Scotland. Gilbert and Sullivan.

What else? Pinafore dresses. More. What? I am the captain of the Pinafore, and a right good captain too. Dah-dah-dah-dah . . . How does that go? And I'm never ever sick at sea. What, never? No, never! What, never? Well . . .

Hardly ever.

Sick at sea. Picking oakum. Straightening the stock. Christ, won't it ever be six o'clock?

He started on the Flowers the next morning.

Roses. Yellow roses, red roses. Daisies. Fields of daisies. Yellow rose of Texas. Fields of poppies. Jesus! No, keep at it. Keep at it. Keep at it.

Roses. Rosé wine. Portugal. The roses on the campus back when he was in college. Back when he was in college. God, he'd never pictured it like this. No! Keep at it. Roses. Roses. Rosey cheeks. Rosie O'Grady. Rosey . . . Many a rose-lipped maiden. And many a light-foot lad. With rue my heart is laden. With rue my heart is laden. With rue my heart is . . .

"Honey, look, I know it's boring and you're on your feet all day, but it can't really be that bad. After all, other people do it all their lives."

"I'm not other people."

"Yes, but it's only a temporary job. And, besides, it's a *job*! You should be glad to be working."

"I know."

"It's just that you're tired and you're standing on your feet all day and you're not used to it. That's all. That's all it is."

"I know."

"Just think of it as a job. And it's not like teaching, remember. When you leave the store, you leave it all there behind you. You don't have to be bringing the work home with you the way you did when you were teaching. Think of it that way."

"Okay."

"Good. Now, come on, don't think about it anymore. Let's get to bed. I'll massage your back for you."

"Okay."

The next day he couldn't go back to his plan, couldn't stand to look at the Flowers at all.

The day passed in a gray nightmare, brain soft, hands trembling—slightly, but trembling—a dampness all around the collar of his shirt, tiny hairs on the backs of his hands tingling, standing up from his skin. The plastic packages of sheets felt clammy.

Evening, long night. And another day.

He forced himself, stomach muscles knotting, to go back to his plan. Go back to the Flowers, stick to the plan you made, it's the only way.

The heat in the department was oppressive, heavy. Like a hothouse. The air was thick, steamy, tropical. Perfect for flowers. Flowers.

Roses again. Daisies. Lilacs. Narcissus. Oh God, not Narcissus. Not him, looking at himself in the water. Falling in love. Seeing himself so clearly that . . .

George's hands were trembling violently as he whirled away from the narcissus sheets. The long stems, the long narrow leaves, were pointing at him, reaching out for him.

He spent half an hour in the men's room, sitting, hunched over, arms wrapped tight around his belly, shaking, fingers knotted into his shirt. Nobody missed him.

It wasn't working. But it had to work. The plan had to work.

Somehow the week passed.

The following Monday he made up his mind to go on to what he called the Sillies. Sheets with a tiger's face and stripes all over them. Sheets with a drawing of a grinning cat. Sheets with a constantly repeated, badly executed, medieval scene, hares endlessly leaping away from hunters, a unicorn constantly peering from behind a tree.

Unicorns. Now there was something to think about. There was a shop on Greenwich Avenue in the Village that sold only things with a unicorn design. Commercial, but kind of nice. Wonder if they have these sheets.

Never mind the cat and the tiger. Think about the unicorn. Careful, he told it. Stay behind the tree. They're hunting for you. Oh, but they can never . . . No, wait, that's only one of the legends. In others . . .

It screamed. The unicorn screamed, leaped, twisted in the air, landed heavily, one thin fragile leg bent beneath it. It pitched forward, eyes wide, terrified. A tiny spot of crimson, just a red dot, appeared on its pure white chest. The unicorn's head went down, snapped up again. The spot, the red spot, was larger, glistening, wet, growing larger as he watched. Scarlet blood pumped, pulsed, from the center of the stain, ran in a thin trickle through the coarse white hair. It stained the pure white, ran in a jagged broken line down one of the unicorn's forelegs. One hoof, delicate, fragile, pawed desperately at the ground, seeking balance. The unicorn's head came up again, eyes blazing this time. Its hoof found solid ground. It lurched, heaved, and was standing. It tossed its head, white mane flying.

Blood pumped from the hole in its chest. It tossed its head again and the dazzling sun glinted off its horn.

The pounding of its frantic hooves echoed in his head, matched the thumping of his heart. He closed his eyes, tightened his fingertip grasp on the edge of the display shelf. The glass was cold on his fingers.

He was gone almost an hour after that. When he returned, the supervisor looked curiously and disapprovingly at him but said nothing. He stayed away from the floor for the rest of the day, stayed close to his cash register, tried not to look at what the customers were buying. One woman bought a unicorn and he charged her the wrong price because his eyes misted over and the numbers blurred when he looked it up in the price list.

"Do you think they'll keep you on after the white sale is over?"

"I don't know."

"It would be nice if you did get to stay. At least we'd have that money coming in. And you can start looking for something else in the meanwhile. But, you know, we should really buy a few things we need while you're still entitled to a discount. Don't you think so? In fact, we could get a new set of sheets. Come on, don't look like that. Anyway, we need them. And at least, after looking at sheets for so long and selling them to everybody else, you should have new sheets yourself. Don't you think so? . . . Don't you think so?"

Butterflies today.

Yellow, beige, blue, green, orange. Large and small, swarms of them, swirling, circling around his head, chirping like hungry birds. Crazy. Crazy. Butterflies don't make any sound. They don't. They don't! Christ, butterflies, don't make any sound!

"Well, don't you have any in the stockroom?"
"No, ma'am."
"But the girl told me on the phone that you had them."
"Well, I don't know what anybody else told you, ma'am, but the fact is it's out of stock."
"But why would the girl tell me you had it if you didn't?"
"I really don't know, ma'am."
"Well, I certainly wouldn't have come all the way down here if I'd known this was going to happen. Why would the girl tell me a thing like that?"
"Ma'am, if you talked to the Order Department, they would automatically tell you we have it if the item is in the sale catalogue. Did you talk to the Order Department or to someone here on the selling floor?"
"I . . . I'm sure it must have been here. When I called, I said, 'Give me Linens.'"
"Or give me death."
"What?"
"Nothing."

Home.
Shivering, hands damp, eyes itchy, swollen. His back ached, the muscles in the calves of his legs were in hard tight knots, sore to the touch. One of his toes was cramped and painful.

Dear God, please let me sleep tonight. Please. I'll stick it out to the end. Please just let me sleep. It's easier during the day if I get some sleep at night. At first I thought it would be easier if I was exhausted from lack of sleep, half unconscious. It's not. I need to sleep. I have to sleep.

He was alone. She was asleep already.

The pillow whooshed softly up around his head. His eyes were open, staring, unseeing in the dark. He moved, shifted his weight, and felt the smooth cold sheets against his body.

Something touched his ear in the dark.

Childlike, shivering, he lay stiffly straight in the bed, heels hooked on the bottom edge of the mattress. With icy fingers, he tugged the covers up to his chin, tucked them in tight against his neck.

It moved against his cheek, fluttered, and was gone.

His head snapped to the side, cheek against the pillow, pressed into it.

It touched his other ear in the dark.

He shuddered. A bead of cold sweat ran, like the tip of an icicle, down his side.

He pressed his body down, down, muscles trembling with the strain, into the mattress. His eyes were squeezed shut.

It touched an eyelash, lightly, like a whisper with fingers. His eyes flew open, as if that could brush it away, ward it off.

Then it touched his nose. No. No, it was another. Still another touched his cheek. His lip. Just brushed against his lip.

Then he heard them. They chirped like hungry birds, rising up from the sheets he clutched so tightly, from the pillowcase that cradled his head.

They were under the sheets now. They were in the

sheets. They were in the bed with him.

Beaks, sharp, pointed, nipped at his flesh, toes, stomach, arm, the back of his neck crushed into the pillow. Their beaks were sharp. They were chirping, hungry, nipping into him, breaking the skin, he could feel them all over his body, in the bed with him.

With a scream choking him, filling his throat, he lurched up, flinging the covers, the sheets, off his body. He sat up and screamed silently, mouth open, wrapped in thick wet darkness, alone.

The pain shot through his body. He twisted, unable to escape it, unable to move off the bed. They were walking on his legs, his back, but the pain drew his eyes to his chest. There, against the gray whiteness of his chest in the dark, the even darker stain pumped, pulsed, grew larger, and ran down his body onto his legs, and slowly soaked into the sheets.

MY FATHER'S HEAD

by

Timothy Robert Sullivan

I pray that Father is already dead. His dim form, blurred by the driving rain, is barely discernible as I approach the muddy hill. Behind him, at the summit, the hill's lone *natoca'abor* tree cowers before the storm, a tendril snaking about his narrow chest.

The tree, I know, is a heat seeker. I renew my prayer. I pray not only for myself, but for my son Abissan as well, that he will see nothing from below, where he is sheltered in a copse with the animals.

No human may see; it is the law.

Father's arm waves, as if to ward me away, and for a terrible moment I fear he is still alive. A thrill of nausea forces a bitter taste to the back of my throat, but I swallow the bile. The movement, I see, is too regular to be the gesture of a dying man. Surely it is the effect of the savage wind, a result of the tree's swaying, and nothing more.

I am nearer now. Squinting through the rain, I study the once-beloved face. It is gray, mottled, bloodless. Water streams from lank white rags that were his hair and beard. My father is dead.

I am relieved, reassured. This is a shadow, a ghost of the awesome man who took me hunting for *dra* when I was twelve years of age. Straight, proud, clean-limbed, then. A strong man. A good man.

A ruin now.

And yet I hesitate, staring at the gaunt figure as it bends gently with the groaning old *natoca'abor*. I begin to see a resemblance to Father's once graceful physique, and, corroded by time and dissipation though they are, the cast of his handsome features. If his eyes were open, I could not do the thing before me.

Now I am close enough to touch him. I hold his stiffening body in my arms, the tendril tensing against me as it senses my warmth.

Although I feel I should, I do not weep. It is better this way.

I shout over the howling wind:

"Father, forgive me. It must be done, at last. . . ." My voice trails away into the furious elements.

I draw my blade with my right hand. My left holds my father's sopping, stringy hair. I cut into the neck. The flesh is soft and yielding, and there is not as much blood as I expected—most of it washes away in the rain—but the smell is strong. I brace my feet against the tree's gnarled, knee-high roots, and press until I feel the spine snap at the base of the skull.

The sound of breaking bone is obscured by a thunderclap. I stumble awkwardly against the tree, bumping the corpse. My father falls forward, one waving arm encircling me in a horrid embrace. The red stump of his neck swings close to my face, but I quickly extricate myself, still holding the hair of his head in my left hand. With a single slice of my tarnished blade, I sever the tendril, and the body sags to the slime.

It is done.

Numbed physically and mentally, as much by the foul weather as by this rite of manhood, I start down the hill with my father's head. I slip as I make my way through the mud toward the copse where Abissan and the beasts hide from the storm. The boles of two crossed *jarlagor* trees shudder as I duck under them, entering a dripping cave of foliage. Abissan is huddled inside with the three *muras*, who lie on their massive, shaggy limbs like dwarfed versions of themselves. They cluck as they sense my presence.

There is a worried look on my son's unlined face. He stares at the head.

"You've done it," he says, a note of uncertainty—not sorrow—making his voice tremulous. I cannot blame him; his whole life has been spent in the shadow of my disgrace. "You've finally done it, Jarrass."

"Yes," I reply, wishing just this once he had called me Father. "But I didn't kill him. He was already dead."

"It doesn't matter," Abissan says, frowning, "as long as you have the head."

He remains where he is, coiled as if he will spring and run away. As though he is afraid of the head.

"Do you think it can hurt you?" I ask, unable to resist taunting him. There is far too much animosity between us for me to calm him in a kinder way.

He looks at me through eyes that sear with hatred. Beautiful, clear eyes—his mother's. I must watch him. His time is at hand; he is seventeen, and will soon no longer be a virgin. Then he will come after me . . . as I went after Father eighteen years ago.

"Don't be afraid of the dead," I tell him. "Only the living. The dead can do nothing to you."

I rummage through my saddlebag until I find a sack, made of woven *mi'itor* fibers and treated with waterproofing wax. I have brought it along for another purpose, but it will serve to carry my father's head. With my free hand, I open the sack. I carefully place the head inside it.

My impression of the head now is of something barely human. It is a strange, pale thing, a gruesome bust designed and executed by a sick artist. Twisting up the end of the sack, I tie it to my saddle horn.

The *muras* croak as I flick my crop across their hunched flanks to make them rise.

"You want to go *now?*" my son demands. "We need shelter for the night—we can't keep going in this storm."

"We must take the head to your mother."

Now?"

"We can be there in just a few days," I say. "The sooner the better . . . after eighteen years."

Abissan is apparently satisfied with this explanation. He would have preferred that I kill Father, of course, but he really didn't expect anything to happen—and neither did I. Now that I have actually decapitated the old man, he is uneasy. The sight of a severed human head has temporarily subdued even his youthfully aggressive spirit. I must act before his nerve returns.

Leading the animals, I go back out into the open. The storm howls like a thousand damned souls, and the *muras* are not so anxious to come out as they were to go in. But by alternately pulling at their reins and cajoling them with a *bu'ulafor* root, I bring them out into the lashing rain. I am drenched to the bone, but it is imperative for us to be on our way. Still, I must not allow Abissan to see how anxious I am; all his suspicions must be diverted.

"Lead the way," I tell him as we mount the *muras*.

"I can't, Jarrass," he says. "I'm lost." And well he should be. He has not been to his mother's house since he was six years old. That is one tradition I didn't break, though Femalwen raved and wept and cursed me over Abissan's wails. I had not killed the child's grandfather, she said, so I had no right to raise him. Two males, sharing the same seed and capable of procreation, cannot exist in the same family under the law. But a male child on Newth must learn about his short life from a man—his father. The law says that too.

The law.

By raising Abissan I hoped to make him understand more than what is required by law.

I point toward the undulating forest. It seems to encroach upon the muddy hill even more closely than it did an hour ago, when we traced Father to this lonely, stormy place.

"Shouldn't we bury Grandfather's body first?" Abissan shouts over the wind.

"He would not have wanted that," I say. Abissan never knew Father, of course, so he must accept what I tell him. "Your grandfather would rather be one with the world of Newth, crumbling into its soil."

My son nods.

We flick the reins, and our *muras* lean into the pelting rain, the third trailing as a pack animal. We plod through the mud toward the nearby forest. As we ride, our cowled heads pulled down to our chests, I have a moment to consider my course. If a single detail of my plan fails, I am a dead man. But if all goes well, I will escape this world with my life . . . and without having killed my father.

Still, Father would be alive now if I hadn't come here. The forest people—the Calcitu'ua—might have let him remain with them. They harbored him in his last days, until he ran away to the muddy hill where he died. Or did the Calcitu'ua cast him out, to avoid trouble with me?

It is difficult to say; their leader, Nath, hates Man, but tolerates individual men. My father and I were always welcome among his people. I have not been to their village in years, however, due to Abissan's passionate loathing for all forest people.

"It's been a very long time since you've seen my mother, hasn't it, Jarrass?" Abissan asks. "What if—if she's not there anymore?"

"You mean, 'What if she's dead?' don't you?" I say. "Well, it's not likely. Your mother is one of those fortunate few women who survived the bloodrot. Nothing will kill her in her prime. I imagine you'll have your birthright very soon."

Abissan says nothing as we ride through the

pounding rain, toward the black branches of the nearby forest. His resentment will not be assuaged by mere consoling words. He has lived all his young life as an outcast—the son of a man who did not act "honorably"; who did not perform this vaunted rite of manhood—and the values I have tried to impart to him have become as odious as their teacher. He sneers at the concept of mercy. All that Homeworld book talk of humanism he sees as the cowardly philosophy that has poisoned his life from the beginning. Dear Father, the "love of man," which you so zealously preached, bears in your grandchild only the bitter fruit of hatred.

I had my doubts, too, when I was Abissan's age. Confused, angry at Father for some disciplinary slight, I went to Femalwen's house. How could I have known she would select me from her stable of young men? There were seven others in her kitchen that night. I drank too much, listening to the suitors' intoxicated boasts and self-consciously boisterous laughter. When she appeared, her voluptuous glory stilled them. And when the virago took me by the hand and led me out of the kitchen toward her bedroom, I heard a chorus of cheers from my rivals. Their fathers would live a little longer.

Once in her bedroom, there was no arguing with Femalwen; she was too much a woman. In my lust I pushed out of my mind all thoughts of the father who had cared for me, who had taught me of the larger world beyond Newth.

Clearly, I recall the gray light of dawn following that night of pleasure. As reason emerged from the incomprehensible pattern of my dreams, I realized that the rite of manhood had begun. Like a somnambulist, I rose and dressed myself, went to the stable, and saddled my *mura*. I rode toward my father's tent, my head throbbing from the excesses of my wedding night. I knew what must be done, but it seemed unreal. As the sun rose, my heart beat more and more wildly.

I drew nearer to his camp, my panic growing. Perhaps I could provoke him into an argument, I reasoned desperately. That would make it easier. If he became angry and tried to punish me for staying out all night, I might be able to do it.

But he waited patiently on a hammock of *ota*-film, reading a book.

"Jarrass, where have you been?" he asked me. "I've been worried about you."

"When I didn't answer, he asked me what was wrong.

I drew my blade, then so shiny and new. I trembled so much I thought I would drop it.

His heat pistol was on the book chest behind him, but he made no move toward it. Instead, he looked me right in the eye, and said:

"So you're no longer a virgin."

His image became insubstantial as the hot tears flooded my eyes. I cried and threw the knife down.

"Run, Father! Run—or kill me!" I shouted. "I have to! I have to! ... But I can't."

As I fell to my knees, he put his hand on my shoulder, and gave me a cloth to dry my eyes. I looked up at his strong face, into his clear, dark eyes, and knew that I could not kill him.

"I'll have to go away, Jarrass," he said. "And you'll have to come after me sooner or later. That is apparently our destiny. I killed your grandfather when

I was your age, and I anticipated the same end. Easier for both of us, perhaps, had you done it! Still, it would have been wrong."

He gathered a few essentials, took up his heat pistol, and opened the flap of the tent. From the threshold, he said:

"Remember the words from the book, from the Homeworld, the words that tell us how to be human. Among them is the command, 'Thou shalt not kill.'"

Then he was gone. Eighteen years he would spend on the run, no doubt believing he deserved it for murdering his own father. I suppose he thought the pressure of society would eventually coerce me into chasing him. To hide from me, he went deeper into the forest.

And now the dark limbs of that same forest beckon my son and me into their moldy world. The curtain of rain thins as we are shielded from the elements somewhat by the restless trees. There is nothing to encourage Homeworld theology in this dank, unlighted place.

Involuntarily, I shake my head, remembering that my father's head is in the sack tied to my saddlebag. I could have put it on the pack animal, of course, but I feel it is wise to carry it to Femalwen myself, so that she and Abissan will believe in me . . . after all these years.

I did not set out to kill him, but I would have, rather than let him die of exposure. I only came to tell him of my plan. When I found him dead . . .

"Abissan," I say, to take my mind off what I have done, "the forest is a str—" My words are cut short as my *mura* rears back, clucking in fright. I am nearly thrown, but manage to calm my mount.

We are surrounded by forest people—the Calcitu'ua—their yellow eyes staring at us from furry heads, their pronged weapons poised for the thrust.

They are silent.

I raise my hand in a peaceful gesture; I know what they want. Peripherally, I see Abissan draw his heat pistol.

"Put that away!" My voice rings out in this enclosed area, out of the wind and rain.

Reluctantly, Abissan does as I say, holstering the blue-steel weapon. Sickened, I realize that he might very well have killed one or more of the Calcitu'ua if I hadn't intervened.

The leader stares at him, tail curling and straightening, curling and straightening. This is Nath, whom I knew long ago. He is a cunning fellow. Without taking his eyes off Abissan, he advances. I can see the pink wound slashing the side of his gray face as he comes closer. They say he received the wound in a battle against Man many years ago. I don't really know if there is any truth to the rumor, but I do know that Nath is not a friend to man, and never has been. It was he who led his people against those Calcitu'ua who wanted to live among humans, back when our ancestors tried so unsuccessfully to impose their Terran sense of order and industry on Newth.

His chief opponent, Tru'ug, abides in Femalwen's house to this day. Among the Calcitu'ua, the animosity incurred by Tru'ug has not diminished, as have the details of the war, passed down orally for three generations. Facts have gradually been superseded by myth as the tribes who once cooperated with the Terrans returned to the forest over the years, while the humans were forced to adapt to Newth. Man's customs changed as he struggled to survive the planet's only gift—the bloodrot.

Thus, Nath is vindicated in his old age. He is a great hero to his people.

He beckons for us to follow. We have no chance to dispute his command. The reins of our *muras* are gripped, and we are led to their village, through the twisting branches of the forest.

We are there within the hour. The village is as I remember it—a maze of living *na'aor*. Neither plant nor animal, but greater than either, according to Calcitu'uan belief. Like hummocks among the dripping trees, the inhabited hives roll softly one against the other. Smoke curls out of partially open clefts in the furrows of the forest people's homes, rising from fires inside them.

"Why did you let them bring us here?" Abissan demands, as we pick our way between the hives.

"They only want to know if it's done," I say. "Your grandfather lived here, you know. They want me to tell them if . . . if he's dead."

"Just the same, I'm glad we have our heat pistols." As he is about to pat his holster, a small, hairy hand snatches Abissan's weapon. My son grabs at empty air. He makes a move toward the diminutive thief, but the heat pistol is tossed to Nath.

Snatching it out of the air, Nath removes the magazine. He stares at me.

"My Jarrass will not shoot?" he asks.

"No. I won't shoot."

"Then give *me* your pistol!" Abissan shouts.

"Abissan!"

Angry, I yank his cloak, pulling his face toward mine. I see his anger drain, as if mine absorbed it. It is replaced by fear in his young eyes—the bright, furtive eyes of a hunted animal. I can almost read his mind. Has Jarrass arranged this situation with Nath somehow? he wonders. Is his own father going to kill him here in the wilderness, so no one can dispute the false account of his death?

"They are angry at you," I say, to quell his doubt. "You've given them good reason to kill you. Better be quiet."

I relax my hold on him. He makes an awkward attempt at taking my pistol. I catch his wrist, gripping it like a vise.

He backs off, and I release him.

"I'd like to kill them all," he says in a voice simultaneously carrying conviction and diffidence. "I'd like to burn this pesthole right out of the f—"

Startled, I see a carpet of matted gray fur swarm over my son, knocking him off his mount. He is pinned to the ground, grunting, by half a dozen Calcitu'ua. Nath, barely a meter tall, scampers up and perches on his chest. The old forest man slips the magazine back into the pistol and toys with it, staring down at Abissan.

"My Jarrass," he says, "what is to be done with this, your young self?" Nath refers to Abissan in the Calcitu'uan way, as a part of the parent. It is only because I know Nath that my son is still alive, surely. Nath waits for me to give him a sign.

I swing my leg over my saddle and dismount. Untying the sack from my saddle horn, I set it on the damp, rich soil. I glance at Abissan, who stares back at me in horrified fascination. The possibility that I might kill him is still in his mind. That he might die rather than me.

I ask myself why my son doesn't know I love him.

Stooping, I open the sack, feeling inside until I touch Father's scalp. I grip his long locks firmly and yank his head out, holding it high for all to see. Slowly it turns, suspended from a rope of white hair. It is cyanotic, shriveled; black drops collect on the severed neck and fall to the ground. Still, my father is recognizable in it.

There is a muffled gasp, then a babel of high voices as the forest people see my father's head. Nath begins to mutter, vowel sounds flowing together, like a recording of a human voice played backward at high speed—a Calcitu'uan prayer.

"This is my father's head," I say. "I have taken it from his body."

Silence, punctuated by the soft collisions of raindrops falling from the treetops.

"It is our way," I continue. "My son will soon do the same to me. If he does not it will bring disgrace on many people—disgrace and dishonor. I plead with you to let him live."

Nath peers at me from his perch on Abissan's chest, yellow eyes gleaming.

"My Jarrass wishes . . . to die?"

"No. But I want my son to live."

Nath ponders this. At last he nods to Abissan's captors. They rise. Abissan flexes his fingers as his limbs are freed, as if he is so full of rage he will leap up and destroy everything he sees. But Nath's long, horny toes still curve over his rib cage, and the yellow eyes burn unblinking into his own. He does not move.

A sonorous hum rises from a single Calcitu'uan

throat. It is joined by others until the entire village harmonizes. One by one, clefts open in the hives, responding to the vibration of the voices. In a few moments, my son and I are alone with Nath.

The small humanoid form leaps from Abissan's prone body, landing softly in the mulch beside me. Nath looks up at my father's head.

"My Jarrass," he says. "You go into the camp of my enemy."

"And are you my friend?" I ask. "My father thought you were his friend, and you turned him out in the storm."

He gazes into my eyes intently.

"It was as he wished," Nath says at last. Again, he looks at the head. "It was as he wished."

I don't know whether to believe this sly old forest man or not. I let it pass.

"Tru'ug is not my Jarrass's friend," Nath says. "He is friend not to Calcitu'uan, not to Man."

"He's been with Femalwen a long time."

"He gives nothing," Nath says, turning toward a small, round hive. "Watch him."

He hums, a lovely, wavering, sustained song. A bubble swells in the seamless mound of his house, thinning until it is clear. The edges of a furrowless cleft bulge like a pair of lips and slowly open.

Nath is gone.

I put my father's head back into the sack and tie it to my saddlebag. The *muras* are restless, shifting from side to side.

Abissan rises, brushing himself off, flushed with embarrassment. The little men with tails have made a fool of him.

"Let's go," I say.

"I'm not going anywhere without my heat pistol," he says.

"Do you think they'll give it back to you now, so you can kill them all?"

"We can't go without that pistol," he says stubbornly.

"We have to." The heat pistol is an incalculable loss, of course. It is perhaps the most valuable possession a Newthian can have. Neither the pistols nor the heat magazines that power them have been manufactured on this world since before I was born. What prestige they bring us! With them a man commands almost as much respect as a full-grown woman . . . or is it just fear?

"Come on," I say, waiting for Abissan. I can see that he is shaken, his ego badly bruised. I don't like to see him humiliated, but I know it's good for him. "Come on before Nath changes his mind."

Stealing furtive glances around him, Abissan goes to his *mura* and mounts up. We ride between the hives, making our way out of the village.

"Don't hate the forest people," I say after we have gone on for some time in silence. "Remember that this was their world before Man came."

"It isn't theirs now."

"More than it was a year ago," I reply, "and still more than the year before that . . . it will all be theirs again someday."

"Why?" Abissan demands. "Because our women die young? My generation may be the first to have girl children without the bloodrot."

"They've always said that," I reply. "That's why the

older generation of males is killed off, instead of the baby boys or the young men."

"Well, they also claim there is a way to make children without women."

"On some worlds, perhaps, but not on Newth," I say, trying to clarify the facts for him for the thousandth time. "Here we rely on women to bear children, and most of the women die when they reach puberty. The bloodrot is an overproduction of certain cells, originally a defense against some disease. It is somehow triggered by a girl's first menstruation."

"So the men must die," Abissan says, finishing my little speech.

"Unless their sons spare them." But I am thinking that the decapitation of my father seemed as hideous as murdering him. It is something I will never forget, I am certain. I can feel my father's dead flesh, see and smell the blood, hear the snap of his spinal column. I remind myself that if it was monstrous, it was also the only way . . . that it *is* the only way . . . that Father would have understood.

Abissan's face is blanched. He has been through a great deal today, perhaps too much for a boy of his age. The end of his disgrace is what he hopes for, the dream that makes him hang on through all the horror. Of course, he will never be free, as he imagines. His is the soul of the fugitive. Someday he will learn that he is always going to be on the run, whether he is with me or not. He is quiet as we ride.

It comforts me to know I have saved his life; I cannot help wondering how he feels about it. Will he revile me a little less from now on? Or even more?

The storm does not abate. We follow the forest path,

though occasionally we wander outside its protection for one reason or another. At these times, predatory *re'evas* circle above, in spite of the storm, their scaly wings slick with rain as they swoop and soar. They smell the flesh of my father's head.

At times the forest is impassable. Once, when I try to hack through a wall of vegetation, a writhing branch suddenly lashes out, narrowly missing my eye. I back away. Abissan suggests I use my heat pistol, but I remind him there is only one pistol now, and it will be easier to go around, anyhow. We are not scaled or furred, nor do we hum well; we will go where the way is unobstructed.

He mumbles something as I mount up, but I cannot hear what he is saying.

The animate growths are sluggish and turgid because of all the rain. Through the fat vines and creepers I occasionally see the yellow eyes of Calcitu'ua. Each time, when I look again, they are gone.

We come out of the forest to travel by a river. Sheets of rain greet us, striking a thousand specks of spattering gray in the water. Since the forest hangs over the river on one side, we ford it. On the far side is a carpet of fungus stretching for several kilometers. A few meters from the river it rolls up into a huge dripping crest, a frozen wave that is melting. The crest extends by the riverbank as far as we can see through the haze of rain. There is barely room enough for us to slosh along between the fungus and the rippling water.

Drawn into myself more and more, partly because it is so hard to talk over the raging storm, I consider the unexpected appearance of Nath and his followers. Did Father have something to do with it? Could he have been protecting me, even after death? Could he have asked Nath to capture us and frighten the boy, so that I could "save" him?

Doubtful, but what else could have prompted the Calcitu'ua to do it?

It is a conundrum—a riddle without an answer. The sort of thing I so easily become preoccupied with. But there is no time for it; to avoid such an obsession, I try to engage Abissan in conversation. The least he can do is talk to me, now that I've saved his life. I make some innocuous comment about the rain.

"Jarrass, do you ever wish I was born a girl?" he asks. He has not heard my comment. Perhaps the incident with the forest men has given him pause.

"No," I say. "Once I did, but in the end I decided that the grief I would have suffered when my twelve-year-old daughter died of the bloodrot is far worse than knowing my son must try to kill me."

"*Try* to kill you?" Abissan sneers. "No one who has sons escapes lawful execution."

"Some do," I say, looking down at the sack.

"My grandfather is the only one I know of."

"There are . . . others."

"Those who kill their sons first," he says. "But they are criminals, to be hunted down like animals and exterminated."

I do not mention those who escape without killing anyone, those who have the means to get off-world . . . a rare thing even for the wealthy, because of the time element. I say nothing more, for if Abissan suspected my plan things would become infinitely more difficult. My son and I are now on better terms than we have been in years. I won't press my luck.

Abissan is a very clever boy. . . . I am reminded of his first hunting kill, five years ago . . . when he was only twelve. He outflanked me to head off a *dra* buck, coolly facing its charge. With a quick series of blasts from his heat pistol, he dropped it in its furious, snorting charge. Half the beast was burned to cinders, of course—hardly an artful kill—but we ate what was left for a long time afterward.

He could outflank me again, lose his virginity when I'm not watching him, and come after me . . . to do the job . . . to kill me.

But the hungry bleat of the *re'evas* wrenches me back to the present. I am reminded that the time when Abissan will be eligible to kill me is still far off, at least in terms of distance. I will be gone before he has the opportunity to penetrate a woman . . . unless Femalwen has changed, and now enjoys the company of other ladies. With all her riches and social position, I doubt it . . . you might even say I'm staking my life on it.

There is something on my side now, however, that I didn't have before. My son owes me his life, and he believes I have decapitated Father to belatedly restore the family honor. When he sees why I have really done it, I am afraid our uneasy peace will be at an end.

By that time, though, there will be nothing Abissan can do—unless he chases me to the stars.

The stars, where Newth and its barbaric customs will shrink to insignificance.

"Is not a man greater than a world?" I say, thinking aloud.

"What?" Abissan asks.

"I'm paraphrasing a quote from Emerson," I say. "I

read the original in one of the books your grandfather left when he . . ."

"Oh," Abissan replies. But he does not offer his usual disdainful sneer. For the first time in his life he has seen me practice what I preach: I begged for my son's life even though I knew he would try to kill me.

"It seems strange that you wanted to take the head to Mother so quickly," Abissan says, after awhile.

"The sooner the better," I reply, "before the head is putrescent." This attempt to allay Abissan's suspicions seems to work.

My real reason for hurrying is that the ship will come in just a few days—the first Terran ship to visit Newth in twenty-one years. When the last one arrived, I was only fourteen; there will not be another until I am fifty-six . . . if I live to be fifty-six.

"Mother will be happy to see it, won't she?" Abissan asks, still speaking of the head.

"There are many heads on the thorn spikes of her house. One more or less will make little difference to her. She will probably be pleased to see you, though."

"Why did you take me from her, Jarrass?"

"Why? Because I wanted to bring you up according to law."

"But you had already defied the law."

"Only in a matter of conscience."

"Conscience?" he says. "I am an outcast because of your conscience." For a moment his face seems scarred with hate and resentment again, his eyes regaining the feral spark of the killer—there is the hint of a demon behind them. I cannot blame him; his life has been a nightmare. Still, I always tried to make him see why I couldn't kill Father. My motives were not entirely self-serving, I am convinced. I have racked myself with doubt, having come to know through a thousand sleepless nights why I did what I did and why I feel as I do. There is only one way to explain it to my son.

"I hoped to make you love me," I say, "like I loved my father."

Abissan looks at me in a way I haven't seen since he was small, since he first understood why we never live in any particular place for long, since he first realized why he couldn't have friends, like the children we saw from time to time playing at the edge of the forest. He has never forgiven me for these things.

But now he is wavering a little, I think.

It pleases me that I might leave Newth with my son sympathetic to, perhaps even sharing, my beliefs. Or is that too much to hope for?

On the last leg of the journey the river widens into a broad marsh. *Otas* spin a film across the patches of rippling water, raindrops like jewels on their spines and ridges. They dance between the spear-tipped aquatic plants on their retractable limbs, searching for food. I see one of them bob; it emerges with a small, wheezing creature in its jaws.

Later, in the distance, we spy a small party of Calcitu'ua. Their hunting prongs are sheathed, and they are building a fire. In their midst is the carcass of an *ota*. One of the forest people is fashioning a net from the animal's glutinous film, scooping the stuff out of a sac at its severed throat. We wave to them as we pass. Their high-pitched voices carry over the stinging, soaking wind for a moment, as they call to us. Soon the sounds fade and are gone.

Only the storm can be heard.

Now, just before the sky darkens completely, we catch sight of Femalwen's house. The bristling, swelling *na'aor* structure is nearly cut off completely by the forest, the heat-seeking trees threatening to choke it, bury it alive. As we cut through their clutching tendrils, we can see the thorn spikes protruding from the roof. Impaled on several of them are the remains of human heads—the fathers of her lovers. Many of the heads have fallen, the skulls littering the mossy ground the house grows from, like round, white stones.

"What a woman my mother must be," Abissan says. He is old enough to appreciate a woman's house now, the first time he has seen one since he was a child.

Thunder grumbles overhead as we hack our way through the last few meters of forest. At the front cleft of the house we dismount and set the *muras* to resting in the inadequate shelter its bulk provides. While I am untying the sack, which is now discolored and oily, I hear a voice from inside—a high, girlish voice. Has Femalwen assembled a houseful of young women on a whim, or for some social occasion, to unwittingly trip me up at the last moment?

A muffled vibration, and a bubble erupts in the spongy cleft, swelling until it is transparent. Through it a yellow eye stares out. It is a forest man—the high voice was his. Is it Tru'ug? Even he is preferable to a woman under these circumstances. My suspicions seem ridiculous now.

There is a sucking sound as the cleft opens like a wound. Behind it Tru'ug stands, a golden ring from Terra around his neck. From it dangle a number of keys, which open Femalwen's many chests. In his small fists is the divider, still ringing from the blow he struck on its stand. Tru'ug never hums to open the *na'aor*. Some claim he has lost the Calcitu'uan gift—the affinity to *na'aor;* others say he symbolically rejects his heritage by using the metal device instead of his own vocal chords.

The vibration fades, and Tru'ug sets the divider on its metal stand.

"Femalwen is in her rooms," he chirrups.

"Is this how you greet me after all these years, Tru'ug?" I ask. "Like a stranger?"

"Jarrass," he says, nodding politely.

Abissan says nothing. Clearly, he fears the forest man. He has forgotten that he knew Tru'ug when he was small. I make a mental note to remind him of this later, but realize I will probably never have the chance.

"I will take you to Femalwen," Tru'ug says.

"That won't be necessary." Femalwen's regal voice echoes through the dark passageway. She emerges from the bottleneck entrance to an adjacent chamber, a vision of fertility and abundance, her pendulous breasts hanging nearly to her waist, her senuous features cushioned in soft flesh. Immediately, I feel desire stir my loins. She is more beautiful than ever.

"Femalwen," I say. "I've . . . come back."

"Yes," she replies. "The news has preceded you."

I feel the yellow stare of Tru'ug on the back of my neck.

"You've brought one of my sons with you?" She turns toward Abissan, slowly, deliberately.

"Yes," I say. "He is a man now. I thought you would like to see him."

She nods solemnly.

"Where is the head?" she asks.

"Outside, on my *mura*. This is the first time it's been out of my sight since . . ."

"Get the head and be done with it then, Jarrass." Is there a note of sympathy in her voice? Has Femalwen come to understand why I did not kill my father?

Without a word, I turn. Tru'ug strikes the divider, the cleft parts, and I go back out into the driving rain. The *muras* croak unhappily at me as I unfasten the sack.

"Tru'ug," I call through the closing cleft, "please take these animals to shelter."

He gazes at me, his wizened gray face inscrutable in the dim light of the slowly sealing cleft.

"I will take care of them . . . Jarrass," he says, as it closes completely.

I wonder if he would be so civil if he knew he's helping me take advantage of Femalwen, helping me leave Newth. I am certain he would hasten my departure from this world if he did. My personal acquaintance with Nath is enough reason to be cautious with him.

Leaning into the powerful wind, I cross a slippery bed of human skulls. Then I begin climbing a ledge along the bulging side of the house, rain pelting me mercilessly. I brace myself against the spongy stuff, my hand sinking in nearly to the wrist. From my free hand swings the sack.

This house has been growing for many generations—Femalwen's mother and grandmother lived here, as well as all her brothers and short-lived sisters, even her father, when he was a boy—and it is immense. I cannot tell if it is burgeoning out to meet the forest, or if the *natoca'abor* trees are closing in on it. Branches reach for my passing warmth as I edge along the swollen side of the house. Inching my way up, I slip on the wet *na'aor* and nearly fall. My gorge rises as I totter, twenty meters high, over the dark, glistening ground. I swing the sack around to balance myself, and the weight of my father's head pulls me back to safety. The rain stings my eyes as I lean back against the convex *na'aor,* panting for breath. Now that I am so close, I must be more careful than ever. There is a good chance that Femalwen will find out what I am up to, and try to kill me. If I am not careful, I will save her the trouble.

My plan seems almost fruitless to me as I crouch soaking wet on this monstrous, inhabited growth, frail and miserable. Even if I make it to the roof, I ask myself, what then? Will I be able to go through with it?

I must.

At last I gather up strength enough to go on. I renew the climb, and soon I am standing precariously on a knob from which the house's summit is easily accessible. Before me, intermittently visible in the lightning flashes, are thorn spikes as thick as human arms. They protrude from knobs and knots on the curved roof, starkly outlined against the roiling night clouds. Many of them are adorned with skulls, jawbones hanging askew in the pounding rain.

The sound of thunder nears as I find the spike whose point is highest. Purposefully, I move toward it until I can reach out and grab it. Pulling myself up, I straddle the thorn spike. I open the sack. I feel around inside. The flesh of my father's head is slack, oily, unlike skin.

It's not human, I tell myself. I can do it. This is the last thing.

I remove my father's head from the sack.

The face still bears a resemblance to his, though withered and blue, drawn to the very bone where the flesh does not hang in folds. My eyes water with something other than rain.

"Forgive me, Father," I say. "There is no other way."

Give me courage, I pray.

I lift the head as high as I can. Looking down at the thorn spike between my legs, I close my eyes. With all my strength, I force my father's head down on the sharp point.

At the jarring instant of impact I hear a thunderclap—but it might only be in my mind.

For a long moment I stand in the cruel storm, eyes squeezed shut. When I finally open them, I see an alien thing impaled on a thorn spike, blue-gray and terrible in the lightning flashes. In it there is the barest ghost of my father's face—and of his soul, it seems to me for an awful moment.

It is finished.... All but one thing. The most dangerous part of my plan, but it will be child's play now. I urge myself to get on with it.

Yet I stand rooted to the spot, unable to look away from the gruesome sight before me, transfixed by the decapitated head, rotten, stinking, of the man who gave me life. Who taught me to read and to hunt. Who taught me about life . . . who loved me.

It was me, I think as if for the first time. I cut off his head. I stuck it on this thorn spike. I . . . I . . . me . . . me . . . So I could get away from Newth. Selfish . . . selfish . . . No matter how long I live, I will never get over this. My heart is a gaping wound, and even if I span the galaxy the wound will not heal.

Look what I have done! Look!

... but at least I didn't murder him.

No, I let him live. I came eighteen years after I was supposed to strike him down, to tell him I had a plan for us to escape Newth ... that we had to get money somehow ... perhaps from Femalwen ... but I never got a chance to talk to him. He ran away. The Calcitu'ua did not expel him. He ran away from me. He ran away from his son, to a *natoca'abor* tree in the storm. I found him there ... and I prayed he was dead ... because I knew what had to be done to ensure that my plan would work.

He made it easy for me.

I turn, making my way across the roof. I do not go back the way I came. I tuck the greasy sack into my cloak and cross over to a thorn spike jutting on the downward slope of the curved roof. Under its basal knob is a furrow, deep and old. I grasp the thorn spike—which is almost horizontal to the ground—and hang. My fingers are numb with the cold and wet as I swing my body into the furrow. I smack into the resilient *na'aor* and scramble inside.

On my belly, I crawl until I come to what seems in this perfect darkness to be the furrow's end. I poke at the spongy vegetable matter with my fingers. I am rewarded as my hand pops through. Then, with both hands I force the soft stuff apart, contorting my body until I am able to slip one leg through, then the other. I wriggle in up to my chest. There is tremendous pressure; I can hardly breathe. I take one last deep draught of air, pulling myself down until my head is covered. Forcing my way with my legs, I worm deeper into the cleft. My lungs are bursting. I hadn't realized the skin of the house was so thick. As I inch further, I despair to find still more resisting *na'aor*. I am too far in to work my way back—I'd never make it before asphyxiating—I have no choice but to continue. My rib cage feels as if it is about to cave in. A dreadful tingling invades my body.

At last! My feet are free! I squeeze through, dropping into an arterial passageway big enough so that I can stand erect in it. Gulping air, I am about to be on my way to a cell hidden in the house's uppermost reaches, just below the thorn spike where my father's head is impaled. Femalwen never knew, but I found the cell as I roamed incessantly through the arteries of the house while she was entertaining suitors. I still know my way around, even though there is some change in the general shape of the house; growth has been slow. The passageway is wider, and the slots of the cells are stretched and distorted. *Na'aor* doesn't hold still.

Neither does time.

I run to the cell, one among dozens along the artery, but I recognize the right one immediately. I go inside, drawing my blade. The cell is cluttered with odds and ends, like a storage space. Tossing aside tools, broken art objects, moth-eaten *mura* skins, I uncover it: a small chest made of dead, hardened *na'aor,* emblazoned with a bas-relief of naked men. With the point of my blade I force the lock. It resists for a moment, then the lid flies off with a cracking noise, clattering against the detritus on the floor. Heart pounding, I freeze—but there is no one in this part of the house, I tell myself. Still, I listen for a moment.

In the chest there are neatly piled crediscs, good on any world where Terrans are known; there is also jewelry, a hundred scintillant colors winking at me. But best of all are the rare heat magazines—there must be a thousand years worth of energy for my pistol here. I'll be formidably armed while I'm on the run. And I'll be able to sell the magazines to the highest bidder before the ship takes off. It may not come to much of a fortune on the more advanced worlds, but at least it will pay my way to one of them.

I will escape Newth in fire and thunder, if only I can make it through this terrible night.

A sackful of loot will be more than enough . . . and Femalwen will hardly miss what I take. No, I'm fooling myself. She'll miss it. Every bit of it. This is her domain, and not much time will pass before she checks her chest of blood money. When she does, this house will become a tomb for me . . . if I'm fool enough to still be here.

I must keep her busy tonight and flee at dawn.

Backing out of the cell, I turn and jog through the artery, the sack of valuables swinging from my clenched fist. I hesitate at the cleft.

There is another way out, with little or no danger involved: down through the stable. That is where I intend to hide the loot anyway, after Femalwen is asleep—the stable. I would have stashed it in the furrow temporarily, and after she was asleep I would have gone back out and climbed up to get it, taken it to the stable and hidden it in my saddlebag.

But if I go directly to the stable, I will save all those steps . . . and I am so very tired.

The only drawback here is that they are waiting for me, and I have been gone—supposedly up on the roof—a very long time. They will be wondering where I am now. If I am gone much longer . . .

Still, they won't look on the roof to see what is keeping me. It is against the law for any human eye to witness the impaling but my own, the same as the decapitation. And if they should be bold enough to ask (Femalwen might do just that), I will tell them I meditated by my father's head—one final lie. The only thing that could go wrong is if someone is in the stable. But Tru'ug has had more than ample time to attend to the *muras*.

I'm going to risk it.

I hurry along the corridor until it takes a curve, easing down a corkscrew spiral toward the stable. In my haste, I almost run into a well-lighted cell. Voices issue from it. I flatten myself against the yielding wall of the artery, wishing I could control my crazy pulse, the pounding vein in my head.

"She won't last the night," one of the voices says.

"The poor child," says another.

One of Femalwen's daughters. How many has she lost over the years? Ten? Twenty? None of them inherited her immunity to the bloodrot. They never do. My father told me all about it. The lucky genes are carried by males, apparently. At least that was what the Terran report said. But the scientific findings of the Terrans have been reduced to the insane law of Newth. The younger generation of males must kill the older to purify the blood, supposedly. That way the carriers will one day be weeded out.

But when?

There is the sound of soft weeping from the lighted cell. I creep by, while those inside are preoccupied with the child's imminent death.

I meet no one the rest of the way, until I reach the bottleneck opening to the stable. Here I am almost directly on the other side of the house from the main entrance, from the cleft by which Abissan entered Femalwen's house with me.

I steal up to the stable and peer inside.

Muras cluck at me, but no one attends them. Tru'ug is gone, as I hoped. I thread my way through the resting animals, until I find my own querulous *mura*.

I pull the sack from under my cloak and take the goods out of it, stuffing them deep into my saddlebag. Then I toss the sack into the corner. Empty now, the sack that carried my father's head. I will never see it again . . . and I will never look back.

And yet I know this night will always be with me.

I take the divider off its stand; the metal is cold in my hands. I strike it against the stand, and the vibration seems to shake some of the numbness out of me. The cleft opens and I go back out into the storm, which seems to rage more fiercely than ever. I can barely stand in the furious wind.

As best I can, I hurry around the rolling extremities of the house. It lies like a drowned giantess in the unending rain, slick and gleaming in the lightning flashes. *Natoca'abor* tendrils extend ominously toward me from the encroaching forest, sinuous, grasping.

At last I fight my way through the elements to the main-entrance cleft. As a bubble swells from the vibration of the divider, I call out:

"It is done!"

The cleft opens to admit me. Abissan wields the still-ringing divider, his mother behind him. Both of them seem pale, distraught, as though they are afraid of me. I know this is a false impression—a trick of the light, or an effect of exhaustion on my perceptions. They must be in their glory now that it is at long last done.

No one speaks.

"The law . . ." I finally say, ". . . has been observed."

Femalwen takes my hand, gently leading me through corridors that wind like the guts of an animal. My son Abissan is behind us.

But where is Tru'ug?

"I wanted to talk to Tru'ug," I say, cursing my own duplicity. "Where is he?"

Femalwen looks at me with sad, dreaming eyes.

"He's gone to fetch some food and dry clothing for you and Abissan," she says. "He'll be back in a moment."

We come to the slot openings in two cells. I crawl into one, Abissan into the other. Inside, I take off my wet cloak and undergarments, feeling very vulnerable—wet, naked, and fatigued almost beyond endurance.

An alien, chirruping sound—Tru'ug. Though he has abandoned the formal Calcitu'uan tongue, his voice belies his heritage.

A fur garment is handed in to me. I slip gratefully into its warm, dry comfort. Through the slot I see Tru'ug's tail curl spasmodically as Femalwen whispers something I cannot quite make out.

I emerge wearing the dry robe, trying not to reveal tension, trying to act relieved. Femalwen smiles as her son's lithe young body slips out of the adjacent cell. She takes each of us by a hand, and leads us toward the kitchen, her skirts rustling on the *na'aor*.

The kitchen is empty, a dimly lit cave full of unused

benches and long, bare tables. Tru'ug and two servants bring us food, and we eat in silence.

When we are through, Femalwen takes us to the sleeping cells, located above. She shows Abissan to one, and then we go together to her room.

"Good night, Abissan," she calls out. "We'll talk some more tomorrow."

"Good night . . . Mother," he says from the shadows.

Femalwen hesitates a moment, then says:

"Abissan, aren't you going to say good night to your father?"

A long pause. Then, as if from far away:

"Good night . . . Father."

Father. This is the first time my son has called me father in years. I am pleased, on this last night I will ever see him, that he calls me Father. I feel a welling of emotion, but stifle it. Femalwen must not suspect I am leaving in the morning.

Through a winding artery we make our way until we reach Femalwen's room. After all that has happened, I almost dread what I must do now. Almost, but not quite.

Inside Femalwen's bedroom, there is just enough candlelight to see the *ota*-film hammock, stretching weblike throughout the chamber. Beneath it are chests full of clothing and amenities. There is no space for them anywhere else; the room is filled with Femalwen's bed.

We lie down on the *ota*-film. As the soft stuff accommodates itself to our bodies, I remember the two *otas* we saw on our way to this house, the hunter and the hunted. I shake myself out of this reverie. It is exhaustion that makes my mind wander so, I tell myself. Do I even have enough energy to make love to Femalwen? I'd better. She is rubbing my back, her long nails reaching under the fine fur robe I am wearing, scratching playfully. Erotically.

The rest is a dream in which Femalwen's voluminous clothing dissolves. She writhes beneath me wildly, her heavy arms crushing the breath out of me. Then I am thrusting again and again, swollen beyond endurance. A helpless moment, my body seeming to float above hers, anchored only at one exploding nexus. Then—blessed, streaming release.

And there in the quiet, suspended above Femalwen's room on her *ota*-film bed, it occurs to me that dying now would have its advantages. I have not killed my father, though I have mutilated his corpse; my son feels something besides hate for me, I think; and I have just made love to my wife for the first time in many years. I could die with a modicum of serenity right now.

But there is another kind of infinity to know first. The eternities of deep space . . . the endless star fields . . . haunted always by the specter of my father's head.

"You still have the same strong touch," Femalwen says, waking me up. She dangles a meaty leg through a rent in the film, picking up a carafe with her toes. It is followed by two goblets.

"And your capacity for lovemaking is still awesome," I reply. I cannot resist this: "Tell me, Femalwen, why are there no young men awaiting your pleasure down in the kitchen tonight?"

She pours wine from the carafe into the goblets—fine, red wine.

"Did you tire of using their father's heads as paving stones?" I persist.

"The heads never meant much to me," she says, calmly setting a cut-glass goblet, an ancient memento of the Homeworld, on my chest. "But those young loins!"

"Don't tell me you've grown tired of them, too?"

"No." The delicate features frown in their plump, symmetrical frame. The smell of her sex is overpowering. "There are younger women's houses within a few days' ride. Most of the boys go elsewhere now."

"Suitors are hard to get these days, are they?"

"Yes," she says. "But that's all right."

"You're tired, Femalwen. You've had too much of everything."

She stares at me as though for the first time.

"You know, Jarrass," she says, "you're the only one of all my husbands who ever talked to me like that."

"I'm surprised you remember so well. I was only here a few months."

"Many of the things you said hurt me, and I didn't even try to strike back at you."

"Oh, yes you did."

"Only when it became clear that you didn't intend to kill your father. You dallied almost a year before I said anything. All that time you continually found fault with me."

"I suppose I was unhappy, dissatisfied . . . but I always tried to be honest with you."

"Honest?" Femalwen smirks. "By leading me to believe you would kill your father?"

"Try not to indulge in self-pity," I say. "It is true that I besmirched your honor, but you have dozens of other husbands who have acted according to the letter of the law. I, on the other hand, have spent these last eighteen years wandering aimlessly. I have no home, and everywhere I go I am shunned. The possessions of my father are all gone now, except for a heat pistol, a few books, and a knife. I have been jeered, stoned, and spat upon. I have existed in abject poverty, because I have followed my conscience. But it is all over now. My father is dead."

I kiss her. Further lovemaking is, incredibly, on my mind, but the wine has made me very sleepy. I must rest. This day has been the most terrible of my life, but it marks a new beginning for me. I can hardly believe I've come this far. When I wake in the morning, I'll be ready to make the long journey to Terra field. Weather permitting, I'll be there in eight days—with a day to spare. The storm cannot last much longer, so I should make good time.

I alone, for my father's sake as well as my own, can and will escape the monstrous tradition that binds us, that makes us at once against nature and against ourselves. . . . I will escape . . . tomorrow.

I close my eyes. . . . I hear Femalwen's regular breathing next to me. . . . I think of our son Abissan. . . . He will be a tough, hard man, but vulnerable in his hatred and violence . . . in his anger and willful ignorance. . . . What will become of him?

. . . tomorrow . . . tomorrow . . .

My eyes are open. I am conscious.

A furrow has opened in the bedroom wall, its cleft slowly widening. As I hoped, the storm is over. The gray dawn is edged with a single, sharp sliver of red.

I want to get up . . . to dress myself and go to the stable . . . to lead my *mura* out into the sun and ride toward the ship . . . to fly away from Newth on fire and thunder.

These are the things I want to do, but I cannot move.

Part of me realized I couldn't move even as I slept. But I thought it was only a dream.

I am not dreaming.

I am awake. I know I am awake. Yet I am unable to twitch the smallest muscle in my finger. . . . I cannot even rotate my eyes.

There is sound . . . and motion.

The bed is heaving; I bob like a boat at sea. Femalwen is having sex with someone—I can tell from the groans, the heavy breathing, the small animal cries of passion.

Has a suitor come to her in the night, while I slept?

A voice, panting. Abissan's.

"Do you think he's awake yet?"

"Umm hmm." The purr belongs to Femalwen.

"Good. I want him to know what's happening. I want to scare him like he had Nath scare me in the forest."

Nath. I should have listened to his warning, I tell myself as Femalwen's round face enters my line of vision. Her fat hands hold the discolored empty sack I used to carry my father's head . . . and later to carry the things I stole from her.

"It was good of you to be so honest with me," she says, smiling in a terrible way. "I am so easily fooled."

Yellow eyes blink behind her.

"Since no human could go with you when you took the head up to the roof," she says, "I had Tru'ug follow you."

"My Jarrass . . ." Tru'ug bows mockingly.

Watch him, Nath said. Why didn't I listen?

As the cleft opens fully to meet the rising sun, I see a shadow on the crawling wall of forest just outside. It is the highest thorn spike, and there is a shapeless, awful thing impaled on it.

And at last my son's face looms up before my frozen eyes. His own eyes are focused purposefully on my throat.

In his clenched fist is the tarnished blade that severed my father's head.

PORTRAIT FOR A BLIND MAN

by

Karl Hansen

We hear the blind man coming for a long time.

As we listen, a pleasant reverie builds its images in my mind, sending a chill shuddering through my bones briefly, before the cold settles deep in my belly. I can hold it there. I will not let a shiver betray my feelings.

I distract myself from my daydreams by trying to detect nervousness in Roxanne as he steadily approaches; she hides her feelings well: no unevenness in her breathing, no tremulousness in her hands, no anxious perspiration, no quaver in her voice. I cannot tell if she remembers who he had been. But she must remember something: his touch, his laughter, his eyes when they were alive. I know she cannot yet realize what I intend to do with him, but I find it pleasing to torment myself with the irrational suspicion she has sufficient clairvoyance to glimpse in my mind the dark fantasy that amuses me. So I observe her carefully for latent apprehension.

I know she listens to him come. The electric whine of motors as he wheels down the hallway is just audible, but we hear clearly the louder surges as he stops and starts. For an interval it is quiet, as he pauses before each door, activates the annunciator, then waits with perfunctory silence for the door to open. During the hiatal quiet, Roxanne closes her eyes. Feeling is still there.

Sometimes the doors do open; we hear the faint hiss of pneumatic mechanisms and the gentle thud as the door seats flush into the wall.

I imagine suspicious eyes peering out of the blurred aperture of the protective doorway—old white-haired women with sagging faces and sharp, chicken-beak noses hiding behind the wavering field, protected from a changed reality by the buzzing ionized force grid, clutching a faded halter top together in front by one blue-veined hand to hide drooping breasts, while the other hand stands poised over the closing stud of the door mechanism, ready to send the door sliding shut at the slightest alarm. The eyes are veiled with ancient resentment, hidden among the wrinkles of the face. The lips are pulled back across shiny plastic teeth.

But the eyes never brighten, even with imagined fear; suspicion fades to dull self-pity when they see him, annoyed by his intrusion into their world of ebbing memories of husbands gone and children lost to war.

Maybe they look away from his dead face, apprehensive that familiarity will be hidden in the sallow features or disguised by the atrophy of unused muscles, and that recognition will come if they look too carefully. Maybe they realize there is something worse than loneliness, even something worse than the loneliness he suffers. Not once do we hear the crackle of the protective field wane, only his mumbled speech cut short by the hiss of the door closing and the grate of old locks snapping shut.

And usually the doors never open; so after a brief silence, we again hear the surge of the electric hum as he wheels down the hall to the next door, and Roxanne once more opens her eyes.

Eadie and Roxanne lie with me on the couch. Not very long ago we made love. Now we lie holding each other close, feeling our skins touching, almost fusing together with sweat mingling, dozing in the lazy glow of used love. Soon I will leave for awhile; others wait their turn with me. In my mind, I can already trace the lines across Eadie's face when it conforms to remembered hurt, and I savor seeing her eyes darkly swollen with tears. She is still a little afraid I will not come back. Sometimes I do delay my return; once I was gone for over a week. But Roxanne knows I must return to them eventually, just as she knows they will always take me back. And the others do not need me quite as much.

For awhile, I linger, waiting for the blind man. Before long, he will wish his mind was once more cradled in the grip of the field, and that he was still sightless. His wish will be futile; he cannot escape the pain that way now. I smile in anticipation.

The dark sky behind the window turns the glass to

mirror—I see our images lying together on the couch. Eadie and I are facing each other; her pale lips move slowly along my cheek. Her legs extend beside mine. They are wrapped with bulging varicosities, as if steel wire meandered beneath the skin. Roxanne curls against my back. Her face is hidden by dark hair. Her hand holds Eadie's breast, moving the nipple in a circle against my chest. The window glass distorts the images; the eyes that watch from behind the mirror are blurred, set in the face of a stranger. But there is a familiarity to the eyes—I have seen them before. Slowly I remember. I feel strands of blue ice pressing into my skin.

With Roxanne and Eadie, I know contentment for the first time since the war ended and my classmates and I left our academy. Now, I sometimes have the secret hope the interval between wars will last— armistice is pleasant. Yet I know peace is temporary and my happiness illusory. War will return, and then I will leave Roxanne and Eadie. They will take their place in my memories, as peacetime life fades to dreams.

Already the past three years have a dreamlike imagery: At first, our faces were flushed from cheering for the truce, and we walked about the streets clapping each other on the shoulders, laughing boisterously, waving to the timid faces that watched us from the windows along the sidewalk. All day we roamed the empty city. So strange and different from the academy it was—the buildings were old and dilapidated, the pavement was crumbling, and instead of everything being bright and clean, glass was dusted with grime and metal was coated with dull tarnish. The neglect excited our senses; there was unknown delight hidden beneath a seamy facade.

But when night came, we huddled in the park that bordered the academy, wishing once more for its security, lost in a world unused to peace after twenty-five years of war, shunned by the people outside, crying with disappointment at being cheated by a few months' time of our chance for glory.

During the night, we each woke alone to shout out in fear. As I lay awake in the early-morning cold, shivering more from the memory of my dream than from the damp in the air, I watched him gathering the flowers that grew next to the fence, hearing the faint hum of motors as he slowly wheeled along the wire. That morning, I understood why he was out so early—he shared our dreams. Although he was safe now and would never again feel pain, he had enough from before to last each night.

Soon the nights were different, as women who had been too long without men lost their reticence, and became shyly eager to share table and bed, not caring that their lover was young enough to be their son. I drifted among them, unable to stay with any one for more than a few days, before I felt compelled to throw off their clinging hands and lash out at their pleading eyes, always leaving them sobbing, never knowing what I sought or needed, until I met Eadie and then Roxanne.

Now only the dreams persist, to disturb the quiet of my life.

The window behind us is open, letting the cool afternoon wind bring fresh air to the room, washing away the musty smells that have accumulated over the winter. Outside it has rained. The machines make it rain every afternoon during the spring and summer, just enough to settle the air. We taste the rain in the air still, although now the clouds are clearing and soon the sun will break through for a few more hours of warmth. The drumming of the rain against the window was very pleasant to listen to, not too long ago.

The whine comes closer, moving slowly along the hall. I imagine the wet imprint his wheels leave on the floor—the water shines from the overhead lights. When the rain wets his face now, I wonder if he remembers how soft it used to feel. I watch Roxanne's face—it shows nothing.

I feel Eadie's breasts touching my chest. Her eyes are circled darkly. She kisses me delicately under my chin; her tongue darts out sometimes to tease my face. With one hand, I stroke her long hair against her back; it feels like soft straw and crackles like *rales* with electricity from the humid air. My other hand rests on her thigh. My fingers outline a dark bruise in the skin. I find remarkable how quickly she has lost the adolescent angularity that attracted me to her at first; in two years she has grown into a woman. Her gravid belly conforms to the hollow of mine; each slow movement of quickening within her womb is transmitted to my body, reaching deep with a visceral shiver. She has settled into the pregnancy now, no longer finding as much hurt in each careless phrase, no longer needing me so much. Maybe soon she will not need me at all.

Roxanne breathes against my back, holding both Eadie and me, loving us both, sharing Eadie's joy. Although she is only forty-one, she has been infertile for five years, her reward for producing ten healthy male babies for placement in military academies. Only once did the technicians at the insemination center err in the separation of Y and X spermatozoa. But she was allowed to keep her daughter and finally become a parent. Soon she will be able to again hold a baby in the night, knowing that darkness will last until morning.

Splatters of rain dry from the window glass as the air warms. The protective grill outside the window breaks the sunlight into a checkerboard on the floor. I close my eyes. My thoughts wander; images form, then dissolve, form again: lips moving close to my ear (Eadie whispering, tempting), walking beside me, pulling me by the hand, leading me to her room; someone sitting in a chair in front of the window, turning with light catching in her eyes (Roxanne waiting); later, my fingers tracing the stria in her skin, kissing her breasts, while Eadie sits away still, with long legs awkwardly crossed and new breasts just beginning to swell, not looking toward us; lying side by side, Eadie finally coming near, shyly touching me, touching Roxanne, smiling once, laughing; a face watching all the time from the wall, the eyes appearing to follow the movements of my eyes.

I look to the wall. I still find the holograph disturbing. The face remains young, unchanging. He went to war almost twenty-five years ago, leaving a young wife and a depot of frozen semen to father his ten sons and one daughter. I let the face age in my mind, pulling the features into a waxy mask. I see it through dew-coated wire. A woman's face appears above his; her face is familiar, she often watches us from beyond the fence. Now her eyes do not notice me. She stands cumbersomely, buys his flowers, then leaves.

Roxanne only smiles when asked his name, the same smile I see in the dark when she holds me after I wake screaming from the dreams.

She keeps a vase of dried flowers next to the portrait. Now the holograph has grown fuzzy at the edges, dimming as time passes, fading as the colors of the flowers fade.

The motor hum stops next door. A doorbell sounds. Roxanne looks at me; I remember her eyes. I think I know what images the machines used to drive his mind out of fantasy.

We hear the old woman creaking in the room adjacent to ours: shiny vinyl shoes crack with stiff bending as she walks, worn floor slats screak comfortably with each step, old joints crepitate with arthritis.

We seldom see her; she must spend most of her time barricaded behind her door, surrounded by the furnishings of another time: chairs and tables of real wood, polished to a dark luster over the years, a sofa with dusty upholstery, a massive old holovision, with the surface polymer peeling into eggshells and black-plastic knobs worn smooth by old fingers, a frayed carpet on the floor, tired plants hanging in baskets near the window, and a rocking chair under a chrome floor lamp, where she sits all day and rocks, the old floor creaking in sympathy. When the creaking stops, we will know the old woman is dead.

I have seen her close only once. We nearly collided on the elevator landing. She was inside, waiting for the door to open, carrying a small parcel. I was outside, thinking of a woman waiting for me in the park and the way the sunlight smelled in her hair, Eadie's red eyes still vivid in my mind. When the door opened, I started to enter, saw her, stopped with barely an inch separating us, stepped aside, and said hello. The old woman looked like a rat a terrier was keeping from its hole—glittering terror in her eyes, yellow teeth bared, fingers with long, cracked nails twisted into claws. And there was more than just fear in her eyes. My face meant something else as well. She brushed past me and scurried down the hall to her room, with my laughter following her all the way.

The creaking of the floor pauses before the door. The old woman stands still, waiting, the only sound her own raspy breathing. The bell rings again. The door remains closed, the old woman still. I know she will never open the door. She is afraid someone has returned belatedly from war, someone she will recognize, but cannot take back now. That fear holds her hand away from the button.

In the evenings she plays life tapes on her holovision, recordings made many years ago before the war. Lost voices seep into our room—the voices of a man and two boys, and the voice of a young woman before it turned hoarse and bitter with loneliness. The rocker creaking rhythmically persists long into the night, many hours after the voices have stopped and the speakers emit only soft static.

I think she sits in a chair, unable to sleep, staring at the empty air, remembering the men who shared her life briefly, dreaming of lost evenings when low laughter filled the room—her memories more vivid than the fading voices and insubstantial images generated by the tapes.

I wonder what the old woman thinks of the sounds coming from our room at night, when my women moan softly with love or laugh when my lips tickle a breast. I wonder if she hears the other sounds, later, and what she makes of them—and I wonder if the old woman truly remembers.

In the early morning, we finally hear her go to bed, as Roxanne holds me after I awaken in terror from the dreams, and Eadie still cries quietly to herself in the dark. It is then that Roxanne sees herself as the old woman, and she holds me tighter, just a little afraid I will leave.

The whine in the hall begins again and then stops before our door. We hear metal fingers fumble for the annunciator button, scratching against the tarnished steel of the door frame, and then the bell sounds, the gentle beeps cleansing the air of the harsh breathing next door. I hope to feel Roxanne stiffen when she hears the bell, but her body betrays no tension. She has been successful at hiding her feelings so far, but now it will be different. She does not know what I have planned. It will be harder for her now. I smile to myself.

I get up and go to the door. With my finger on the stud, I look back to Roxanne, watching her face, waiting for her features to reflect the turmoil she must feel. But her face is quiet.

I open both the door and the protective field and stand naked in the doorway, anticipating who is there.

The blind peddler stands in the hall, carrying bunches of flowers in the tray in front of his ambulation unit. He begins his speech when the door opens; his lips remain immobile in a frozen face. Dead eyes are hidden behind dark prosthetic lenses. Still Roxanne is unresponsive, her face as flat of affect as his. That will change soon.

He is one of the only survivors to come back from the war. He had been one of the first to be caught in the edge of a neuromotive field that dampened neural energy. If he had been entirely within the field, he would have died painlessly as his heart and lungs stopped functioning. But at the edge of the field, the damping effect was weaker, so only his peripheral nerves shut down, and the man lay alive in total sensory deprivation, entirely unresponsive to external stimuli. The damage from the field was permanent, so the medmech attempted to use the brains of the survivors as cyborg controls in war machines, bypassing the ruined peripheral nerves. But the brains would only perform basal functions; the minds could not be roused to do more complex tasks.

To determine the cause of this autism, the medmech grafted prosthetic visual and auditory apparatus directly to the blind man's cerebral cortex, and implanted efferent transducers, then drove his tortured mind back to reality with noxious stimuli. They found he had withdrawn to an autistic state during the psychosis of sensory deprivation, fleeing from the fear of total isolation by regressing to the security of early infancy, and the gratifying memories held there. Unfortunately, his brain was damaged by the procedures, so he would never be suitable as a war cyborg.

He is not totally blind—he sees with glass eyes, barely able to distinguish form from shadow. He hears with audiotransducers. He no longer has smell, or touch, or taste. His body is cradled in a wheeled ambulation unit that also tends his bladder and bowel; he is fed through a tube implanted into his stomach. He has control of one mechanical arm. His speech occurs through an electroacoustic speaker.

Instead of giving him euthanasia, because of some inscrutable machine logic, the medmech returned him to civilian status, but they felt no need for nuances; sophisticated cyborg servomechanisms were needed for war. He would have to survive with only basics. But they had determined what had happened, and they knew what to do to prevent it from recurring: if there were no secure place to hide, the retreating mind would drive itself back to reality, no matter how grim that reality was.

As I listen to the blind man's flat voice, my thoughts return to the academy: I entered the simulation chamber, lay on the couch. Suddenly I was alone—no light, no sound (not even my heartbeat), no feeling, just me. No body, no arms, no legs, just me. Memories surfaced. Always running, we were always running. Crying as we ran, sometimes too tired to cry. Our names were never known to each other. The sharing of names was much too difficult, much easier to use the white numerals stenciled to the backs of our shirts. At night, too tired to resist the blows, tasting blood from split lips, submitting at last, barely noticing the pain that rippled deep inside with each thrust, later taking the fecal-stained penis in my mouth, almost asleep before tasting warm semen. A number sitting in the corner, arms wrapped around his knees, staring blankly, lost in disconfirmation. Someone pulled him to the center of the room. They stood around him. Urine splattered against his face. They began kicking the silent body. Broken teeth lay scattered across the floor. I grasped the memories as they passed, holding each image, but they slipped by, one at a time, becoming lost. Twelve years passed by and were gone. I sat alone, surrounded by broken toys. One by one the toys disappeared. I crawled aimlessly about. I cried for endless hours, then closed my eyes. Warm milk filled my mouth; I suckled contentedly. But something was wrong. I opened my eyes. I was clinging to a wire framework, sucking on a rubber nipple protruding through the mesh. The cold metal etched white lines into my skin. I was alone—so alone—forever. I cried in anguish. A drop of milk formed on the underside of the nipple and fell to the floor. I fled; my memories returned; my life slowly rebuilt. I opened my eyes and sat up on the couch. That night, for the first time, I awoke in terror, and sought a younger boy, making him soothe me. The next day, at recess, I joined the older boys next to the fence, where we threw rocks at the blind man as he gathered flowers, laughing with them when the stones sounded hollowly from his metal body.

The blind man has finished his speech and waits. His face is unchanged. I stammer for a moment, not having heard what he has said. Not that it matters. I know what he wants. But he does not expect to get what I intend to give him.

I turn, as if to get some money. Eadie is sitting on the couch, with Roxanne behind her, combing Eadie's hair. She has parted it in the middle, with the two halves pulled in front to cover Eadie's breasts. The dark nipples peak through the strands of hair. Eadie smiles.

I look quickly back to the blind man. He stands passively in his ambulation unit, face lax, unable to smile. I wonder how much he can see, how much form the shadows have. I do not want him to miss the fun.

Eadie is sitting back between Roxanne's legs, her head resting between the woman's breasts. Roxanne's hands rest lightly on Eadie's abdomen. Her fingers play in the soft hair of the girl's mound. The light from the open window silhouettes them in diffuse radiance, envelops them in tawny haze. Roxanne's eyes seem distant, but I see no concern in her features. Maybe her feelings for him have faded. Maybe she has no emotions left to conceal. I hope not; that would ruin my game.

A smile hides in her face.

I think of the fantasy that has amused me since we first heard the blind man coming: I have brought him into the room and have closed the door. He stands in the center of the room. Rain has washed the grime from the sides of his ambulation unit, but the water has left streaks down the metal. The light reflects in prismatic colors from his vision lenses. His pincers still hold a bunch of flowers, while his speaker voice still mumbles rote words. Roxanne and Eadie sit together, not yet realizing what I intend. I go sit beside them, taking Roxanne's hair in my hands, and pull her face toward my lap. She resists at first, but my grip is too strong. She is slowly drawn closer. My erect penis touches her lips. She twists her head suddenly, almost pulling away, but as she turns she sees the blind man watching. His face is still waxy, unable to reveal his feelings. His eyes are still dead. She looks away from him, remembering the way he used to be. This time her lips find my penis themselves, and her mouth surrounds it, taking it greedily. Her fingers dig into my buttocks as she holds me. I release her hair. Eadie stands beside the blind man. She leans over, brushing her breast against his cheek. Her hand strokes his matted hair. She straddles one of his wheels, rubbing back and forth with the wheel between her legs. Then the blind man acts. We hear a surge of electric power and the whine of gears. Eadie jumps away. He wheels ponderously toward us, with his pincer arm raised. I stand up, with Roxanne still clinging to me, and easily catch the arm and hold it. His face remains lax, unmoving. He is helpless in my grip. For a moment, I am tempted to batter his unfeeling face with my fist, then I realize that I cannot hurt him further; the pain he remembers is more vivid than any I can inflict. Disappointment touches me. The fantasy fades.

I know I will not bring him into the room; it would be futile, he is safe from me. The machines have cheated me of my amusement.

He stands patiently before the open door. I leave, find some money, and return to the door. I drop the coins in his tray and take a bunch of flowers. I close the door. The hum of motors is heard once more.

I remove the dried flowers from the vase on the shelf, replacing them with the fresh. The shriveled petals crumble into powder in my hand. I almost turn to go to my women, then pause and look at the holograph. The face watches, the eyes are the same.

Momentarily I glimpse the dream: I prowl a ruined countryside. It is night, but my vision lenses collect the starlight and turn it bright. A life form moves. I fire. All is still. The ash shatters quietly beneath my treads.

Eadie pads over to stand next to me, slides her arms around my waist, and pulls me toward the couch. I drop the old flowers to the floor. She kisses me, tongue slipping past opened teeth. Her swollen breasts bounce as we walk.

We reach the couch. Eadie eases me on top of her.

Roxanne sits away, listening, eyes fixed on the broken flowers on the floor.

The springs of the couch begin to creak with my thrusts. Eadie arches her back to receive me deeper, and wraps her legs around my torso, pressing her firm abdomen against me. I bring my lips close to her ear and whisper. As before, I tell her of my other women and describe the babies they have borne me: heads lacking faces, twisted limbs, fused fingers, bellies not sealed, with entrails hanging out.

I continue the rhythm of my thrusts, watching her face, waiting for her to cry. But this time she does not cry. She has become less vulnerable to me. She closes her eyes, not listening, not responding.

I withdraw and kneel above her. She lies still, with eyes closed. I slap her face with an open hand and watch a red outline form on her cheek. Her eyes stay closed. I slap her again; this time my hand remains raised. A drop of blood forms in one nostril, then trickles down to wet her lips.

She rolls to lie on her side, hugging her knees to her breasts to conceal the bulge of her womb, knowing where I will hit her next.

Roxanne moves over to kneel between us. She says nothing, still listening. My arm descends. The edge of my hand glances along Roxanne's jaw. I hit one side of her face and then the other. She remains upright, with Eadie curled into a ball behind. The sunlight through the window grill casts a fishnet of shadow across her body. I hit her low, in the midsection; air whistles from her nose.

I finally stop when I hear the sound of crying, not realizing at first it is just my own.

Roxanne holds me close. I bury my face between her breasts; the flesh muffles my sobbing. Tears streak her skin. My lips find the nipple; my mouth surrounds it, tasting salty tears. My cheeks are pulled flat against my teeth as I suckle. She is warm.

In the quiet, we hear the old woman breathing, still waiting in front of her door.

I close my eyes, seeing a holograph of myself sitting on the shelf, already dimming about the edges.

NIGHTBIRD AT THE WINDOW

by

Pat Murphy

I used to wake up to the sound of my brother's screams. Sometimes he would shout words—"No! No, not me!"—but most of the time he would wail without words, yammering in panic at terrors in the night that I could not see. He would scream until I shook him awake.

For sixteen years, we shared a bedroom, and for sixteen years I shook Jimmy awake to save him from the horrors that invaded his dreams. In the seventeenth year, that changed.

"I battle the Devil in my sleep," Jimmy told me one day. "I scream when I'm losing. And I always lose."

Jimmy squinted at me with his curious, sly eyes. We had the same face—Jimmy and I; we were twins.

We had the same face, but Jimmy stretched it in ways that I never could. I tried once when I was very young. I watched myself in the mirror and tried to grin as Jimmy grinned—an impossibly wide smile that seemed to involve every muscle in his face. I tried to frown as Jimmy frowned. I couldn't.

"Don't you ever battle the Devil in your dreams, Tommy?" Jimmy asked. "Don't you ever lose?"

"You know better than that. You know I never dream." After sixteen years of Jimmy's harassment, I knew better than to rise to his bait. He could turn me inside out with words if only I gave him a chance. I had learned never to give him a chance.

"Wouldn't you like to try it sometime, Tommy?" Jimmy picked up his guitar and played a series of notes that tumbled and quarreled as they sang from the strings, then ended where they began—nowhere. "Are you sure you wouldn't like to dream sometime?"

"What a stupid question. If I dream, I dream. If I don't, I don't. It's as simple as that."

"No, Tommy, it's not as simple as that. It's not nearly so simple." He picked out the notes again, stringing them together in a wandering melody. "Nothing is ever that simple."

Jimmy had found the guitar in the attic. When he found it, he told me that it had belonged to our father. I told Mother what Jimmy had told me, and Mother slapped him. Our father had left Mother before we were born.

Jimmy wasn't allowed to play the guitar when Mother was home. She said Jimmy's music made spiders creep up her back. She said she couldn't stand it. But when she tried to take the guitar away, Jimmy threatened to burn the house down while we slept. So she let him keep it, but she warned him she would take it away if he so much as touched a string when she was near.

Remembering what Mother had said, I could feel a careful spider stepping slowly up my spine, touching each bone in time to Jimmy's music. "Will you stop playing that thing?" I snarled.

"No, I don't think I will. Mother's not home, and I think I'll just keep right on playing."

"Suppose I break the guitar?"

"I'll hum the notes."

"Suppose I break your neck."

"Then I'll haunt your dreams, rattling my chains in a tune that will drive you nuts. And if I die, Tommy, you'll have dreams." He grinned out of a face that was my face, but my mouth would never stretch so wide. He stopped playing the guitar and watched my face intently. "You see, I've got a theory, Tommy. I think that when you die, you'll just turn to dust and blow away. You know why? Because you don't have a soul. Because I've got my soul and I've got your soul. And you've got none." He studied my face, as if attempting to judge the impact of his words. "Doesn't that bother you?"

I shrugged. "I always suspected you were crazy, Jimmy. Now I know it. Who says I even believe in souls?"

"I guess it would be hard for someone who never had a soul to know what he was missing. You can't feel without a soul; you can't dream without a soul." He grinned. "But maybe I'll let you try out what it'd be like to have a soul." He said it as if he had just thought of the idea—but I knew better. I could tell by the gleam in his eyes that he had been planning this. "How about tonight? Would you like that?"

"You're nuts, Jimmy. What do you mean—you're going to let me see what it's like? You mean you're going to give me bad dreams? Brother, if living in the same room with you doesn't give me bad dreams, nothing can."

"Oh, I can, Tommy." He smirked at me. "And I will. I can give you a dream you'll remember forever."

"Don't be stupid, Jimmy. You can't scare me. You never could." When we were both little, Jimmy had tried to scare me with elaborate threats. He promised to put leeches on my face when I slept, to rub me with a lotion that would make beetles crawl on me, to lock me in the attic with the one-eyed ghost he claimed lived there. When Jimmy described the ghost, he made it seem more real and vivid than anything I had ever seen. But I didn't believe in ghosts and I didn't believe Jimmy's threats.

For as long as I could remember, Jimmy and I had been enemies. When we were six, Jimmy had pushed me off the barn roof and I had broken my leg. When we were eight, he had killed my cat, drowning it in the creek and abandoning the carcass on my bed.

When Mother was home, she slapped Jimmy if he wronged me. Jimmy was a demon, but Mother was an avenging angel. An angel with long, black hair and skin as pale as the ivory keys on the piano in the living room. But when Mother was gone, Jimmy was king, taking my toys, taking my books, taking everything and leaving me with nothing. He always acted as if I had something that he lacked, something that he could steal from me if he tried hard enough.

Jimmy started the spider walking up my spine again, holding each note, forcing the strings to quaver and cry. "Wait until tonight, Tommy. Just wait until tonight."

I didn't believe Jimmy had any power over me; I didn't pay any attention to his threats. But that night the crickets creaked in a ragged, nervous rhythm. The sound of Jimmy's even breathing mocked me from across the room.

I watched him by the moonlight that streamed through the window. For once, he slept peacefully. In repose, his face was my own. Watching him was like watching myself sleep, watching my own chest rise and fall with each breath.

Watching him, I started to drift into the darkness of a dreamless sleep. A breeze rattled the window and I woke up, startled by the sound. The crickets jittered out of tune and I could not relax again.

I did not mind the darkness of sleep, but I didn't trust my mind to stay dark. How did Jimmy's dreams begin? With a flare of light, a stab of pain, a crash of sound? Would a dream hurt, would I cry, would I scream in terror? I didn't want to know. I wanted to sleep with the darkness of my mind undisturbed.

Looking out the window, I watched the full moon rise high in the sky, until it flooded the yard with silver light. Gradually, my eyelids drooped and, despite the nervous crickets, my eyes closed and I drifted away into darkness.

Suddenly, the screaming began. For an instant, my

heart seemed to stop its steady beat. Was this how Jimmy's dreams began? Did he hear a desperate keening that burned his ears until it compelled him to join in and howl his pain? Then I recognized Jimmy's voice in the screams, and the crickets in the yard seemed to change their song to a steady, comforting beat. The dream was for Jimmy, not for me.

Jimmy screamed in a high, harsh voice that sounded as if it would soon rasp dry in his throat and fade to a whisper. But I knew from many long nights that the screams would not stop, would not fade. Jimmy gulped air in shuddering gasps, then screamed again. He would shriek until morning or until I shook him awake.

For a moment I ignored Jimmy's screams, savoring my relief that the dream was Jimmy's, not my own.

Abruptly, Jimmy stopped screaming. And the moonlight at the window was blocked by a shadow, a piece of the pit, the Devil's courier who had come for Jimmy's soul. A carrion-eating bird, a raven with eyes that glowed gold with hate, beat its wings against the window. She had come for Jimmy. I could hear the rustle of her feathers, the scratch of her talons, the rattle of her beak against the thin pane of glass. The moonlight edged her feathers with silver.

Behind her beating wings, I caught glimpses of a world painted silver and black with moonlight and shadows, a world of sharp edges, a pointed, painful world. Each piece of the world—the barn, the fence, the grass in the yard—each had a vibrancy about it, a biting clarity, a piercing intensity.

This was not a dream—I knew that. The raven was real; the sharp-edged world was real. I had lived my whole life in a twilight state—half alseep. At last I had awakened.

I shouted at the discovery, a whoop of pain and exaltation. At the sound, the raven's eyes met mine. The golden eyes glittered in anticipation of a feast. No! She had not come for Jimmy; she had come for me.

The window shuddered when she hurled herself against it. The glass rattled from a blow of her beak. The bird would get in—I knew she would get in.

She would fly at me and peck out my eyes and feast upon my brains, hauling strands of sticky gray through the holes that were once my eyes. My brain, my mind, would go to feed the raven. I would be lost, forever lost.

I screamed in a voice as harsh as Jimmy's had been. My heart pounded—urging me to run, to escape, to hide. I leaped from my bed as the raven attacked the glass in a frenzy.

I ran from the room, but even in the hall, I could hear the rustle of every feather, every scrape of the bill. More clearly than I had ever heard any sound, I heard the sharp crack of breaking glass, as a solitary skater hears a warning crackle when thin ice begins to give way beneath him and he knows that he will drown, swallowed by an icy lake.

The raven burst through the window and I heard the glass splinter. Dark waters closed over my head and I screamed. Darkness entered me through my open mouth to choke me. Darkness flowed in through my ears, a deafening darkness that thundered like wings.

Like wings! I turned to escape, but an ivory claw caught my shoulder and whirled me back. Mother stood in the doorway to her room, awake and alert. I held my arms out to her, trusting my avenging angel to save me from the Devil's courier.

"Shut up, Jimmy," she rasped. "Shut up."

Her nails dug into my shoulder like talons. Her eyes glowed gold in the moonlight. Golden eyes—I saw them and knew why the eyes of the raven had seemed familiar. She clutched my shoulder, but I tore myself free. I turned to run and the thunder of wings was upon me.

I heard the first rap of the raven's ivory bill against my skull and the grating of talons on bone. I saw a flash of white in the darkness when the beak plunged at me again, and I heard the snap of my skull giving way. I heard the rustle of feathers as the bird drew back to launch the final blow, the one that would split my skull and lay my brain open for the bird to devour.

The third blow was inevitable. Giving up, giving in, I sank to the floor and an ivory dart flashed through the night. It caught the side of my face and my head rocked with the slap, a slap that stung like ice. My mother slapped me again to be sure I was awake, then hauled me to my feet.

I hated her. In the last moment of that dark reality, I hated her. And I took a fierce delight in my hatred, a delight that burst on my mind like the pealing of wild bells on a silent night, like a lightning flash in a pitch-black room.

The golden light faded from Mother's eyes as the darkness faded from mine. She released my shoulder and snapped on the hall light. "Tommy," she called into my room. "Why didn't you wake him up?"

When he stepped into the hall, Jimmy looked shaken. But his sly grin returned quickly, pasted in place over a pale mask. "Wrong son, Mother. You've got Tommy right there."

"Tommy?" She peered into my face and I drew back. I shrugged off the hand that gripped my shoulder. "Honey, are you all right?" My shoulder ached where her nails had clawed me. I nodded silently. If I had attempted to speak, my voice would have cracked and I would have started to scream again.

Mother's voice grated in her throat when she spoke to Jimmy. "What happened? And why the hell are you grinning?"

"I'm grinning because for once Tommy got what he's missing. Serves him right." His voice held the mocking tone he used to make Mother angry.

Mother's hand whipped across his face in a ringing slap and I winced. Jimmy kept on grinning. And now I could guess what lay behind that grin—wild bells pealing in the dark night behind his eyes.

"Go to bed," Mother snapped. "I'll take care of you in the morning." She turned to me and her voice changed to a soothing tone. "Poor Tommy." She reached out to stroke my face and I backed away. My face still tingled with the memory of a cold slap.

She hesitated, then dropped her hand. "We'll talk in the morning. You'll see better by sunlight. Go to sleep now. And this time, don't dream."

I turned and stumbled back to my bed. The window was not broken. The room was not sprinkled with splintered glass. Not a feather had fallen to mark the passage of the raven with Mother's eyes. I shivered and crawled into bed, wrapping the blanket around me for protection against the night. Moonlight still streamed in the window and I was grateful for the light.

"Tom," Jimmy whispered. His voice sounded tired. "Tom, is it always that bad?"

"What do you mean—that bad? I don't dream; I don't have nightmares. I just . . . " In the middle of a sentence, I realized that something was wrong. The fierce delight I had felt in the hallway had faded. I could remember the feeling, but I could not recapture it. I could remember how clear and intense the world had been—but the world had changed. "I just . . . " I repeated. I could not finish the sentence.

"The world was out of focus." Jimmy murmured. "I couldn't see. I couldn't feel—my mind was stuffed with fog. I couldn't think. You don't really think, Tom. You remember things and repeat them. But you don't think." His voice gained strength. "And you don't sleep, Tom. You die every night. I thought if you didn't dream you . . . I thought you . . . I don't know what I thought. I didn't think that sleep could be so cold. It was like entering a tomb, it was like being buried alive in the hard, bare earth. Or like sinking into the ocean and watching the waves roll over your head and knowing you would never see the day again."

I shuddered and pulled the blanket tighter around me. "Stop. . . . Don't talk about it. I don't want to . . . " I didn't want to see the mouth of the grave gaping before me each time I drifted into sleep.

"All right. We won't talk." Jimmy's voice was softer, gentler than I had ever heard it. "Don't worry, Tom, I won't inflict my dreams on you again. Not if it means I have to go through what you go through. Good night, Tom."

"Good night."

We lay in silence for the rest of the night. And I remembered the raven. She had been like Jimmy's description of the one-eyed ghost—vivid and complete.

I remembered the glow of her eyes and the ivory sheen of her beak, and I realized I had never seen anything as clearly as I had seen the raven battering at the window of my mind.

Jimmy was right. He had my soul—he could love and hate and laugh and cry and live in a world of nightmare visions. I lived in the real world only, and slept like the dead. I did not even hate Jimmy—I couldn't. I remembered the dreams and I knew how hatred felt. I did not hate him; I disliked him.

Mother had said she would talk to us in the morning—she never got a chance. When the first gray light of morning touched the window, Jimmy slipped quietly out of bed. Silently, he packed a few clothes into his canvas book bag and picked up his guitar. Then his feet whispered down the stairs and he was gone. He slipped away in the dawn with my soul in his pocket.

Things had changed in the night and it made no sense to stay. I could not see Mother without seeing the face of the raven, the only being I had ever hated. Before the sound of Jimmy's footsteps faded, I packed my own bag and ghosted after him. By the tracks in the dew on the lawn, I could see that Jimmy had headed west. I headed east.

I never saw Mother again. I never heard from Jimmy. But I know that he's alive because my night thoughts are empty—a black, blank expanse, dark as a graveyard at midnight.

It doesn't seem fair that our dreams should be so unequally divided that one mind burns in Hell by dreaming with the intensity of two, while another mind longs for a touch of warmth. I can't be angry about it, but I know it's unfair.

I listen for wings, but the sound never comes. I remember the sound—angry and dangerous, but clear and intense, sharp enough to pierce my soul. I remember the scrape of talons against bone and the snap of a shattering skull, but mostly I remember the thunder of wings—the sound that deafened me while embracing and overwhelming me.

The sound of wings held a promise—of feeling, of seeing, of hearing. To feel pain is better than not to feel at all; to see the eyes of my destroyer would be better than being blind. All my life my eyes have been clouded. Except for one night in my seventeenth year when I saw clearly in a dream.

I wonder if Jimmy misses the silence of the grave. I wonder if he'll send me a messanger from Hell some night. I hope he will. I wish I could dream of that other world of clarity and feeling, but I don't dream.

At night, the darkness closes over my head like the waters of an underground pool—dark and impenetrable—and I listen through the silence for the thunder of wings.

COMETS AND KINGS

by

Somtow Sucharitkul

When you are a boy all the trees of all the forests seem to stretch up forever, to merge into a leaf-dark zenith as far away as the sky. When you're older, I suppose you laugh at yourself. But there is one forest of my boyhood whose trees, I sometimes fantasize, have kept pace with my growing. Even now, when I stand at the edge of the universe, the shadows touch me, across Greece, across Persia, across India.

Do you believe in hubris?

But of course you do. Yet it is a far more complex issue than our ancients could possibly have imagined.... Well, I shan't philosophize. This isn't even my story; and I am no visionary, as Alexander is.

There was a forest in Macedonia where we played at being men, in an autumn much like any other. He was a pretty princeling with a crazy fire in him; and I had only just found out how terrible it is to love the great.

"Hephaistion!" he called me, and flashed into the forest, his gray chiton crisscrossed by the evening sun. He ran ahead, I caught up, we walked arm in arm, we laughed together, senselessly; we wrestled, we sank, panting, onto the damp moss.... Then he got up, without a word, and went off by himself in a unknown direction.

Already I knew better than to follow him unbidden.

"Hephaistion!" he cried out again. I could not fathom the emotion. I saw a strange man lurking in the shadows; Alexander had practically walked into him.

A sudden terror seized me. Did he only seem to be a man? "He's harmless," I said. "Just a peasant of these parts, I bet."

His body was blurred against the trees, shimmering. My eyes smarted. Alex was cautious, so I stayed frozen too. The glare forced my eyes away from the bearded face, from the blood-chilling eyes, down to the chiton, woven of some alien stuff, like the stuff of rainbow.

Perhaps he was one of the forgotten gods of Macedon, driven into oblivion when civilization came to the North.

Alexander showed no fear, as always. He didn't flinch at all from the alien's gaze.

Past the old man's head, in a little gap between the trees, stood a structure of polished bronze, something like an inverted amphora. A field of metallic reeds protruded, waving delicately in the breeze. It was perhaps large enough to house the stranger. I thought it quaint, a prop in a satyr play, perhaps.

Alex spoke first. "Are you a god?"

"It might be expedient to think of me that way, yes," said the stranger. He laughed suddenly, but his eyes remained expressionless. "Call me Ectogeos—'outside the earth.'" He spoke Attic atrociously. His sibilants lisped, and he didn't contract his verbs, which gave his speech a peculiar, mock-Homeric quality. "You wonder why I come to *you*, Alexander?"

Nothing was being addressed to *me*. I was just an insignificant witness to some key event in *his* life. I tried not to be jealous.

"I am an observer," the ancient continued. "All my kind are; incessant observers. And here there is surely something to observe, even if he is only a boy as yet!"

Alex was drinking it in. I don't know how, but he seemed half to recognize the stranger. . . .

Ectogeos said, "You stand out against your human background like a supernova against the stars. Observing you, one sees the whole world; influence you, and one could—well, it is forbidden of course. Even my visit here is a little risky." Had he said too much? "Think of me as your guardian from above."

Alexander nodded. "But," the old man said, "I wish to ask you some questions, in the name of research—or you might call it curiosity. What do you plan to do in your life?"

"Conquer the world." This without hesitation.

"The world?"

"When I was born a comet came."

I had to interrupt, then. "Why are *you* asking him

questions? *Are* you a god then, or is he? Is it your place to question him?" Then I said, "Are you or are you not a god?"

"A god?" I saw he had no intention of answering me.

Alexander said: "If you are a god of these woods, your kind is dying. Soon they will forget you, and you need worship to sustain you. Times are changing. . . ." It was true enough.

The man laughed again. It was a throaty chuckle that seemed to grow out of the forest depths. "It's kind of you to worry about me." It *was* kind, I thought; he had always been concerned about the aged. Was he destined never to see age, then? "But I am more than capable of seeing to myself."

My eye was drawn again to the structure. Softly the silvery reeds rustled. I wanted to dare to go up to it and peer inside. . . .

"It is forbidden, Hephaistion!" he said sharply.

He has read my thoughts! Fear and guilt shot through me. I withdrew my thoughts, shielding them. They were deep in conversation, those two; it was boyish stuff, about conquering the Persians and the rest of the world. Alexander had always been extravagant; I found it charming, but Ectogeos looked very grave.

Finally the alien said, "Thank you for your information," and made to return to his inverted amphora.

"Not yet!" It was a challenge. "You have not told me who *you* are." Alexander . . . the forest sunlight mottled his face. My heart almost stopped beating.

"You tempt me, earthchild," said the stranger. "We cannot, as a rule, reveal our identity to the worlds we observe... but there is something special about you, and... no, no, I doubt you could accept what I am."

"If you don't tell me, I won't rest till I've found out. My father is King here." Alexander's eyes flashed, defiant.

"I know." The stranger spoke reluctantly. "But you could not imagine what I am. Perhaps, though, at the end of your Quest... when it no longer matters..."

"My Quest?"

"Well, it won't hurt to tell you what you know already. The world is yours."

"*All* the world?" said Alex, wonder creeping into his voice.

"Why not?" And he had gone into the structure.

He seemed bewitched as we walked home; he moved ahead, striding rapidly, crunching twigs, not looking in front of him. It was hard to keep up with him. And now the twilight seemed to settle. Of a sudden we had stepped out of the forest; I picked the leaves from my cloak and wrapped it around his shoulders as he paused. It was chillier now. The breeze and the half light toyed with his long, untamable golden hair.

"Don't be so withdrawn, Alex," I said. "How can you hide so from me?"

"You saw. My dreams are coming true, faster than I can cope with them." He looked steadily at the dark earth. Only when he had said it aloud, I thought, did he know it was true.

I knew he would sulk tonight, and be surly to our tutor, Aristotle; that he would sit alone at the edge of his bed, dreaming dreams, excluding me—not by design, for he would not do that, but because the dreams transcended me. "Who was the man?" I asked him. "What was the dream?" The name, 'outside the world,' does not ring true. Alex did not answer me; I do not think he knew.

"Alex," I said, breaking another silence, "was it a visitation from a god?" I felt the shadows of trees, and was uneasy.

His eyes were on me. I wanted so much to give him everything, if I could reassure him just a little. . . . To love the great is terrible.

But he turned to me on impulse. Without a word he embraced me in a desperate clinging, like a lost child.

Many images follow in the memory: the stench of blood, the sun eclipsed by black blankets of arrows . . . and Alexander and I growing tall together.

They have all merged for me, these images: all the forests and woods and taiga and sweltering jungles, the towers and pyramids, the ziggurats and obelisks, the empty tombs, the wide-trousered dancing boys, the kohl-eyed priestesses, the satraps with beards like terraces, the camp whores with bosoms spilling out of gaudy corsets, and the countless Kings, overdressed, like life-size dolls, dwarfed by their golden thrones.

But he conquered Persia and became Great King, and we sacrificed at the tomb of Achilles and Patroklos.

And after, flushed with wine and victory, he stormed into the tent. Our friends were posturing drunkenly at one another; and after awhile they staggered home, and the Persian domestics vanished like a magician's coins, and we were alone.

"Aren't you ever going to turn back?" I asked him. I was not the first to ask; well, perhaps the first to ask to his face.

He flung down his empty wineskin. "What do you mean?" His speech unslurred abruptly; his eyes flashed clear in the half dark.

"I mean, consolidate your empire. . . ." I was always more practical than he, not a visionary, as I have said.

"I have no *time* for that!" He began to explain: "There's so much of the world left, and I have to have all of it! It's nothing personal, this conquest, it's just . . . I *have* to. It's a destiny." He said the word with a funny self-consciousness.

"By now you ought to have seen reason."

His voice slurred again. "Don't you remember? In the woods, with the god . . . ?"

I struggled to place the memory. It was hazy at first: a shimmering old man, an autumn haze, dreary conversations in the half dark—

. . . the forest sunlight mottling his face.

It was an image of fragile transience and cutting clarity. Like a magnet, it drew the memory to the surface. But I tried to laugh it off. "It was just a practical joke, or something. . . ."

"*You* don't believe that." Alexander was right. I turned away from him, watching the fire and the dance of shadows against canvas. I heard him say, urgently, "He came to *me*. And he gave me the world."

"Maybe it wasn't his to give," I countered with involuntary sharpness, although I was trying to humor him. His confidence had always terrified me—and convinced me, by its sheer intensity.

So we argued, for the sake of form, a few minutes longer. *It's a mistake*, I thought, *to judge him by values which* he *has rendered meaningless. And we both know how such arguments usually end.*

In the flickering orange light he touched me, touched my hands, my face.

How can I refuse you, I thought, *what is yours by right of conquest?* He yielded to me as marble to a sculptor; giving, he only became more and more himself.

The night he burned Persepolis....

Towering, fantastical spires of flame were lapping at the corners of the sky, and in our noses was the suffocating stench of incense and charred flesh.

We followed Alexander into the empty, endless throne room. As they cleared a path through the rubble, he wielded his torch like a fury, staggering toward the Great King's throne, clambering up the hundred giddy steps of solid gold. Across the vastness of the hall, I heard him shout for a footstool—he was too short—and then he became like the other Kings, countless Kings, deposed and dying, dwarfed in their own thrones. *They were living gods,* I thought, *and now he has cast them down.*

The wild laughter sounded small. Soldiers were hurling their firebrands into the splendor. A courtesan was screeching elegantly, quaffing from a looted wine cup. From the foot of the steps I watched him; the brightness of his eyes still cowed me, even at this distance.

I thought: *This fire rages so he can breathe life anew into the defenseless city.* The fire evoked a sense of wonder, with columns snapping like lyre strings overtaut. For a moment we were all openmouthed, like children at our first funeral.

I heard him call me, so I went up to him, almost stumbling over a severed arm.

Urgently I asked him, "Why are you burning Persepolis?" But he sat impassively on the throne.

Then he said: *"Because no God has visited me since I was a young boy. I make this fire so they can see me."*

A great palace burning . . . a great man, burning with desire . . . ; a great man, desperately feeding on the love of so many, yet knowing they cannot touch his solitude . . . the brightness hurt my eyes. Then, after some hours, it flickered and smoldered and was spent. The morning came: gray, rainy.

Always I shall remember this night, not only because the brilliance of the flames made day where night should be, and usurped the functions of the Gods, but because there sprang to my mind unbidden the sound of a chuckling forest, and the sight of an alien personage in front of an unearthly structure of polished bronze.

Perhaps it was some kind of purging for him. I hoped it was a fire to drive out fire; inside, I hoped for an ending, though all our hopes would be transmuted by the catalyst of his personality, and we would become mere aspects of him.

And then, more merging images: white sand that blinded, pyramids that littered the sand like a child's building blocks. Nilos, which runs backward, strange gods, strange rites. Soldiers, digging up mummies from the sand, mummies whose faces glared stone-hardened across unimaginable time.

There was an oracle in the desert, in an oasis. We waited while Alexander went to consult the strange gods that had become his own. It was an idyllic time, without bloodshed; soldiers' children played at the desert's edge, and there was water and grain toward the river. It was a place of luxurious plenty, sprouting out of a devastated vastness.

One day a Bedouin scout, shouting frenziedly, whipping his camel, rode into camp. *The oracle has declared Alexander a God, the son of Zeus!* Alexander would return, perhaps in a few days, perhaps a week, to receive the homage of his subjects.

The scout did not say that Alexander had met Ectogeos again. . . .

We were alone together, and it was one of those times—increasingly rare now—when he talked freely, almost as though we were still boys together. "Let them believe that they deified me!" he said, laughing. "The priests, muttering in their weird languages, the incense everywhere. At least it was cool there in that temple under the rocks. I listened to their god with great courtesy, but . . . there was another meeting, too."

I stared at him, already guessing. An oppressive tension fell out of a clear blue sky. "I'll tell you a secret!" he said, half laughing like the old days; but it was not the same. You'd think he had become an oriental, with all the bowing and scraping. . . . I waited as I was supposed to, listening to the date palms rustling.

Finally, "Well, what?"

"Relax! I'll tell you!" His eyes sparkled.

After a sufficient pause, he told me. He had gone off by himself in the desert, after the fuss at the Siwa Oasis was over. The others must have been frantic trying to find him. And, just as he knew it would be, *he* was standing there, beside the comical structure. "He says it's a flying machine, but won't elaborate."

"What," I said, "is he a Daedalus too, as well as a peasant and a guardian from above and a wood god?"

"After I spoke to him, he got into it and flew off," he said matter-of-factly. His eyes were distant. "Well, say something."

"I don't believe it." But I believed every word.

"Oh, nonsense, Heph. Do take me seriously. He said many things which tempt me to believe, you know, that oracle. We played questions and answers again. He was very ambiguous.... I think, you know, he tries to cover his tracks...."

As though he might be reprimanded if caught? I thought.

"You know what the first thing he said to me was? Go on, guess."

"How should I know? 'How you've grown,' maybe."

"Exactly so! You see, you *can* read my mind."

We both burst out laughing. Almost at once, the tension returned.

"Actually, he said: 'How you've grown; you shortlivers always surprise me,'" said Alexander.

Shortlivers? And what had he called Alex before: *earthchild?* These were not the sorts of words gods used of mortals, exactly ... and then I thought, what if someone had invented a flying machine? Many of the wonders that had assaulted our senses were no less implausible.

Alex said: "He said to me, 'I hear they have given you divinity now. How does your halo fit?' I said I wasn't at all sure. 'Ha!' he said. 'Isn't sureness a measure of one's divinity? Of course it is!'

"But I said, 'If I'm to be a god, then I am one of you, but you see, I can't fly.'

"'What's bigger—flying, or conquering the world? I didn't invent this contraption, you know. Someone else—let's call him Hephaestus, so as not to distort your world perception too much—makes all these things.'"

"So what came of it?" I asked him.

"I said to him, 'So you still maintain that I'll conquer the world—even though my army doesn't want to go on? They all miss home, don't you know that?'

"'I maintain nothing. Actually, *they* keep telling me not to interfere.'

"'Who're *they*?' I was insistent. I don't like riddles.'"

Alex was very serious. I tried to see the mystery of the story, but it was broad daylight, the breeze was blowing softly through the trees, children were playing "leap-the-steps" on a little step pyramid (they've looted it since). . . . Somehow it was not as terrifying to me as it might have been brooding by night on a battle's eve. He sensed, I think, that I was trying to hide something from him, not disbelief exactly, but . . . the delicate tension of our relationship had drifted away.

Looking at him, sitting on a rude bench, travel soiled, I saw he had battle scars but there were no lines under his eyes. He had shaken off the foreboding of warfare like a sea lion erupting from the water. His eyes reflected the sky.

Even when I looked away, his presence was something palpable. "Don't you want to know, then, what he said next?" he asked me.

"Of course." I did, really; I did not know why it came out so offhand, so blasé.

"Well then. He didn't answer. In fact, he just looked at me, the way Aristotle used to peer at a specimen. A sandstorm was brewing, but I had to wait, even though it wasn't funny anymore. Abruptly he said to me, 'Define a god.'

"I was stuck for an answer. He chuckled, the way he had done in Macedonia long ago; you could hear it echoing in the wind and sand, and then he walked up to his structure and sort of faded into it. Fire leaped from under it. Then he poked his head out, as though tempted to say one final thing:

"'Go on! *Be* what they say you are! Isn't that what *being* is all about?'"

Alex assumed that distant look again. The conversation was not satisfying; it had all the logic of a dream, and all the essential reality of one.

I fell to thinking, under the scorching heat:

I have known him intimately, in the most profound sense that a man can know, ever since we were boys.... How old were we now? I had lost track, not yet thirty, though. And now that he was elevated to godhead by an oracle, I was left a poor relation, like Polydeuces to Castor. How did they manage these questions, after we were dead?

As I watched Alexander, locked in his terrible solitude, the thought of death fell like a tree's shadow across my mind. *Does he still think of conquering the world, of absorbing the universe into his fiery corona?* In the final analysis, the vision was his alone. Even I could not see it.

Ectogeos had called himself an observer. I did not understand why he should observe. The gods see everything anyway; they did not have to send someone down to gawk. Were the gods voyeurs? There are men and gods. . . . Was there a third category?

I wished *he* would come and talk to *me*.

More images, from the last days of the great conquering:

The world grew wider, wilder.

There were markets reeking with strangers' sweat, great green jungles, serpents of myth coiled around nameless trees of emerald . . . and everything growing, upward, outward, inward, downward, in a frenzy of growing as we neared the edge of the earth. There were whirlwinds, assaults of rain; the horizon never moved any closer, and black Ganga coursed sluggishly beneath a lowering sky. There were faces so alien that I forgot *the alien*'s face; there were the giant gardens of King Poros, green, now dipped in the purple of bloodshed. And the animals: elephants, rhinoceroses, dolphins, tigers, unicorns, and women with diamonds in their noses, women naked from the waist up, their breasts dangling like ripe mangoes that glisten in the sunshine, brown children leaping into rivers, widows leaping into funeral pyres—

Amid the amazing fertility, the armies came to rest, perhaps only eight hundred stades from the other shore of Oceanos, the boundary of the world—and were on the brink of mutiny.

"Pull down the tent flaps, shut out the noise!" Alexander screamed.

"Can't you see, Alexander, they want to turn back?" I was pleading with him.

He talked like a child, sure of his reward, but

knowing he has to play a silly begging game first. "But I haven't *seen* yet!"

I was irritated. By then I knew exactly how much of this conquest was due to his charisma, and how much merely to his understanding of the mob.

"If you don't turn back, they'll mutiny and leave you here." They were outside the tent, cursing, demanding, the old veterans, making threats in Macedonian. "Can't you hear them?"

"They would never leave me," he said. Then, with a quiet, terrible intensity, "I *must* see this through to the end! I *must* fulfill my destiny!"

"Destiny? *Hubris?*"

I had stung him. He turned to me and said, with a strained calmness, "I know he will be there to meet me."

"You mean you think you'll run into that man who claims to be your guardian from above? What a farce! In the desert, back in Egypt—I wasn't even there with you! Prove it!"

He flared up, then fell back, speechless. I pressed my advantage. *"I'll* send them back, with or without you!"

"You!" He was livid. "By what authority do you flout your surpreme commander?" He reached for his weapon, then put his hand down, staring at it dully, not knowing where to put it. "Who do you think you are?"

I said, very softly, *"He, too, is Alexander."* Those had been his words to the mother of Darius (they are history) when she had prostrated herself before me, the taller, by mistake.

He was about to speak, but his voice was drowned by the clamor from outside.

"Yes, Hephaistion," he said. An admission. "But *I*

must see it, the limit of the world, the horizon extending until it merges with Ocean, the boundary of our cosmos. Send them home; it's only eight hundred stades from here and I can catch up...."

"But—why leave me out?" I said. I should live up to this blurring of our identities....

He planted a single kiss upon my cheek, this boy with his face mottled by the forest sunlight.

In history, we turned back; and what is not in the records does not constitute history. Truth does not enter into it....

He was standing by the seashore in the twilight, beside the shining structure. We tethered our horses to a tree. Hands touching, feet sinking in step in the warm wet sand, we approached the alien.

The wind at the world's end howled over the sea. There was no horizon; sea and sky merged into one gray. You could not tell where the end came, for the gods are masters of illusion.

I saw recognition burst out on Alexander's face. He left me running behind in his eagerness to meet the ancient.

"Rejoice," he greeted him, like a friend.

Ectogeos said nothing. His eyes were closed, his lips moved soundlessly as though he were in communication with something far away.

He woke with a start and saw us, smiled broadly.

"Now that your destiny is accomplished," he said, "I have been liberated from observing; I am free to answer your questions."

I expected Alexander to ask the questions one asks of gods: questions like *when will I die?* or some such.

But all he asked was: "Is there not more?"

"Why? Does your Quest's ending disappoint you?"

I saw how perceptive the alien had been, though Alex would never admit it to himself. For I understood him, how he was driven by the desire to push forever into the unknown. We all followed him, of course, but our desires were limited: a little treasure, a little land, a kingdom, a satrapy, even a little sexual adventure . . . and we were content.

For him, ending was catastrophe.

Ectogeos turned to me. "Well, Hephaistion, are you not satisfied? I did not come to observe *you*. You could have asked me anything; I have been reading your mind always."

I didn't know what to reply. He shrugged. His rainbow chiton shone brilliantly in the dusk. A shaft of light from the structure fell on Alexander's face, and I saw for the first time that his eyes had become lined. Alexander repeated his question.

"Come into my *spaceship*," said the alien. He had coined a strange word, full of power. We followed him in, and all the while the world's-end ocean sighed and heaved in the world's-end wind.

The interior of the structure—I cannot describe it; I have no referents in my experience of the world . . . a mirror curved into forever. Hazes that became solids. Lights without source, shifting like lights of a faceted crystal.

"This," said the ancient, "is a space-time scanner." There was a square mirror of highly polished silver. I was struggling with the name of the thing. "Don't bother to understand," he said to me, not unkindly.

Alex accepted without question the old man's

assertion that the mirror could show all places in the cosmos, and all times.

First we saw the world's end, but from a peculiar distance, as though suspended far above it.

We saw a round world spinning crazily like a top in the nothingness; and on that world countless nations springing up wildly, everywhere, in its most inaccessible corners, immense buildings crashing into the firmament on an undiscovered continent where Aztecs built pyramids to bloodstained Helios and starfarers leaped into the sky. The moon was full of people.

Alex clenched and unclenched his fist.

"So there's more. Our cosmology is wrong," he said tonelessly. "I haven't achieved anything yet! It isn't over yet!"

"My poor child! Your whole world doesn't begin to contain the totality of life!"

Rushing past our eyes at a continually accelerated rate—the seven planets, and a few more besides, crowded with life forms, microscopic, macroscopic, insubstantial, massless, waveless, thought forms . . . I gave up trying to understand.

Alexander watched, engrossed. I felt his heart sinking.

The solar system shrank to a point.

We flew past thousands, then millions of stars, all full of life: green, purple, gold, black, ultraviolet, X-ray-colored life. The galaxy collapsed into a single point.

Alexander looked up, relieved that it was over. "So that is why it could never be mine," he said, almost reconciled.

The scanner was black for some moments; then

another galaxy swam into view. The same process began again: a cluster of galaxies shrank into nothingness, a cluster of clusters, a cluster of clusters of clusters . . . the universe shrank into nothingness.

The mirror was empty for perhaps ten minutes. Then, to his horror, another universe began to form, and another, a cluster of universes, a cluster of clusters, a cluster of clusters of clusters. . . .

The alien said: "And now you have the truth. I wanted to spare you the pain of looking more."

It was midnight. The wind had never ceased to howl; we were outside the structure. A pale, cold light from the structure illuminated Alexander's face, and I saw the despair in his eyes, and the innocence.

"I may have mocked you," continued the stranger. "If so I apologize; there are so many rules governing scientific research. I wish I could have helped." His garment glowed faintly.

Alex was silent, so finally it was I who asked the question that I had wanted answered for so long:

"Who, in all truth, are you?"

"My name is Zethtep," he said; "in your language, 'Watcher.' My friends call me 'Meddler.'" Already he was going into the spaceship.

Alex and I watched, alone together on the shore. The ship streaked into the blackness of the sky. In the distance, against the stars, it blazed like a comet; then slowly, like the dying of a plucked lyre string, it faded and melded with the night.

We found our horses. Alex was silent all the way to the camp. But I was not as shaken as he, for it was not after all my vision. . . . We rode in a darkness further darkened by compound shadows of strange trees. Wind gusted, damp and warm.

I remembered the ship, splashed out across the sky like a living fire. *Are all comets born this way?* I thought.

Alex was spurring on his horse, impatient. I could not see his face, and for once I was glad I couldn't.

I remembered how he had told the alien, that first time, in the forest in Macedonia: *when I was born a comet came.* I remembered the casual pride of that statement. But—

Had they come, even then, to observe him? Had they gathered round, like students round a specimen?

I sped up to a gallop. The wind streamed on either side of me; and I abandoned myself to it, hardly noticing which way we went.

I think it has broken his heart.

ALL THE STAGE, A WORLD

by

Dave F. Bischoff

I like similes.
Nothing wrong with metaphors, mind you. They have a savory heft of their own on the tongue tip, the epithets especially. 'Swine,' 'cur,' 'bastard,' delightful lumps of acidic phlegm to hawk up from the back of the throat, splatter into the despised one's face. Many a rival actor has felt the sting of my vocal mucus, to be sure.

But all the same, similes are my weakness. The words 'like' and 'as' are, to me, not unlike prefatory tongue drum rolls to the execution of the exquisite image, the delightful slash of razor words.

I start this performance with a simile:

"Puppetlike, actors dangle on the words the play demands. They may worm and squirm between the walls of their text prison, and gaze out dolefully through the bars of their speeches, rattling their chains—but there is no escape." I explain all this in my personal prologue, alone on the stage. "Tonight, upon the behest of the Co-Ordinators, the Players shall perform a play of our choice, without puppet strings. We have chosen Shakespeare's *Hamlet*. We are actors. We know the words. But we are also artists. We shall improvise variations of the words, in variations of scenes, in a variation of the play."

I look up into the darkness surrounding the circular platform which serves as the stage—up, around, behind is only blackness. I know they are there, watching. I know that the appropriate holography equipment is trained on the stage, recording.

I know. Oh God, what I know.

"Now, as we are but acclaim-poor souls, hungry for recognition, we ask only for the food of your applause, the wine of your laughter and terror—if what you see presented here today meets with your approval."

Almost immediately, a cascade of tinny, loudspeaker clapping breaks the silence around me.

With as much dignity as I can muster I bow—I bow again.

"Ladies and gentlemen—*The Tragedy of Hamlet, Prince of Denmark.*"

More canned applause opens up.

The lights dim. I depart, to await my cue to reenter in the character of Hamlet.

I take my seat below the stage, and quietly regard the

action, preparing myself for the emotional rigors I must encounter.

From black, the lights fade on to a murky shade. There are no props. But the Co-Ordinators have the script of the original. They know the play is set at Elsinore Castle.

It begins poorly. The guards improvise badly, sticking principally to the text. Slaves. Simon Marshall, the Ghost, is a serviceable actor, but he only walks across the stage in the first scene. Only Stuart Stakowski as Horatio shows any verve, any flair at all, and that is precious little.

They stick me among incompetents, and they expect true artistic expression.

Scene one ends rapidly, for which I am grateful. I am nervous. I long to plunge myself into the play, wrap Hamlet around myself, and myself around the role.

Scene two begins. I enter with my fellow actors.

William Albright makes a creditable Claudius. He has attired himself in a plain twentieth century-style suit, and has had himself made up to resemble President Richard Nixon—a leader of this country when it was called the United States. He opens with a clever variation, pretending that his marriage to Gertrude is the result of more electoral-college votes than his opponent. He flashes many victory signs, kisses many imaginary babies, pats my head.

"Well, young man. It's good to be your father," he says.

"Then you are mistaken," I snarl. "The only pleasure a man gets of a son is generally in the begetting of him."

The Co-Ordinator machinery approves. I get a brief burst of laughter.

Albright seems piqued. I have received favor in my variations before him, who had the first chance. He strains and strains, but he tires too hard, and there is no response. In the end he has no more to say other than how he hopes Hamlet will cheer up over the death of his father. He must now leave the stage with the rest of the players, so that I may do my scheduled soliloquy.

Here I pause a moment, rallying my creativity, letting it well up in me, so that it may burst out violently in the direction I choose, thus giving me the upper hand in the course the play takes, the thrust of its layers of meaning.

Having the principal role, I of course become the main mover of thematic content. But I have been in this position many times before, and know that I must be strong in my approach, firm in the execution of my brilliance, lest my fellows upstage my genius. The power struggle in these 'creative interpretations' is tremendous. All of which makes the Co-Ordinators quite pleased. And those of us judged most successful in each are allowed extra comfort in our cells.

Now I stand quite still, letting the viewers take notice of the apparel I have chosen for the part: the plain jumpsuit of a Class-C citizen.

I begin: "Oh God, I really feel drippy."

I have chosen my variation on Shakespeare's line— "Oh that this all too too solid flesh would melt, thaw and resolve into a dew!"—quite well, netting a barrage of chuckles from the invisible speakers.

I launch myself into a long harangue on how rotten I feel, interspersed with occasional off-color Lenny Bruce-type jokes, and a soft-shoe patter, to illustrate my range. But this is merely for their amusement—I sum up with powerful variations of Shakespeare's image of life as an overgrown garden, an offshoot of a similar spiel I did in *Richard II*. My virtuoso performance obviously stuns the Co-Ordinators' reaction machinery—a gurgle of laughter mixed with awed, frightened breath intakes issues forth—I have overloaded it. I am pleased.

The play proceeds. I have gained the upper hand, and maintain it, despite a heavy bid for attention from Fred Rossillini as Polonius. Fred is a formidable contender in any role, but as Polonius he is superb. I must exert my all against his portrayal of the role as a dippy librarian, reading his speeches out of books. A brilliant piece of interpretation, if I say so myself.

Simon Marshall is also effective, choosing to wear an Uncle Sam costume. But I allow him to upstage me while he is on, because his interpretation is in harmony with my own. Besides, his role is such a short one—there is no threat.

But there is a slight difficulty for me in the second act. Several of the actors have obviously formed a conspiracy to make the play a nihilistic, even existential, tract. The characters of Rosencrantz and Guildenstern have dubbed themselves 'Tom' and 'Stoppard.' Scott Homa in the role of Laertes is obviously the ringleader in the bid for takeover of the play.

He spews out unaltered passages from Beckett, Sartre, Barthelme, and Woody Allen between his lines. He picks his nose while I respond, and wipes snot on my shirt. Once, he almost breaks me up. I almost collapse into laughter, but bring the discipline of my art and craft to bear, and steel up under the considerable pressure. Even despite the outrageous attempt on the conspiracy's part, I succeed in diverting the play from the dead end of absurdity, placing it clearly back on the track despite their most clever ploy—spelling Hamlet with two *t*'s, alluding of course to Ionesco's travesty of *Macbeth, Macbett.*

I do this in act three, with the famous 'To be, or not to be' soliloquy:

"Tee vee, or not tee vee: that is the question.
Whether 'tis nobler in the mind to suffer
The slings and arrows of outrageous radiation
Or take a sledgehammer and smash the set . . ."

My version is *most* successful, a long *tour de force* questioning the role of the individual in an oppressive society, debating myself on the duty of power in the hands of the artist.

It is the center of my version of the play, the core of my creative interpretation of Hamlet. At the end of it, I am so overwhelmed with my own speech, I almost rush off to destroy Claudius. But if the words do not halt me, the course of action we wind our way around does. I must wait two more acts.

During the course of this brilliant speech, the actress who portrays Ophelia, a lady I do not know who wanders about with a bag of heroin and a syringe humming a Rolling Stones song between her lines, has attempted to interrupt me. A hurried whisper to her suggesting that she go jump in a lake brings gales of laughter from the speakers—neatly dispatching an almost-successful bid of the absurdist faction.

And I persevere, preserving the thrust of my speech despite the interruption, and finally triumph gloriously.

This advantage is carried through to the 'play within the play,' which I, as Hamlet, am able to direct.

Just as Hamlet alters the action of the Italian tragedy the players present, so I adjust the proceedings to suit my stratagem. The player king wears a sign reading: 'The People.' The player queen bears one reading: 'The Government.' Lucianius I have left unlabeled—allowing a bit of subtlety into the affair. They perform their actions well under my command—Lucianius poisoning the sleeping player king in league with the player queen. Claudius is guilt stricken (here it is necessary to divert from truth for the sake of the action of the play) and darts away. Hamlet is now sure of himself.

But is he? He comes upon a penitent Claudius sprawled before an altar. Albright has succumbed totally to my desired direction, and assumes a vulnerable position.

Hamlet can skewer him, but holds—here I add a detailed, soul-searching speech full of self-doubt. Will Hamlet, in avenging his father's murder and by that act becoming king himself,—will Hamlet make a *good* king? Or will he be the tyrant his uncle, Claudius, is? He remains undecided—and allows the king to keep his life.

The following scene is one of particular relish to me—the confrontation of Gertrude and Hamlet. I play it to the hilt, thus exorcising some of my anger at my own mother.

And the sword stroke through the curtain, through Polonius, is almost as satisfying as one might be through Claudius.

All fares well—the play flows along the ditches I

have dug.

The actor as *auteur*.

When Hamlet is sent away to England, I have a brief respite from my efforts, and sit in my folding chair below stage, sipping reconstituted orange juice, charging myself for the final scenes.

As I tend to do when stationary, unacting and unacted upon, I brood. I wonder if my efforts will be rewarded, if they will have any affect at all on the Co-Ordinators. This is my goal—my most earnest desire. I strut and fret across the tiny stage, making my body a mirror of my soul, my voice a trumpet of my anguish, my message a direct link to their minds crackling communication across the great gap.

I ponder their procedures—question their rationale. It is my fantasy that the recordings of my plays are beamed across the nation to holo sets, that my genius is seen eventually by millions, that I am broadcasting myself, not to darkness, response machinery, and technicians, but to living, thinking minds like mine.

It is an illusion I steadily cling to, but nonetheless it *is* an illusion.

No—I suspect darker, more clinical reasons for this inspired insanity they force out of me and my fellow actors.

I vaguely note that Laertes is pulling absurdist stunts again, attempting to gnarl the play, but Albright has long since settled on an interpretation of Claudius well within the boundaries of my design, and handles the young man quite well.

Quite suddenly a thought, a revelation, dawns on me—and I see my purpose in the play. I am not merely exercising my gifts for approval, for favor, for my own ego's sake—no. All the time, in all my performances, I have struggled to unify us artists, to direct the force of our creativity toward one point, vectoring all our energy to one goal. That goal is Art, and there is nothing holier.

The lights dim, and the stage manager touches my shoulder. I take the stage for the graveyard scene.

I decide to utilize the Yorick sequence for a long discussion of death—in the individual and in society.

My rest has done me well. I soar on the wings of my words, touching down occasionally on the waves of the great empty ocean of death. I ramble on and on, rolling the words out, flowing philosophy, faster, faster, weaving a rapid web of meaning—

—and suddenly pull a Pinter pause.

The effect is devastating. The reaction machines have not been geared for such—the brilliance of contrast between the rapid, lively, animated, energetic monologue on death, and the sudden cessation of it all, leaving only catacomb silence below the spotlights, between the darkness. Laughs, giggles, cries of despair and agony—a veritable Dante's *Inferno* of sounds spews from the speaker—as though not so much in reaction to my trick, but to cover up the terrible silence.

I wonder if I have gotten through to the Co-Ordinators.

Regardless, I am jubilant.

I word-pirouette neatly into a pun session with the grave digger, and segue expertly into stunning displays of grief upon hearing the news of Ophelia's gurgly death.

I almost leap feetfirst into the final scene, so filled with exaltation am I. I am in the midst of my most inspired performance ever. My blood has turned to fire—I am in a controlled skid of my exultation. I have absorbed the barrier between the Melancholic Prince and myself. I rush forward to cut the rottenness from Denmark, knowing that the action, so long delayed, will be my doom.

By now all the players are in the palm of my hand. Even Laertes is in awe of my energy, the dazzling, encompassing charisma I have gradually built up over the course of the play.

I chuckle inwardly—perhaps we will all get steak for dinner.

But this cynical little voice is speedily snuffed. I lunge into the duel with Laertes. The queen drinks the poison cup. Laertes wounds me, I wound Laertes. He tells me of Claudius' treachery.

I turn on the king, direct my rapier for the climactic plunge of revenge, of outrage, of rebellion, treason, hatred—

And suddenly wheeling up the ramp to the stage, a robot comes, its steel pincers gleaming in the spotlights as it reaches for me.

I have gone too far—

But I must complete my action or all my work, all the energy of defiance I have worked up into the evening's art, will be meaningless, anticlimactic.

Albright senses this, and tries to move closer to speed my psuedothrust.

But the robot is too fast. It grabs my arm, shakes the plastic sword from my hand.

The others of the cast are dumbstruck. Nothing of this nature has ever occurred before at an Institute play. They break out of character, shuffle away to their cells.

"The rest is silence!" I scream, but there is no response from the reaction speakers.

The robot drags me back to my own small cell, shuts me in, promising that a Technician will be here soon to sedate me.

I should never have let them bring me here, I think.

I should have died first.

I sit quietly in my cell, my head in my hands, my unconsummated genius a dead albatross around my neck.

THE FACES OF MEN

by

Glenn Chang

Around them the sea was calm and still. Only the gentlest motion stirred the boats: a lazy roll over the surface making them bob in a slow ballet under the hot cloudless sky. Those in them sat silently, except for the standing helmsmen—tall, rail-thin, narrow-headed and skull-faced, their skin burnt brown by many days in the sun—watching the mirrored plane for the telltale breaks. The Earthman, Versola, sat with them, as silent as the others; his eyes were not quite as good, but he too searched for the ripples on the water. He was dressed as they were: the briefest protective loincloth, with the addition of his own utility belt. Though as tanned and weathered as they were, his shorter, wider stature and broader facial features set him apart.

Now and then he would glance back at Selaam, the helmsman in his boat, as if to ask something. Yet each time he would hesitate, glance quickly over the waters where the helmsman's steady gaze was directed, then back, and finally decide against it. No one else moved or spoke; they watched and waited, stretching the time out until it had no meaning.

"Eh-yai!" The sudden shout made the Earthman sit up quickly. All the helmsmen pointed out over the water with their short, hook-ended clubs.

At first there was nothing. Versola squinted against the glare and finally saw a shadow gliding under the surface, at an angle away from them.

He began to turn, but sudden movement caught from the corner of his eye made him stop. The shadow had grown larger and more distinct; now it broke through the surface about fifty meters away. Versola caught a glimpse of something, gray mottled with white, amidst the foam, before it slipped beneath again.

At a signal the rowers began stroking, and the boats seemed to leap forward after the submerged shadow. They spread out in a shallow arc—six boats in all—following the quarry's wake as it surfaced and submerged periodically, almost in a teasing fashion. As they rowed, the boatmen began a chant, a deep-throated rhythmic litany. Versola recognized it as their archaic ceremonial language, the one he had not yet learned. All the songs and chants of their rituals were done in this language; it was considerably more complex than their vernacular dialect, and despite the prolonged time he had been on this world, he understood but little of it. Nevertheless he tried to follow carefully the words, phrases, and rhythms in his head.

The chase went on. The rowers steadily urged the boats over the glassy surface, relentlessly pursuing the quarry. The afternoon heat caused the Earthman only slight discomfort, nothing near the ordeal it had been during his first days on the planet. Now he was able to immerse himself in the totality of the ritual: the low throbbing voices, the hiss of the boats through the water as they pursued the flickering grayness farther out, a tableau that to him was like a dance playing itself out in timeless motion on a hot, bright stage.

Suddenly the shadow was not there. Selaam barked out an order; the chants and rowing stopped, and they backed water with their oars to bring the boats to a halt. The arc the boats formed had pinched together, now a not-quite-closed circle; there they waited again, this time poised and ready, the helmsmen leaning slightly forward as if expecting something.

Then the sea before them seemed to explode. Spray and foam founted upward; the boats rocked violently in the water, and the boatmen were shouting out orders and exclamations, their voices a confused babble. Versola, hanging onto the gunwales for support, saw the great gray shape in the midst of the geyser surge up out of the water, tossing the boat nearest it into the air. The upended boat spun once, spilling its boatmen into the sea, then came down end over end—so slowly, it seemed—and fell back into their midst with a cannon slap against the water. Then the creature itself was falling, and another booming sound filled the air as it completed its breach, sending out backwash that threatened to swamp them all again.

The waves subsided and the boats leveled out. Another order came from Selaam, the chief helmsman, and the rowers turned their boats toward the scene of receding turmoil. A great fluked tail was just slipping beneath the surface; three boats, Versola's among them, raced toward it, while the other two slowed to retrieve the floundering boatmen.

Now the helmsmen of the three pursuing boats reached down and traded their short clubs for the long barbed harpoons. The tail slipped under, and the wide expanse of the creature's back began lifting up out of the water. The boats moved swiftly closer. The back was now a great, gray, exposed hump; Selaam gave another command, and all three helmsmen lifted their harpoons and threw.

Two struck true. The third went slightly askew and only lodged loosely. The back shuddered, then spasmed violently several times and disappeared below the surface. The lines connected to the harpoons grew taut and, slowly, the boats began moving after the quarry.

On they went, the creature towing the boats, the boatmen again waiting, more harpoons in hand, for their quarry to surface. For a long time, though, it seemed virtually inexhaustible, pulling all three of the boats steadily. The sun slowly crept lower toward the horizon as they waited it out. The waters became rougher, and Versola had to grip the gunwales again and squint against the stinging spray as the boats bucked and slapped against the frequent whitecaps. They were heading toward the chilly southern seas, he realized; how much farther would they continue?

Eventually he noticed a perceptible slowing in their progress. Now and then the lines slackened; the beast was tiring.

"Soon now." Selaam spoke informally to Versola for the first time, in their vernacular language, so close to the Earthman that he started. "Soon the dance will end."

"You'll finish him off?" Versola asked.

"Or he us. Whatever is written in the deep this day." The lines were now completely slack in the water. The helmsmen turned and called to the other boats, and they spread out a bit, the rowers backing water.

Versola turned his attention back to the sea, now gray and choppy. As he did, he saw the lines grow taut again, so taut they hummed and threw off gobbets of water. The bows of the boats dipped, almost under the surface of the water. Versola braced against the sudden shift of gravity. Then the lines suddenly slackened, and moments later the sea exploded again, spuming a furious spray that drenched them all, with that mottled-grayish shape suspended in the midst of it once more.

As he watched, it cleared the water, twisted in midair and ponderously flicked its tail. The frail-looking harpoon shafts jerked on the lines, then the loose one sprang free and the other two suddenly broke off near their heads. With a tremendous slap, the creature breached one last time; the water surged and swirled in its bubbly wake, and it was gone.

Slowly the waters slowed their swirling motion, the foam subsided, and then the three boats were alone on the sea.

"So be it." Selaam's voice broke the silence. "We have a reprieve today. All of us."

The others quietly murmured their assent.

Versola turned toward Selaam. "That's it, then," he

said. "You don't plan—"

"Not this day. It wasn't meant to be."

Versola made to answer, then fell silent. He remembered the many times he'd watched from the shore as the boats came in at twilight, sometimes with the great burden lashed between the boats, sometimes bearing no catch at all. It would all be rationalized, he thought, whatever happened. Of course. A hard and hazardous life—but it was their life.

"Now we return," Selaam said. The chief helmsman turned and called to the other boats. The other helmsmen answered, the three vessels turned northward, and the rowers began stroking them toward home.

The voyage back seemed shorter to Versola. Perhaps it was because there was none of the anticipation and waiting they had done on the way out. Also his mind was filled with the images, sounds, and smells of the day's event. He ran it over and over again in his head, recalling all of the experience, feeling more enriched each time. It was a singular occasion: in all the time he'd spent with these people, this was the first hunt on which they'd consented to let him accompany them.

When he finally came out of his distracted state, he was mildly surprised to see the dark strip of land against the horizon, outlined by the light of near dusk.

A movement behind him caught his attention. Selaam stood up straight at the helm and pointed toward the sky ahead of them. "Something comes. From the sky."

Versola looked back at the helmsman quickly, then squinted upward where he had pointed. Against the colored, suffused sky, something flashed, tiny and metal-bright, several times.

"No," he whispered, almost to himself. "Not yet." The Earthman had reverted back to his native language. "It can't be time yet." He stared at the winking dot, then he blinked hard several times, as if trying to clear some intruding vision from his eyes. When he stared again, the dot was a steady point of light; as he watched, it slowly made its way across the now dark-maroon sky, then began dropping lower and lower, toward the land.

"They have come," Selaam said. "Yours." The Earthman turned. The helmsman's head and body formed a dark outline, featureless except for the golden eyes reflecting the residual light. "They have returned for you."

Versola nodded. He did not speak.

"We go home," the helmsman said, and turned his gaze forward again. The Earthman remained silent, his eyes staring fixedly toward the shore. None of the other boatmen paid any attention. They continued rowing, and the boats moved steadily toward land.

It was just dark when they pulled up onto the shore, guided by the torches lit and placed in the bows and by those held by the party waiting for their return. Versola sat silently regarding them as they did the boatmen; their faces flickered into distinguishable features in the uncertain light, expressionless as always. The Earthman could not recall seeing anything other than that visage of calmness on their faces, no matter what activity they were engaged in. Perhaps they had no facial muscles to express emotions. Perhaps they expressed them another way.

The others quietly stepped out of the vessels and beached them far up, almost to the tree line. The crowd parted before them. As always, nearly all the villagers had turned out; only the very old, the heavily bearing and their midwives, and the very young staying behind. At first glance they all looked the same in their sleek-muscled, lanky-limbed physiognomy—even the youngsters scampering about among the adults' legs—save for the occasional crippled or diseased one, and here and there a stocky ancient. That had intrigued Versola in the beginning, even despite their hermaphroditic nature, and had provided not a little confusion before he developed the ability to distinguish individuals among them. Now there was usually little trouble—except in moments of reflection when he considered how different he was. Like now. He thought of the descending ship.

Selaam spoke softly to the waiting crowd. He paused, and a murmured chorus came from them. Then he spoke again, a bit longer; another pause, another chorus. The other boatmen stood by quietly. Versola heard only snatches, but he knew what it was: the ritual announcement, in the vernacular, of the day's events. Then would come the final litany in that difficult ceremonial tongue. As he thought that, their voices grew louder, and then joined in that selfsame archaic chant. Then the sound died away, and they began to head back toward the settlement.

Versola moved slowly, his head full of thoughts, when he became aware of someone by his side.

"You will go to them tonight?" Selaam asked.

"Yes," he said. "I suppose I'd better."

"Do you require us to accompany you? There is no

knowledge of how this is to be done. None of it is remembered."

No, Versola thought, I don't suppose it would be. "That's all right," he said aloud. "I'll meet them myself. I'll try to make it brief and be back shortly."

"Back? You will come back tonight?"

"Yes, I'm pretty tired—" Versola stopped, aware of something slightly askew, on the verge of going awry. "I need some rest," he said carefully. "Tonight I will only greet them and talk with them for awhile."

Selaam stood silently for several seconds, then made the slight movements of his head and shoulders for assent. "Yes," he said. Without another word, he increased his pace and walked away toward the settlement.

Versola considered the brief exchange. There was a sense to it that made him apprehensive, but it was not clear. He shrugged, filed it away in his mind reluctantly, and looked for the long-unused path to the landing field.

Purple-leaved creepers and the ubiquitous scraggly underbrush had almost totally reclaimed the path. He struggled along, using a thick wooden branch he found to clear out most of the confining vegetation. Under the canopy of the inland forest it was dark and shadowy; he could barely see the night sky, sprinkled with stars, through the overhanging branches, and hardly anything ahead of him. He moved mainly by feel, roughly gauging where he was by the level of the land, the memory of this once well-traversed region slowly coming back. Even so it was a mild surprise when he topped the last gentle rise and abruptly broke through to the clearing.

The tableau, softly illuminated by the reflected light of the three moons overhead, was in sharp contrast to the recent near-total darkness. The shuttle craft was a dull-gray construction, its precisely engineered struts and contours a jarring image in its surroundings. Already the peaked shapes of the outdoor shelters had been set up, and lamplights aided visibility. He could see figures moving around, sitting, standing still, obviously conversing with each other. There were six by his count—not quite a full complement. Perhaps there were more still aboard.

He remained where he was for a little over a minute, trying to breathe calmly, steadily, composing himself. Then he stepped out into the clear and hailed them.

The figures stopped what they were doing, and he could see their heads turn toward him. Lights were trained in his direction; in their glare he began walking down into the clearing.

"There! Is that him?" he heard one of them say. A new one, he thought, and wondered which world he had come from. "Yes, it's him all right," another one said; Versola recognized the voice and, in spite of the misgivings he felt, had to smile.

"DeVet?" he called out. "DeVet, haven't you retired yet?"

He heard laughter, and then the other's voice again. "No, not yet. Not lucky enough to find paradise yet, I guess. Put those lights down," the voice ordered, and the glare became a glow and Versola could see the figures again. One of them stepped forward as Versola came to a spot a few meters before the group and stopped.

"Well," DeVet said, "the prodigal returns." He stood

before Versola, feet planted wide apart, fists on hips. He was short and stocky: broad in the chest, thick waisted, just beginning to run to fat. He had a huge squarish head, close-cropped hair, big jaw, a great hooked nose, and was grinning toothily at Versola. "Going native seems to agree with you. You look healthy, vigorous—"

"Liar. My hair is gray and I'm as stringy as a piece of dried meat." He paused. "You look the same."

"The same, hey? I'm not sure whether that's a compliment or an insult."

"Ugly as ever, DeVet. But still young."

DeVet's grin faltered, seemed to transform itself into something else. He licked his lips once, quickly. "Yes, well—" he began, then faster, "come on then. Come into our conference room and meet everyone." He turned and walked fast to the largest shelter, glancing over his shoulder once and waving Versola on almost brusquely.

Inside, the light of the lamps was garish, reflecting intensely off the durafabric walls. Versola entered just after DeVet, and the others filed in and stood as if at attention, expectant, around the portable metal table. There were seven now, one short of the standard complement. To Versola they seemed so different and varied: thin and portly, pale and swarthy, tall, short, lanky, compact, bright- and dark-eyed. He stood next to DeVet at the head of the table, his feet shifting slightly on the packed-earth floor, unsure what to say or do. DeVet glanced around, then bent to whisper into one of the others' ears, and the latter nodded and stepped outside.

DeVet turned back to Versola. "Well," he said again,

too heartily, Versola thought. "This is the team now." He swung his left arm out expansively to indicate the others. "Starting from here: Jacobi, Centaurus; Primaverdi, Wolf; Jan-Kusawa, Sirius. . . ." Versola nodded as DeVet announced their names and origins. He would never remember them, he thought. Not because he wouldn't be able to—because it wouldn't do any good. Not if he never saw them again.

Two others stepped into the shelter. "Ah," DeVet said. "Tokala, Barnard's Star—" That was the one who had been there before. "And Andreyevitch, Luyten 726-8 B."

Andreyevitch was a small, dark, intense-looking woman who stared at Versola directly. "Amin Versola," she said in a loud, clear voice. "So you're the one."

Versola felt sudden shock, then defensiveness. He tried to mask it. "Amin Versola," he said, smiling thinly. "The very one."

The woman Andreyevitch nodded once in acknowledgment and continued studying him, unafraid. DeVet stepped forward as if to shield Versola.

"Nearly all new members," he said, grasping Versola's arm. "Just enough to fill the complement. Very lucky this circuit. Jedda and Harding got off at Sirius, Devallier found religion and began the Sol-world pilgrimage—" He paused, and his voice was graver when he resumed. "We lost Mamau and Chagai on an uncharted world—named it after both of them—and Pughi to the worms on Domicile."

Versola turned toward DeVet. "But you're still around, Nathan," he said.

The latter shrugged. "More luck." He paused, then

said, "And then there's you."

"And me," Versola agreed. "But the me of that time is gone, too." He spread his hands and smiled. "The curse of relativity."

"Enough," DeVet said with mock brusqueness. "No morbidity. We have a stock of Eridani wine—remember? Learned how to make it; we grow the grass stocks right in the pods now. Surprised, hey? Well, we can deplete our supply a little; gather round and have a celebration. These young neophytes are tired of my stories. They need some new ones. Come, we can take care of the formal reports tomorrow. . . ."

Later Versola would marvel at how easily he'd reassumed the old behavior patterns, how quickly he'd become part of the world he had watched fly away many years ago. It was curious that the traumatic shock he'd felt earlier on the incoming boat, watching their shuttle descending to the land, was now gone. He wondered about that too. Perhaps he had braced himself so strongly for their presence he was inured. Perhaps he still hadn't been on this world long enough; the milieu of the old one springing up and enveloping him almost unbidden. That bothered him. He had thought it forever excised.

But the Eridani wine was good, and the younger crew members' curiosity strangely stimulating. And smiling, loquacious DeVet wove them skillfully about each other with anecdotes and interjections that drew more of the same from Versola, and he found himself telling more and more about the world here.

"They're hermaphroditic. Estrual periods are every other year, and they're always single births. Since there's a strong parental instinct, the infant-survival rate is quite high. Of course, the life is also pretty hard, but still they do remarkably well."

"What do they do? Gather food, hunt, swim, eat, that's all?"

"Practically all. But it's not a utilitarian practice totally. It's almost ritualized, interwoven with their myths and the chants in that ritual language of theirs."

"Isn't that just another type of simple naturalistic religion?"

"It's not that simple. Theories are fine, as theories, but useful only as a starting point when you run into a new culture on a new planet. That's what the Service is supposed to teach you, right?"

"Do they have a culture, then?"

"I'd say the remnants of one that was once at a relatively high level. I think they're quite an old race, and descendants of a people who set on a great migration. The initial expedition—I'm sure DeVet briefed you—found no artifacts beyond their present-day designs, at least on this island. No explorations were done on the continents on the other side of the world." Versola paused. "I assume some of you intend to do that."

"Have you found out anything further?"

"Found out anything?" Versola smiled. "I've lived with them, eaten, talked, gathered food. They're a remarkably accommodating people."

"And today was the first time you've been with them on their hunt?"

"Yes," Versola said.

"Is there any real reason for that? Did they tell you?"

"I'm not sure. The hunt is seasonal, and seems to be a sort of ceremony too. A rite of passage, perhaps. A lot of the younger ones go out with them." Versola paused. "They're accommodating, but not outgoing."

There were more questions, more wine, but eventually Versola had to beg off. The hunt had tired him more than he thought. They broke off, bade him good night respectfully, and he stepped outside. DeVet accompanied him to the edge of the clearing.

Both moons were out now, bright and sharp edged, chasing each other in the sky from east to west. Their light was a ghostly glow giving the tableau behind Versola an ethereal cast. Before him the path was pale, leading into the gloom.

"So here we are again," Versola said quietly. "Your timing is impeccable."

"Timing?" DeVet asked.

"Never mind," Versola said. "So you're going to explore the continents?"

"That was the plan, yes. They're a good crew. Bright, energetic—"

"The cream of the crop. And all psychopaths. Who else would crew on a Service ship?"

"We were there, too."

"Yes, we were." Versola nodded. "Some of us had enough sense left to get off."

"Is your opinion of the Service so low now?"

"I haven't thought of the Service at all in—" Versola stopped. "I can't even tell you how long. I don't know. You couldn't relate to it. Five years? Ten? Twenty? What would they mean to you? Look at yourself, DeVet. Then look at me. How long has it been *to you* since you last saw me? A couple of years, perhaps?"

DeVet bit his lip and looked away. He said nothing.

"Ah," Versola said, and nodded again. "You see

now. Here they are, the bright young ones in these Service ships which practically take care of themselves, fulfilling what? Vicarious thrills, perhaps. Their neuroses. And all the while the universe shrivels and dies away, and they remain young, until sometime or another they become a little curious about how the universe lives rather than what it looks like. Who knows, maybe that's what the ships were built for in the first place—therapy."

"Amin," DeVet said slowly, "I know our arrival was sudden. It's understandable you're somewhat upset. I'm sorry. I was trying to put you at ease before—it has been a long time for you, I realize—and it seemed to be all right. You seemed to be almost enjoying it."

"I was," Versola said. "That's part of the problem." He stepped forward suddenly onto the path, paced a few meters, turned and walked back to where DeVet stood. He breathed slowly, long and deep, as if to calm himself.

"I'm not saying things right," he said. "It's hard—so long since I've used *these* words to speak with. I'm not used to this language anymore." He looked directly into DeVet's face. "You see? By staying here these many years I have become more a part of this world than of yours. Or thought so. Easier to think so, perhaps, without a choice. Now it appears not so clearcut."

"Do you know what you want, Amin?" DeVet asked. "Now—any better than you did when we first left you here?"

Versola nodded slowly. "I know, DeVet," he said. "Which may be irrelevant. What I want and what I'm compelled to be are two different situations."

DeVet sighed, and his shoulders slumped slightly. "It's still difficult to understand you, Amin. But you have to work things out yourself, so I'll respect that. We'll not intrude. It's a big planet." He paused. "Do you think—" Then he broke off, and made a small embarrassed laugh. "No. It's hard for me to talk to you, too. I know you, and yet I don't know you."

"At least," Versola said, "you understand that." He regarded DeVet's silhouetted form for several seconds, then turned and made his way back along the path toward the dwelling places.

But the calm he had felt before, that had settled into his life during his stay here, was gone, and in its place was the old uneasiness.

The next day Versola rose early and petitioned Selaam for another seat in the hunt, and the chief helmsman consented. This time they were lucky: they found their quarry before midday, and the threshing excitement of the chase and the catch put the uneasiness out of reach. It was still light when they rolled through the breakers of the inner reef, their quarry lashed between two of the boats with the ropes woven out of the dried vine fiber and thick as Versola's forearms.

It was a fine big catch, enough to feed the village for at least a sixday. Versola helped them carve up the carcass—their acceptance of his help being previously the most overt acknowledgment of his presence, before his acceptance of the hunting boats— but refrained from joining them in the low, rhythmic songs they sang as they worked. They portioned out the meat, giving him some from the lower back of carcass, the most flavorful part; he thanked them and made the preparations to preserve the bulk, saving a small part for his evening meal. By the time they were done it was dusk, and one of them lit the torches on the beach for them to see while cleaning up. In the failing day and the flickering light their tall black forms bent and turned, and finally moved away toward their homes.

Not a word had been said by Selaam about the arrival of the Service ship.

Versola sat in the doorway of his hut, staring moodily at the path leading down to the main settlement, separated from his area by several hundred meters. Thinking of that brought the uneasiness back again. He wondered what the helmsman's thoughts—what all their thoughts—were about that. He wondered—

He shook his head abruptly in irritation. That was the trouble, that he was thinking about all of this. Had the arrival of the ship and the others affected him that much—after all this time?

He looked down and was surprised to see his hands clenched tightly in fists, the muscles in his thighs tensed. Slowly he forced himself to relax.

It had been like a dream at first. The world was lush, perfectly suited to support them—yet no better than dozens of other ideal-parameter worlds they'd seen in their Service travels. (Decades? Centuries?) Yet Versola had stayed. A combination of so many things, undefinable and intangible—the ambiance of this world, Versola's own disillusionment and malaise, a thousand irritations in the Service life. And the natives here, who accepted the presence of these strange uniformed outsiders and their gleaming metal ship with perfect aplomb, as if they were just another natural phenomenon. Living close to their world, flowing with its changes rather than brutishly manipulating it—somehow that struck a responsive chord in Versola, something he could not articulate. When the Service crew became bored and wanted to explore elsewhere, Versola stayed behind.

How long—he thought of the tritium-decay timepiece he'd once had, something he'd kept from his early days growing up in the Centauri worlds. The only reminder of that time, in fact. Each half-life was four Primus years—a little over twelve and a half Earth-standard years and thus that many ship standard. After one half-life he had taken it, and all the other vestiges of his former life, up into the hilly jungle and buried them in a remote spot. He could not even guess how old he was; he had got out of the habit of counting his years after the third time he visited Centauri Primus and found it had aged three of its centuries since he had left. Since that symbolic casting off of the trappings of his Service existence, the pulse of his life had slowed, blended into the timelessness of this world.

He got to his feet and walked out several meters onto the path. It was just dusk; the torchlights before each household in the dwelling place were lit, shining palely in the fast-fading day. They would be preparing their evening meals soon, early for them, so they would have ample time for the rituals later on. Versola had already eaten; he would still have to hurry to go through the motions of preparing a report for DeVet, then come back to observe them.

In the first few years of his stay here he had kept himself apart from these others. It was a wholly personal decision. There were feelings within himself he had to confront, feelings he could not even name. Yet he believed they were as real as the substance of his body, and he could only see them by imposing upon himself a period of solitude—getting away from the self-enclosed Service world, away from these indigenous people for the time being, away even, at times, from the awareness of the natural world about him. The ship personnel were surprised at first, then fatalistic; to them it was just another defection of a Service worker, one disgruntled with the transitory life and wishing something more stable. In Versola's mind he knew his case was not that simple. When he tried to say so and explain himself to them, he met only with incomprehension, and knew then how different he was.

Time had passed in uncounted days, constant as the perpetual semitropical weather. The regimen of Service life gradually evaporated; the absence of that world's artifacts made its disappearance from his consciousness easier. He could not have told anyone precisely when he first drifted down from his hut into the native dwelling places, nor what the feeling was that told him to bring his solitude to an end. When they accepted him, made room for him in their life, he knew then that he had found what he was looking for.

Now his discovery was being threatened, by the reappearance of that other world and the obsession with the passage of time that came with it. They might go on to the continents half a world away, but that would not be enough; as long as they were on this planet, they would be as close to him as an intruding insect lodged in his ear.

He stared down at the rough houses, their outlines becoming more indistinct as nightfall began to shroud them. Then he set off down the path and turned sharply toward the clearing and the ship, driven by a vague urgency to do something—the exact nature or details of which he did not yet know.

"That's it, then." DeVet's voice was flat and noncommittal. "That's not much, Amin." He looked up at Versola, his face expressing slight surprise and a hint of dismay.

Versola shrugged. "It's not that easy to get to know them. You establish a relationship and it only goes so far. There it remains, for a long time."

"A long time...." DeVet turned back to the portable screen, now blank. The audiovisual cassette on which Versola had logged his report whirred to an abrupt silence, signifying it was rewound. DeVet reached over and plucked the cassette from the player, weighing it in his hand.

"I don't understand," DeVet said slowly. "You were one of the best ethnologists around. So much better than most of the rank amateurs we get now—nearly as good as the best of the first generation of Service people, back when they were still based in the EarthSol system. That's what everyone said." He looked down at the cassette in his hand as if not quite believing what he saw. "This—there's nothing here, Amin. Oh, vague things, general observations—but not much beyond your preliminary account, back when we first made planetfall. Where are those insights? Those conjectures on these people's evolutionary development? The importance of religion and ritual in their lives?"

"Maybe I've lost the touch. Or there's not much there beyond what I—we first observed."

"Well, which is it?" DeVet almost demanded. His eyes narrowed in scrutiny. "Or is it something else altogether?"

"Look," Versola said, "maybe all this doesn't matter anymore. I can tell you right now it doesn't to me, not much. Maybe I just think it's not important compared to certain other things. That's why I'm no longer the keen-eyed observer you once thought me. That's as good as any, isn't it?"

"What should we do, then? Leave someone else here to spend who knows how many more years to do it right?"

"No," Versola said—too quickly, he thought. Recovering, he continued, "Just forget it. Chalk it up as a loss, a dead end. Don't even bother logging it in the Survey records."

DeVet's face set in a determined expression. "You know we can't do that. That's not what we're in the Service for."

"Oh, DeVet," Versola said wearily. "What are you in the Service for, then? Can you tell me that?"

"You need me to tell you?" DeVet's expression changed to one of surprise. "You haven't forgotten the Expansion Theory, have you? I mean, even after all this time—"

"Don't give me that Service Charter drivel. The idea that we have to keep finding enough worlds to house the outward-expanding human population is just a clever piece of romantic propaganda to ensure there will be enough people clamoring to enter the Service. How big is the Sphere of Man now? Thirty thousand cubic light-years? That's only a radius of, say, twenty light-years. And how many centuries ago did they develop the fusion engines? We're hardly spilling over into the rest of the galaxy. The last time I looked at the survey charts not even half of the Prime worlds were claimed by colony ships, let alone all those hundreds of Good and Marginal ones. I hardly think it's changed much since then. I'd bet the Service could be nonexistent tomorrow and the rest of the habitable worlds in the charts wouldn't even be touched five hundred standard years from now."

"Does that mean we're useless, then? Should we all give up and make our own permanent planetfalls?"

"It doesn't really matter to me what you do," Versola said. "As long as things here remain undisturbed."

"Oh. I see." DeVet's eyes widened slightly, and he nodded several times. "This, then—" He hefted the cassette once, then tossed it onto the table. It clattered, a startling, sudden sound, then was still. "This is your way of telling us to leave you alone."

Versola said nothing. He continued to look at DeVet directly.

"Well, shit—" DeVet uttered the expletive angrily. "Just what exactly have we done to you so far? We've been down hardly more than a day. Is our presence that abhorrent to you now?" His sudden anger seemed to dissipate, and he continued in a more subdued tone. "Look. We're all the same, underneath our individual differences. We're all human. Grant us that common basis at least. We'll be moving over to the continent in several days anyway; is it too much to ask that there be some semblance of contact between us?"

Versola did not answer for several seconds. "I don't know," he said at last. "I don't know if we're able to talk to each other anymore."

DeVet's mouth tautened, and his eyes narrowed slightly as if in pain. "All right," he said, his voice barely more than a whisper. He sat back in his chair and exhaled audibly, studying Versola. A defeated expression was on his face. "We were close friends once," he said softly. "Even compared to the others in that group, not so long ago. Could you have changed so much—could things have changed so much, things I couldn't see?"

"That's the problem," Versola said. He walked to the door of DeVet's tent and paused. "It was a lot longer ago for me than it has been for you." He turned and went outside into the night.

They were gathered in the sheltered hollow, dimly lit by the moonlight; only two of the planet's satellites were out, but the small lake which they fronted shone like a pool of fresh quicksilver. Versola guessed that all of the natives were there, young and old alike, divided by age into several curved rows. They stood and swayed back and forth, slow and somnolent; a low murmuring chant drifted up to him on the cliff, wordless yet rhythmic, counting cadence for their shifting bodies.

The first time Versola had watched this ceremony he was overcome by a sudden impulse to preserve it on film. He was on his feet and about to run back to his hut for the long-unused recorder, when a slow realization came over him, dampening the impulse; then it gave way to a great calm, and he turned back, returned to his place on the cliff overlooking the hollow, and watched silently. It was the next day that he took all the tools of his former life and buried them on some unknown hillock. The only recording he had now of this was in his mind.

The chant shifted from its slow singsong into a more strident pace. Now muted phrases in the ceremonial language could be heard, uttered at random among the wordless rhythms. With the change came an increase in tempo of their swaying, and now it was becoming a dance: the natives turned, wheeled gracefully, stamped their feet and shifted their rows past each other in perfect rhythm to the chant. Its sound was suddenly louder, an insistent throbbing that seemed to attune itself to the beating of his own heart, awakening some urge within him that rose in anticipation.

The voices joined in a sudden shout, and the urge seemed to leap within Versola. The rows of people gave way slightly before the lake, and the surface of the water rippled, then broke as something rose from it, stepped onto the shore, then began its own swooping dance among them—long, silvery, a graceful torpedo shape weaving about the dancers now encircling it.

If Versola looked carefully he could see the feet of those inside the costume of the sea creature as barely discernible shadows underneath it. Most of the time he preferred not to; in his mind he made this ritual more than a reenactment of the day's hunt. To him it *was* the hunt, the creature diving and turning about its attackers, who fell back when wounded or disabled, only to be replaced by a new circle of hunters. They pursued the creature anew, stabbing at it with invisible harpoons, while it twisted and lunged at them in counterattack.

The pace increased. The dancers whirled in a frenzy of action. The throbbing chant ululated in the air, and

Versola felt himself charged with the excitement, felt the beginning dampness of perspiration under his arms.

Then abruptly the creature fell to the ground, mortally wounded. The chant surged into a shout of triumph; the circles of the people came together and closed in upon the supine "corpse," hiding it from view. They linked arms together tightly and fell upon their knees as one. With a final shout their song suddenly ended, and the still silence settled upon their crouched, unmoving mass.

Versola sighed involuntarily, as if it were a release. He got to his feet, looked down at the huddled worshippers, then turned and began making his way back to his hut. It had been a good ceremony, he thought, one worthy of the great catch they had made that day.

When he rounded the turn in the path leading to his abode, he looked up and saw a shadowy figure standing by the entrance to his hut. A sudden surge of anger and irritation went through him; was it someone from the ship? He quickened his pace, words of rebuke on his tongue, then abruptly slowed down when he saw it was none of them, but instead the chief helmsman, Selaam.

"You were not at the worship place?" Versola said in the vernacular language.

"I did not take part tonight." Selaam's head, looking like a hood in the moonlight, inclined slightly forward. "I am to do other things."

Versola did not say anything, expecting Selaam to continue. Yet the chief helmsman also remained silent.

"Come," said Versola at last. "Sit with me in my

house and we will talk."

Selaam gestured acknowledgment. Versola entered, and the other bowed under the doorsill and followed.

They sat on the smooth dirt floor, Versola cross-legged, Selaam with his legs tucked underneath. Moonlight through the two small windows partially lit the interior, but not enough to show more than the outlines of their seated figures.

"They danced well tonight," Versola said by way of preamble.

"We were blessed today. We had profuse thanks to give."

"You have never visited me here," Versola said carefully, "not in all this time. Is there a special reason for this?"

Selaam gestured. "In the seasons you have been in our world you have expressed a desire to remain alone. We have respected that wish. Now the other ones like you have returned from the sky, and you are again together." Selaam paused. "Does this mean your time alone is ended?"

Versola smiled in the darkness. "I don't know if it will ever be ended," he said, "no matter where I am."

"Please explain."

"Ah—" Versola stammered slightly. "Well, it's—it's a personal problem. One that I have, not the others. They are a people, together, just as you are here. I did not feel a part of them."

"So you remained here to be alone."

"Yes," Versola answered.

"But now you will go with them when they leave again?"

"No," Versola said quickly. "I have said—" He

stopped and thought. "It's a season, a season of my life. Before I spent one in the company of men, because that's what it was for. This one, the one that guides me now, is my season of solitude."

"There are seasons of the world," Selaam said slowly, "and the upward climb of the people from the sea to the sky is also divided into seasons. But I have never heard of seasons in the life of a man." Selaam shifted somewhat restlessly. "We have no songs to tell us this. We have lived by them since the world began, when Those Below called the waters out of nothing to cover them, then floated the land on its surface to use as ladders to the sky. They placed our brothers in the sea to remind us on the land of our former seasons, and we dance to celebrate our kinship. The sky is the Last Place; the songs say the seasons will turn into the final one, the season with no time, and in the sky we will remain.

"Now you say you come from the sky back to the land. Are there new songs we must learn in the sky to follow? Are all men to do what you have done?" The chief helmsman's voice was tinged with distress.

"This hasn't worried you before," Versola said. "Why, then, did you accept us—accept me? I thought—"

"It was a new thing. We thought it a part of the coming season-with-no-time that one from the sky would return for awhile, and thus an indication that we would soon be stepping upward from the land. In our minds you were an emissary, a traveler, who would introduce to us the ways of achieving the Last Place." The tall shadow shifted again. "This was not easy to accept in itself. There is no mention of the exact way the time between seasons passes in our songs, either."

The shadow abruptly rose and towered over Versola. He involuntarily got to his own feet, quickly, and stepped a short way backward.

"My presence here—" Selaam's voice was halting. "It is against the way of life as told in our songs. But the return of the others from the sky was an omen that your time on the land would now be short. With nothing to guide us, the decision was made to come forth and petition for the words to the next song."

Versola tried to speak, but found that he strangely could not. His tongue felt thick and dry, blocking the words from coming forth.

"Now you say they will leave, but you will not." The figure of Selaam swayed suddenly. "Something is not proper. We must decide now how to repair the course of our life."

With no further word, Selaam turned and stepped out of the hut. Versola strode quickly to the door, but then stopped. The other's tall form glided down the path, then was lost in the darkness. Versola stood a long time, staring into the night, past the dimly visible path into the hushed shadows.

He kept to himself for two days, away from the natives and the ship personnel, and thought.

They had never really conversed or got to know each other. Even after all this time, the only one among them who had spoken more than words of courtesy to him had been Selaam. Versola assumed it was because that was the other's duty, spokesman of the natives as well as chief helmsman of the hunt, which made sense: combining all the leadership roles in one person was a common enough practice at any social level.

Yet even Selaam had offered no more than small, perfunctory snatches of their life in this world. Versola realized this when he thought back on the conversations they'd had. He didn't really have a complete picture of them; the lazy timelessness of his existence here had fooled him into thinking so, thinking he really did know them, even at times that he was a part of their lives.

Yet it was foolish to think it could have been otherwise. He'd begun with no assumptions or expectations; since then he'd been, if not happy, then somehow satisfied with his sojourn on this planet. Had he really wanted a kinship with them? Hadn't such relationships been precisely why he'd left the Service and, essentially, the world of man? He was still a creature of solitude, maintaining his personal domain apart from the others, preserving his own moments of privacy.

It should have been enough. Until now it had been enough just to visit with them occasionally, not live with them, to see them as part of the world about him and not an encroachment on his own life. He'd told himself that repeatedly and it had seemed right.

Now it did not ring true. It was knowing that the barriers were there that was disturbing.

The return of the ship was proving precipitous. Time and events seemed to be hurtling forward in its wake. He wondered what they would do now, and in turn, about himself.

He walked the shoreline, blanking his mind of thoughts, concentrating on the sensation of his feet sinking into the soft-packed sand. Water and foam hissed about his calves with their sudden wet coolness, receded, then hurled themselves forward again. One moon was out tonight, showing the shore break as pale ghostly foretops of the small waves. Against its weak light the backdrop of star set in darkness shimmered more brightly than usual, inconstant beacons in the night.

He heard a splashing behind him, then the slap of bare feet against the wet sand. Unconsciously he stiffened. It would be one of the ship personnel; none of the natives would have been so noisy. He continued walking, not looking back when he felt the presence of the other a little behind him.

" 'No more tonight/The stars are all fallen. ' " The voice was soft and musing, a female voice.

"Actually, they're not." Versola spoke in a casual voice. He kept his gaze steadily forward, then looked up and pointed. "See: stars beyond number."

"And all our worlds among them—dead, changed, mutable." A slightly mocking tone came into the voice. "We're the lucky ones, aren't we? We get to stay the same."

Versola felt a sudden surge of irritation. He turned slightly and regarded the other with a sideways look. "You're—Andreyevitch, is that right?"

Her head bowed in acknowledgment. "You have a good memory."

"It's the way I was trained—once."

"Once?" she said quickly. "How long ago was that?"

He ignored the question. "Do they still teach the poetry of Lu-Yang in the schools of the Sphere of Man?"

"They did when I was in school. He was still a hero

then. Maybe he's still alive, heading in toward the Core in that stolen ship." He saw the shadows of her shoulder lift in a shrug. "Now—who knows? Maybe they've all forgotten him."

"Where is your star?" he asked.

"A hundred light-years from here, on the edge of the Sphere." Her voice became musing again. "It would take us over three standard centuries to get there from here. It may as well be a thousand centuries away. No matter to me."

"Oh?"

She looked at him levelly. "When I left school for the three-year mandatory Service apprenticeship on Centanrus, the Great Pact between the Sphere of Man and the warring tribes of Luyten Inhabitus—the star's only planet—was barely five years old. My Fourtime Father drove me to the spaceport in a pneumatic car he'd gotten free from the dealers for landing the exclusive concession for them. This from a man once chieftain of the greatest tribe there, who had led the last great war against the Sphere's takeover." She paused. "Now he's dead and rotting in the ground. Along with the world he built. If I hadn't opted for apprenticeship, I would be too."

"And this is better for you?"

"Isn't living always better than dying?" she demanded. "Why should we chain ourselves to worlds that decay and fall apart? This way we live decades, centuries longer. We can go on almost forever."

"No, you don't. You only think you do, because you can see everything else outside your ship age and crumble. It doesn't add anything to your life. It only presses those outside closer together."

"But the result is the same, isn't it? While you're slowly turning to dust, we'll be going on to the next star."

"And will you be that much wiser?" Versola replied. "How much more will you know?"

Andreyevitch's face was a dimly visible mask staring at him. "Maybe all the secrets," she said. "Maybe nothing. But at least we'll have the chance to find out." She stopped abruptly and stood straight, still looking at him. Versola came to a halt several meters away and half turned toward her. "Better to take that chance than to condemn yourself to such an ephemeral life as yours," she declared flatly. "I thought you of all people would remember that."

"Why me? Because of DeVet's stories?" He moved closer. "Did DeVet send you to try to convince me—"

Her sharp laugh cut off his words. "DeVet has nothing to do with this," she said. "I wanted to find out myself what made one of us opt out of the Service."

"Then call it a coming to one's senses," Versola said shortly. "That should be enough. A lifting of one's delusions."

She made a mock-sad sound. "What a shame. Perhaps you've been out too long already."

"You thought it would be simple to persuade me to come back? What do you think I am?"

"A man," she said simply. "Like us. Not anything more or less." She turned and began to walk back the way they'd come, then paused. "Perhaps you'd better look more closely and see which is the delusion and which the real thing." Then she began walking away. Versola stared at her receding figure until it was hidden by a land rise.

He resumed his own strides, then forced himself to slow down when he realized he was pacing along the sand rapidly. The pulsing of his blood sounded in his ears, louder than the roar and hiss of the sea. Every time, he thought. Every time he came in contact with them it was upsetting. No more, he decided. Abruptly he turned inland and made his way over the soft sand to the grassy expanse. Let them fester among themselves in their imbalance, but not him. Andreyevitch's expressionless face came to him again, lingered in his mind. Insane, insane, he thought, and the words and her face whirled about as he made his way back up the hill.

That night Versola dreamed he walked a long, winding stairway of metal, curled into a spiral, like the catwalks on the ships he had once signed on. The gravity felt a little less than standard, so he didn't worry about drifting off, if he stepped too hard, into the weightless area down the axis of the spiral. Beyond the stairway were indistinct shadows; as he walked farther they came closer, their edges sharpened, and he could see the faces of men and women, the crew members of the Service ships he had known in the past—light, dark, thin, bloated, asymmetric and dissimilar; twisted into expressions of joy, anger, surprise, bemusement, sorrow, fear, apathy, pain. He looked ahead and saw the stairway come to an end; his steps came with more difficulty, and when he looked down at himself he saw his hands wrinkled and bony, his body shrunken, and somehow his own face withered and ancient. He kept walking toward the end, and then Selaam and the others stood there, identical as blades of grass. The faces began spinning about the stairway, now and then coming close and receding like a throbbing organ, yet he felt no vertigo. He reached the end and stopped; Selaam and the others made way for him. Beyond them was nothing; the faces spun faster, their mouths open as if shouting. He stepped off the stairway into the nothing, then awoke.

The inside of his hut was very dark; no moons were out. He lay on his back, staring upward, for several minutes. Then he slowly rose and, naked, felt his way to the door and stepped outside.

A slight breeze came up and cooled his skin. All about him was darkness, so he could barely see the brush or the path under his bare feet. He looked up, beyond into the clearing of the natives' houses, and saw tiny points of light that showed their torches were lit. As he stood there he became aware of a faint low murmur of noise, like a wordless conversation.

He moved further along the path. The noise was now somewhat louder, and he could discern that it came from the native dwelling places. They were up and— talking? No, it was more rhythmic. A chant? Which ceremony? Versola had never seen them performing any rituals this late at night. Was it something new?

He listened carefully to their voices for awhile, then gave up. It was their complicated ceremonial language, therefore unfamiliar to him. He'd tried learning it once, but its difficulty had proved much greater than their vernacular dialect. It had been no great disappointment at that time that he couldn't know the meanings of those archaic words. Now he found himself wishing he did.

"I know you, yet I don't know you," he said aloud

softly. In the clearing the points of light flickered. The sounds of their voices continued to drift upward to him. He stood there for several moments longer, then turned with sudden decision and went back inside. He lay down, closed his eyes, and eventually slept. He dreamed no more that night.

The ship gleamed in the middle of the clearing, reflecting the early-morning sun. All the crew's tents and other artifacts had been packed away inside. Several of them busied themselves about the site, performing last-minute cleaning duties.

"We'll be there at least fifty of this planet's days." DeVet spoke somewhat stiffly to Versola. He looked awkward and cramped in his tight-fitting tunic and pants. "The coordinates are logged in here." He hefted the portable communicator in his hand. "Just turn it on and the signal will automatically home in on wherever we set up our receiver—"

"I remember how it works," Versola said.

DeVet pressed his lips together and looked irritated. "All right," he said shortly. His expression softened a little. "Maybe you'll want to talk to us a bit, now and then. Who knows? Or to the rest of us up there." He jerked his chin toward the sky. "We've got a geostationary satellite over this region. Just in case."

"That's fine, DeVet," Versola replied.

DeVet studied Versola for several seconds. "I hope," he said, "you find what you're looking for." He continued to regard Versola, then nodded curtly and walked away to the ship, leaving the communicator beside Versola.

Andreyevitch, standing by two crew members

carrying life-support modules toward the ship, spotted Versola and began walking toward him. She stopped several meters away and placed her hands on her hips, looking at him directly.

"So you really are staying," she said matter-of-factly.

"I always intended to," he said.

"What if you change your mind?"

He shook his head. "I don't think so."

"The next time we come through here—after we're done—might not be too soon. You may be dead by then."

"Good-bye," Versola said.

Her face froze into an expressionless mask. She let her arms hang loosely, and without another word turned and stalked off.

Versola picked up the communicator and walked slowly to the edge of the clearing. There he paused and turned. Everyone was aboard the ship; it would only be a few minutes now. He walked more swiftly over the edge and down the path. A moment later a sudden loud booming noise came, and the ground shuddered slightly. He halted again and looked up, and watched the silvery craft climb higher into the air, growing smaller, until it was a bright dot in the sky.

He turned off the path and made his way through dense brush. Under a small fernlike tree he began digging a hole with his hands. Soon he had one about a meter deep; in it he threw the communicator, then shoved the dirt back in on top of it, packing it with his hands and feet. He brushed the dirt from his body and wended his way back onto the path.

He felt relieved and a little lightheaded, as if he had successfully weathered an ordeal. His step was almost jaunty as he followed the path down to the natives' dwelling places. New energy seemed to come to him, and he began to feel pleasant anticipation throughout his body.

The settlement was very quiet. Versola stepped into the level area and looked about; the huts were still, no one was about. Were they still asleep? How long had the ceremony continued the night before? Had it tired them more than usual?

He went to the nearest hut and cautiously peered into the open doorway. No one was inside; there was no sleeping or eating pallet on the floor. Versola frowned slightly and moved on to the next hut. Inside, it was the same. He began to feel apprehension, and strode swiftly across the avenue to the others.

Several minutes later the apprehension had become near panic. The huts had all been abandoned. All their articles were gone. None of the natives remained.

Versola stood in the middle of the dividing avenue, lost and disoriented. Where had they gone? Why? He had never seen the village completely deserted. Could they have all gone on a hunt? But there was—had been—plenty of meat, hadn't there?

Abruptly he began running, down the path and through the brush, heedless of scratches and whipping branches, toward the beach.

He broke through onto the sparsely vegetated sand and looked upon the expanse of the shore. None of the boats were lined up on the beach; they were all gone.

All gone. He looked out to sea, squinting against the sun and the sparkling brilliance of the water. Nothing—no, wait. Out just beyond the first reef, there was a darker blob on the water. He peered at it until his eyes began tearing; though it was surely too far to tell, he imagined he could perceive a boat, and a lone native sitting in it.

He stood indecisively for a long moment, breathing hard, his blood pounding in his ears. Then he ran forward, stumbling slightly in the soft sand, moving more surely in the hard-packed region, and splashed through the shore break and the bobbing waves. Keeping his eyes on the dark blob, he began to swim out toward it.

The inshore waves buffeted and abused him. He tried to ignore the beginning ache in his arms as he stroked further out. Occasionally a sudden surge of water would slap his head, and he would shake the water out of his eyes and spit it out of his mouth. The strong riptide helped him considerably, but he could feel the tightness growing in his muscles.

Eventually he was past the rough area and into the deeper calm. It was easier here—but it would be easier for the boat to move away, too, he thought, so he began to stroke harder. He could see his initial hunch had been right: it was a boat, and the rower was steadily stroking it further out, toward the deep.

His arms felt heavy. His breath came in gasps now. He turned on his side and began sidestroking, using his legs for most of his exertion, always keeping the boat in sight. The boatman did not acknowledge him; Versola was not even sure from this distance whether the boatman had turned toward him or not. He did not think he had the breath to cry out for his attention.

They continued outward, the skimming boat and the desperate swimmer. The sun climbed higher in the sky. Versola didn't even consider the possibility of failing to catch up with the boat; the panicky energy still held fast in his mind, though not in his body. He struggled to keep his head above water; a hot wheezing pain began in his lungs. Now he stroked hard with his arms, then kicked with his legs when they became tired. The boat seemed closer now; Versola could see the paddle in the boatman's hands. It urged him onward, and he painfully renewed his efforts.

Out past the reef, into the deep blue; the boatman paddled more slowly, and the head turned this way and that, gazing before the boat as if searching for something. Versola's arms felt leaden and numb, but he somehow continued stroking; his lungs were aflame with agony. A muscle in his calf and thigh was threatening to cramp, and he fought to keep it stretched out while still kicking with his other leg. Even in the slow gentle swells his head dipped in the water often, and he vomited up the brackish gulps he involuntarily swallowed. But he was making headway; he could see the native boatman clearly now, paddling much more slowly, as if this were some drawn-out ritual. When the head turned once and gave him a half profile, Versola saw that the boatman was Selaam.

"Selaam—" He tried to say it loud, but his first attempt was swamped by a sudden swell. He gagged and spit out the water, then frantically paddled closer. With great effort he raised his head higher above the water and called out his name as loud as he could. To his own ears it sounded like no more than a hoarse croak, but it seemed enough; the boatman's head swiveled about and Selaam saw him.

The effect on the boatman was dramatic. Selaam raised the paddle as if to ward off an attacker; it slipped from his grasp into the boat. Then he stepped backward, stumbled, and sat down heavily, back pressed against the bow, hands on the gunwales, staring at Versola as he crawled through the water toward the boat.

"Selaam—help me up—please—" Versola gasped out his words in the native's language. The boat was mere meters away. Selaam sat there, as if hypnotized, making no move to lend Versola aid. Versola moved closer, and then his outstretched fingers brushed the side of the boat. His limbs suddenly cramped and his body sank below the surface; frantically he kicked out, and his head rose. He kicked harder and moved against the boat, then threw his arms up and over, hanging on the gunwales near the stern.

"What is this—where are—people—" Versola's breath came in a painful wheeze and he could barely enunciate the words. "Why—you left?"

Selaam said nothing. His hands gripped the gunwales tighter, and the muscles in his shoulders rippled as if with tension.

"I—I have to rest—" Versola heaved, got halfway out of the water, fell back in. He tried again, finally got his torso on the gunwale, and painfully scrabbled over. He collapsed in the stern, exhausted, his mouth open and gasping, and stared at Selaam.

At that point Selaam stood up and sprang at him, hands outstretched and grasping. Versola registered it, too late, and tried to roll away. The native's body crashed into his, and the hands slapped against his head. Versola ducked and tried to slip under and away; long fingers clawed at his neck. He cried out wordlessly and shook free. He stepped backward and fell across the gunwale; Selaam fell on top of him, hands striking at his face, and under the sudden weight Versola felt pain in his side, then even greater pain as something snapped and gave way. He rolled in agony, and Selaam's fingers laced about his throat and forced his head back. Versola struck upward desperately; the fingers loosened and he could breathe, each breath thrusting a knife in his side. He felt blows on his face, and something broke there. His arm was caught in a vise; it was pulled upward, his body following it, and he felt himself turned over. He kicked backward and the weight lifted; then it fell on him again, and his arm twisted on the gunwale and he felt it break.

Versola fell onto his back in the bottom of the boat. Selaam stood over him, the paddle in his hands; the amber eyes seemed to glow, the face more skull-like with the lips drawn back. The native raised the oar; Versola closed his eyes briefly, but could not keep them closed. He stared up at the native as if captivated.

Selaam stood as if frozen for several seconds. Then his head turned quickly to the side. He was staring at something in the water.

Versola turned his head. The calm surface broke, and a grayish-white expanse rolled into view, then slipped back into the water. There was a brief flash of a tail, then it disappeared.

Selaam lowered the paddle. He seemed greatly calmed. He looked down at Versola, then uttered several words in the ceremonial language.

"What—" Versola spoke with difficulty. His mouth felt swollen and full of detritus. "What are you saying?"

Selaam spoke again. His tone was serene and formally cadenced, like a chant. He pointed toward the sea, where the creature had been, then indicated himself. He gestured toward the sky, spread his arms outward, then uttered a long speech, all incomprehensible to Versola, who could only stare dumbly.

Selaam stopped. His eyes searched the sea again. Several meters away the creature's back again broke the sea calm, and it turned slightly so the mottled flipper came partly out of the water. Selaam uttered a sudden burst of words, climbed atop the gunwale, then dived into the water. Versola saw his feet kick twice in the water, then he was gone.

"No." His voice was barely a whisper. He dragged himself to the gunwale and leaned dangerously over the side. "You can't leave. Not without telling me." The sea creature was gone; the surface smoothed over again. "Where are they? You have to tell me." His voice rose higher and cracked. "Where are you all? What is it you're doing? What is it?" He stopped and stared silently into the water, bright and burnished as a mirror, rolling gently, lazily, with the calmest of swells.

They found him two days later when someone did a routine check on the observer satellite, throat raw, jaw broken, arm gangrenous, ribs threatening to knit wrong. In the intensive-care unit they patched him up nicely—new grafts on his throat, cleaning up the infection, resetting the bones.

"You'll be all right." They were solicitous and concerned, their voices sympathetic. "You're safe now. You're with us. How do you feel?"

But he did not know them, any of them. They were all strangers to him.

READING DAY

by

Bill Pronzini and Barry Malzberg

Again and at long last, it was Reading Day.

Once every chronum the Reader comes to our Unit. He stands before the thousands of us assembled in our individual viewing cubicles, and with the aid of the amplificators he practices his strange and wondrous art. This is so arcane that it is difficult to state, but I will do the best I can. By the exercise of his great powers, the Reader is able to convert mysterious printed Symbols into understandable Words. He Reads the Words to us from an object called a Book and they follow one another in the proper order. Thus, they become a Story.

The Story is not quite so interesting or exciting as what the amplificators or cinematic sensors can give us, but on the other hand Reading is a remarkable experience. On its own terms it is to be venerated. We are in awe of it, or at least most of us are in awe of it; some of the young ones are restless, but that is because they do not have the maturity and wisdom of the elders.

The Reader stood before us in the amphitheater. He was a unique and somewhat shriveled man, forty chronums at least by his bearing and demeanor, perhaps even forty-five—a true elder. Through the visiscreens which brought his image before us in our cubicles, we were able to perceive him closely: the wizened features, the large and staring eyes, the powerful jaws for speaking. It was the eyes which fascinated me. Does Reading make one so sad? I wondered. I thought of the mystical lore and craft of the Readers, which set them apart from the rest of us, and felt that this must be so.

We were very quiet during the customary ceremonies and introductions. We have little to say to each other in the Unit, being occupied for the most part with the stresses of vocation and needing the individual attention of the visiscreens during our hours of rest; but this is what is known as a general cultural pattern. The specific individual pattern is that the power of the Reader exerts its power over us. For the Reader remains a mysterious figure; his skills are holy, his name is holy, and we know his holiness. It is not possible to be other than solemn in the presence of those who possess the gift of transmitting printed Symbols into spoken sound. I have heard that the visiscreen technicians themselves are hushed at their work on Reading Day.

"I will now commence," the Reader said at last. "The Selection will be of approximately four centi-chronums duration and I will appreciate your fullest attention."

The young ones do not have the wisdom of we elders, as I have said, nor do they have the ability to concentrate as we do; this is why the Reader's caution is necessary. Chronums ago it was not necessary, but then chronums ago we were not faced with what many of us believe to be intrinsic social deterioration. As few as thirty chronums past there were reputed to be nine hundred Readers; now there are only seven hundred. They are seldom replaced. They are, in fact, virtually irreplaceable, for few of today's elders have the intellect required to learn the great skills of Reading. The seven hundred must travel almost twice as much now, and there is only one Reader per sector. Which is why the once-per-chronum visit to our Unit is a day of festivity, courage, celebration, and occasion.

In his powerful voice the Reader began his ritual. The Word-Symbols rolled through the amplifier and through all the spaces of my cubicle. I listened with reverence; the power of the Reader is always fresh and marvelous. He is not to be taken lightly.

But then, of a sudden, his voice was stilled and I heard other sounds over the amplifier—the sounds of a disturbance. An instant later a new figure appeared on the visiscreen: a young one who had raced into the amphitheater, brandishing a staff and shouting mad imprecations.

"This is apostasy!" he cried. "Reading is a lie; Reading is vile! Death to the Readers!"

I knew at once who and what he was. His newly

shorn head and bulging eyes marked him as a member of the dangerous New Cultists, who not so many chronums ago had started riots during the Reading Days. The Sweeps and Leveling Actions had reduced their numbers considerably, but they were fanatics and as such fearless of death and reprisal.

"Pagan!" the cultist screamed. "You despoil the modern way; your printed Symbols are wicked and debased! False gods, false scripture! Death to you all!"

He launched a terrible blow with his staff, but the Reader avoided it with surprising and thankful agility. Before the cultist could strike again, the Securities were upon him and soon had beaten him to the floor. Seconds later, he was carried from view.

Attendants came and swabbed away the blood. It had been an ugly and terrible incident, one which had left me quite shaken, but the Reader seemed composed, almost serene; he stood quietly at the podium. The visiscreen reflected the pain and knowledge in his eyes and I understood that similar things had happened to him before.

At length all order was restored. The Reader turned a Page in his shining Book with willowy and steady hand, and as if there had been no interruption he said, "I will continue."

He commenced again to Read. The Word-Symbols carried through the amplificator in my cubicle and once more I could feel their tremendous power. So moved was I then that I fell to my knees and closed my eyes and clasped my hands at my breast.

Once every chronum we are granted this day. Once every chronum it *must* be so, for that is the way it has always been. The New Cultists do not understand this;

the New Cultists understand nothing.
   Reading Day is more than just a Chronum's Feast.
   Reading Day is a prayer.

A LONG, BRIGHT DAY BY THE SEA OF UTNER

by

Cherry Wilder

Before dawn the young girl, Maire, climbed up to the masthead and looked out through the narrows into the Western Sea. The caravel rode at anchor and the masthead wheeled in a lazy figure eight: Maire sat braced against the mast, astride the crosstree, and saw the water turn from blue-black, to green, to yellow-green as the sun rose. She looked back toward home waters, where the sea was blue and commonplace as the bustle on the deck below, the voices of the gulls and sailors. The Western Sea was shadowed, even under a cloudless sky; it was landlocked and old; its shores were hollowed out into caves and fragmented into islands.

Maire was watching for the boat, coming back; in the hot light of morning she could not help looking for movement under the waves. She dozed off for a moment and heard a voice in her dream, resonant, yet conversational. Then the ship woke her up and she heard her brother calling from the deck below. Maire would not answer; she was trying to recreate the voice in her dream.

When I went on retreat to the Sea of Utner I lived in a cave with a good clearance above and below the waterline. There was a spring of fresh water just beyond the cave mouth on a sandy cape. One morning I found a legendary creature drinking at the spring . . . a minmer or nipper. It was long as my middle-foot nail and had black skin. I watched it for nearly the whole of the day; it drank several times and slept curled up in the lee of a stone. Toward evening it began hunting for food and speared a winkworm which it cut in pieces . . . with its nippers, I presumed . . . and stored what it did not eat beside its sleeping stone. When the light had gone I channeled quickly through the sandbar and this was enough . . . the minmer was there next morning on an island.

To my surprise it had sloughed the black skin and laid it aside. The underskin was a smooth brownish-red and in places downy, like a sand flower. Unfortunately it had become dimly aware of my presence. The odor of its fear was sharp and distinct; it had no directional sense but seemed rather to guess the cave as a possible source of danger. It crawled behind its stone and as the sun rose higher a blue-green aura shone out from the minmer's body. There were jerks and breaks in the aura which made me investigate further and sure enough the minmer was making sounds, attempting some kind of sonic contact over land with the interior of the cave. I allowed the gentlest altered echo, a soothing whisper, and it registered, to me at least, as *ah-lo*.

The effect on the minmer was so great that I knew my reduplication had been very imperfect. The creature became erect, like a snapping shell; it advanced boldly to the very limits of its island and peered into the darkness of the cave. I magnified more than I had dared and saw two distinct eyes under a tuft of down on the nub of the animal. More arresting still was the single "nipper"... a metal spike, firmly grasped, giving off its own spectrum.

What is the measure of a true sentient intelligence? What are the lower size limits? The verts and dagomils, infinitesimal creatures, accrete vast habitations under the sea and tunnel busily on the land. But they operate under the rule of a blind patterning, without range, without color, without sonic impulse or spectral vision. I specialized one sensor and allowed it to come closer to the island. The minmer had a listening attitude. I listened, generally, and heard the sea, the sky, the local pulse of the land through the walls of that excellent cave. I listened with more particularity, through my sensor, and heard some approximation of what the minmer might hear. A grating of the waves on the island shore, a sucking as the waves washed into the cave mouth nearby, the cries of sea birds, a distinct susurration from within the cave, which I identified at once and took measures to correct. This sound came from my own body.

I drifted my sensor closer still and climbed it upon

the beach. The minmer attacked at once in an access of terror; the sparkle of its "nipper" mingled with its bodily aura. I closed out sensation but not before one or two sharp blows had penetrated. I prostrated the sensor and perfected its single eye and a coating of down. I writhed it in the sand and gave a little supplicating noise, half whistle, half groan, like a piron shell when it is forced open at a feast.

The minmer, which I now saw more clearly, drew back and did not attack again. It remained planted in the sand on a divided limb; after some moments it approached the wounded sensor. It made sounds that I judged were soothing ones; indeed I found them so. I whispered through the sensor a pleading "ah-lo." The minmer came very close, laid aside the metal nipper, then held out its upper branches, empty. I made a gesture of submission, flattening, crouching; it was not misinterpreted. The minmer cast off almost completely its aura of fear and anger; it became tinged with a pearly light about the upper half of its body. I soon learned that this denoted curiosity.

The minmer made sounds and I responded, mostly imitating. Then I slid the sensor back into the sea and returned quickly, from my own feeding seines, with winkworms and shells appropriately small. I laid them before the minmer and it thanked me, bending its body and repeating several sounds. It insisted that the food be shared and opened the shells with its nipper. I feigned eating, when I observed how the minmer ate, and looked my fill, for my single eye was now functioning at a better level to observe my mythical beast.

Now at this first meeting it had become apparent that the minmer had a distinct patterning of sounds . . .

a speech, a language. Leaving aside for the moment the question of any distinction between these two modes, speech and language, I decided to learn the pattern as quickly as I could. The minmer was only too ready to comply; it had nothing but friendly curiosity for the one-eyed amphibian, tall as itself. We accomplished the feat together in half the time it took to shed my skin. I feel a prickling sadness, now, at the memory of those summer days.... I have been influenced by the minmer's preoccupation with the passing of time, the actual passage of single days and nights in the continuum.

There was a harsh materialism about this minmer that grated at first, like sand in a duct. If I probed for sensibility, for breadth of feeling, I received "hard facts."... The minmer had been forced into the Sea of Utner by a storm... or figures spewed forth from the microcosm: the distances, in minmer terms, between the stars.

I was troubled by the deception I was practicing, even if the investigation were proving so successful.

"We don't come to the Western Sea," the minmer explained, "because there are tales of great sea monsters."

"What form might such a monster take?"

As the minmer replied it gave my sensor a strange look and a tinge of the old fear crept into the air around it.

"Who knows the shape of a sea monster?"

"Have you no legendary beasts?"

"Of course," said the minmer sitting up on its lump of sand. "The dragon—there is a great deal of material about dragons, not to mention the Leviathan, the

Kraken, the Behemoth. . . ."

It described all these creatures, then cocked an eye at my sensor.

"Have you seen anything of this sort in this Western Sea?"

"Of course," I whispered, "but you have not described them exactly."

"These are legends," said the minmer, "and off-world yarns at that. Perhaps the shape is nearer that of the plesiosaur, the ichthyosaur, the giant squid. . . ." And it was off again, speaking more wildly than before.

"Minmer," I said impatiently, "your brain is like a boru shell, full of little numbered grains of sand."

"Forgive me," said the minmer, "but I am nervous. I can't get off this island, my boat is gone, I am lost. Yet it is worth all my pain to talk this way with another life form."

"Agreed," I said. "We must speak further."

My retreat was nearly done; that night I made shift to provide the minmer with a new boat. It understood at once, for with daylight my sensor found it bailing water from the sloughed skin of my middle foot, washed up on the island beach. The minmer was active but not untinged with fear.

"What is that?" I asked. "The skin of a dragon's foot?"

"Something like that," growled the minmer. "Do you know how it came here?"

"Perhaps."

"Well, I am thankful. It will make me a boat."

"Come back," I said. "Come back if you have the spirit for it. I will be here again when the stars are overhead . . . including the one with the blazing tail . . . in exactly the same position."

"Whew!" said the minmer, looking up into the daylight sky, where I doubted that it could see more than the morning sun.

"That will take some doing. But truly I will come. Are you sure to be here?"

"I am sure."

The Sea of Utner was calm. The minmer had patched up a device to catch the wind from the black skin it had worn at first. It climbed into the boat and sailed off to the east, with an assisting breeze from the mouth of the cave.

The boy, Paddy, kept watch from the lookout in the afternoon. He ate a red "rogue apple" to keep himself awake; down below, the captain was snoring in his cabin, the crew were drowsing in heaps upon the deck. Suddenly he saw something to the northwest; he knew it could not be his father's boat. A broad furrow curved about in the purple water of the Western Sea and then was gone. Paddy shivered, but it was only the breeze that had come off the black slip of water in the narrows. He had been bred not to fear anything the Western Sea might bring. He remembered his grandmother, pacing the bridge of her ship, intent upon the patterns of the stars.

So the pattern was set and the minmer kept its word with fussy exactitude; I was forced several times to rebuild the island and reintroduce the spring of water. The minmer came in a new craft, towing the tattered relic of the "dragon's foot" as some sort of safe conduct. We talked.

"Minmer, what is the measure of intelligence?"

"Using tools? Building?" The minmer had erected a wooden shelter on the island, neat as a soft crab's nest, and was mending it with a set of metal nippers.

"The larger sea creatures do not 'build' precisely, though they may reform their environment."

"Friend Ash, the monsters may be quite stupid," said the minmer. "There must be some upper size limit for an intelligent life form, even in the sea. They are simply too large."

"Or you are too small."

"What?" the minmer stared into the round eye of my sensor.

I was tired of this equivocation.

"Do you not know, minmer, that a sea creature lives in the cave?"

"It was thought so, once."

"Perhaps you mistake the part for the whole."

"Yes," said the minmer and it looked at my sensor very closely. The stink, the blue-green aura of its fear, washed over it.

"Tell me," asked the minmer, "what is the meaning of that name . . . Ash?"

"It means a tentacle." I slid my sensor back into the water again, across the warm sand. The minmer ran to the water's edge, mastering its fear.

"Come back!" it shouted. "I will not be afraid." I fixed it with my sensor's eye from the shallows.

"Then see . . . minmer."

I reared up the full extent of my sensor to form a bridge leading into the cave and the minmer endured the test. It clambered onto the bridge, marched into the cave. It looked down into the swirling tangle of my seines, up into the darkness, where my eyes and scanners glowed of their own light, out to the forest of my sensors, coiled against the cave walls. But the sight was too much; the poor minmer reeled and could not take it in.

"Ash?"

"Minmer..." I replied as softly as I could but the sound bore down on the minmer like a blow. It fell senseless against the nearest of my three land feet, planted against the cave wall.

I thought it was dead; I felt a grinding sadness, as if one of my own limbs had been lopped off. I bore the minmer back to the island with my adapted sensor, its own friendly one-eyed sea beast, and laid it on the sand. Presently the creature revived and seemed to have learned something... though not much... from its experience. We resumed our relationship through Ash, the adapted sensor; the word "monster" disappeared from the minmer's speech. At our next meeting the minmer put its senses to the test again and visited the cave; it became part of the pattern. The minmer confessed to an extreme difficulty in making the connection between my sensor and my whole body, yet at the same time insisted that it had "known all along," "suspected from the first" or "solved the mystery."

"Minmer, how is your city building?"

"Very well. We number a thousand."

"A thousand minmers!"

"Don't sneer. We are an ancient people. Our ancestors came from the stars. We are alone on your world. We have lost our technology."

"Is self-pity the mark of an intelligent life form?"

"Why not?"

And so we would speak and part until the tailed star rode in the sky again, over the Sea of Utner. But the cycles have passed until this time when I speak; I must divide and forget and be forgotten. When I told the minmer, it was sad and showed more pity for me than ever for itself.

"Ash, you cannot die. You are my heritage.... Your words are repeated in the city. We are comforted by this communication...."

"Go well, minmer. The retreats are over."

"But need that be? The dialogue could continue...."

"How is that?"

"Send another in your place. There must be other beings like you ... hundreds...."

"Minmer, I cannot live as you do, numbering my companions, my days, like grains of sand."

Indeed my retreats, my dialogues with the minmer seem to me like one bright day by the Sea of Utner, a project half begun, a dream, a challenge. The minmer has set sail again, in its red wooden boat, heading east toward the narrows. We cannot allow this creature to return to the world of legend; it has without doubt the beginnings of intelligence. There is more to it than fear and vanity. I have the feeling that there is some part of the pattern missing, some linkage that I have failed to connect. So I have entrusted my records and this preamble to the residual portion of my brain, to go to the repository for the earnest consideration of the council. It might be enlightening to allow these dialogues to continue under exactly the same conditions.

* * *

The long day was almost over; the light of the setting sun reached through the narrows into the Western Sea. Maire and Paddy still sat in the crosstrees, watching keenly. Suddenly Maire swung upright and gave a long, loud hail. Far to the west a sail grew in the half light; the caravel slewed about in the water as the crew shouted a welcome and crowded to the rail. Brian Manin O'Moore, fifth hereditary envoy, stood at the helm of his red boat Dragonfoot III. *He came in closer and was taken aboard.*

GODS IN THE FIRE, GODS IN THE RAIN

by

Jay A. Parry

Daddy's hands shook just a bit as he took the box from high up in his closet and carefully opened it. Jodi leaned close and looked inside. Two blue ribbons. Daddy smiled and drew Jodi closer. "Here," he said, "I want to see how they look." He drew a wad of hair together on one side of her head and tied the ribbon around it.

"Where did you get these, Daddy?" Jodi asked, scratching above her ear where Daddy had pulled too hard.

"Just part of the things I put away," he answered. He turned her so her other side was facing him and gathered another wad of hair in his large, rough hand. "Mommy," he said, "go get that little mirror, will you?" He tied the other blue ribbon on her hair, then held her back at arms' length and looked, moving his head back and forth slightly as he looked from one side to the other.

When Mommy came back he stood and met her at the door. "What do you think, Mommy?"

She reached out and touched Jodi's hair softly, carefully fingering one of the ribbons. "It's beautiful," she whispered.

She handed Jodi the mirror and Jodi looked. Suddenly she was like the little girl in the photo Mommy had. Suddenly she wasn't a homely girl with strings holding her hair in place; she was a princess with blue ribbons. She looked at Daddy and realized for the first time that he was really the king of the land, that he would fight any enemies that came and kill them all. The street would be filled with bodies, and Daddy would stride boldly through it, the king who protected his princess.

She asked in a soft voice: "Can I wear them for awhile?"

Then the king was gone. Daddy's answer came gruffly. "Give them back, girl. I don't want you getting any ideas."

Mommy touched him on the arm. "Can't she just for awhile, Daddy?"

He shook his head, shook her hand off his arm. His face was cloudy. "I said no. No means *no!*" He stretched his hand out, palm up. "Now give them back."

Jodi pulled one off, dropped it into his hand, pulled

off the other. He put them back into the box. Then, taking the box with him, he left the room. He hid the box in the kitchen. Jodi watched, but she was back upstairs when he came back up.

"We mustn't wear those except at special times in the house," Daddy said. "Just like your Easter clothes and those vinyl shoes we gave you."

"They're irreplaceable, Jodi," Mommy said.

Jodi nodded. "Okay," she said. But she didn't mean it.

Later that evening James came in from his chores. Jodi told him that she'd worn the blue ribbons.

"That's stupid," James said. "Who cares about blue ribbons?"

Jodi pretended not to hear his rudeness.

That night Jodi lay awake until everyone else was asleep. Finally Daddy's light, quiet breathing became deep and loud. She crept downstairs into the kitchen. She took down the box. Then it slipped, fell on the floor, banged too, too loud. Jodi waited. Daddy will be very angry she thought. He will wake up and . . . But Daddy didn't wake up. No one did. She picked up the box and opened it. One corner had been smashed in the fall; it was a little difficult to open. But it opened. Inside were two blue ribbons, black in the moonlight. Jodi took them out, closed the box, replaced it, and crept up to bed. Daddy would never know.

The next morning she stopped at her favorite hiding place on the way to school: the old county courthouse, empty since the Collapse. She hid behind one of the huge stone columns and took the strings out of her braided hair, replacing them with the ribbons. I'll be the princess, she thought, and the other children will be my slaves. I'll send them to scavenge the countryside and we'll all live in luxury and plenty.

When she got to the schoolhouse everyone else was already there. Carl Schweitz saw her first. "Hey, looky there!" he shouted. "Jodi's got on some fancies!"

She smiled and walked a little faster. Then Reuben Schweitz came up and began to circle her, being careful not to stumble in his old, too-big pants. "Blue ribbon, blue ribbon!" he chanted. "Jodi Jodi's got some big blue ribbons!"

"I don't like them," Mary Holmes said, her eyes bright. "Why should she have nice new ribbons? All we have is old stuff."

"I don't like them *on her*," Ruthie Schweitz said. "Why should she have them and not us?"

Reuben nodded and began to circle faster. Then he reached out and slapped Jodi on the face, leaving red marks on her cheeks. He slugged her in the stomach; he pulled her pigtails. Then he pushed her to the ground and sat on her back. "Who wants a blue ribbon?" he called out.

The other children tightened their circle around the pair. Nearly everyone answered, shouting their affirmative, surging forward. But one held back. Shy Betsy with green eyes. She said nothing, but she held out her hand.

Reuben saw her. He grinned and smoothly pulled the bow loose, ignoring Jodi's silent head twistings. "You can have one, Betsy," he said, "and you can keep the other one, Jodi. See, doesn't it feel good to share?" He spoke jovially, but there was a certain edge to his voice.

Jodi bit her lip and stiffly backed away.

Then Mrs. Bolton came to the door of the schoolroom and shouted, "Bell time! Ding-a-ling-a-ling!" just as she had every day since the Collapse silenced the school bells.

Reuben was the first into the schoolroom. Betsy walked in slowly, hiding her new ribbon in a clenched fist. She kept her eyes down, not looking at anybody. She sat at a table toward the back of the room and slowly opened her clawed fingers and looked at the rich blue in her palm, shielding it with her body.

Jodi stopped at the doorway and paused, staring at Betsy. She tried to stab her with her eyes. I send darts to cut and hurt you, she thought. You'll fall bleeding to the floor and no one will help you because I give you a *disease*. Then Jodi slowly pulled the other ribbon from her hair and dropped it into her pocket. She unbraided her pigtails, shook her head, and walked into the schoolroom with loose and fluffy hair.

That afternoon Jodi was afraid to go home. Reuben was the first out; he hit Ruthann on the back of the head with his fist, then stopped only briefly to shout an obscenity at Carl. They both laughed and then both were gone. Betsy stood near Jodi for a few moments as though she wanted to say something. But her lips could never quite speak in harmony with the feelings in her eyes. Jodi, she seemed to be trying to say, please forgive me. But a blue ribbon! You would have done the same.

Jodi ignored her. She was thinking about Daddy. She lingered at her table, absently flipping through an old book, until Mrs. Bolton came to take it and lock it up in the safe. When Mrs. Bolton came back into the room Jodi was still there. "Go home, girl," she said. "Your folks will worry."

Jodi touched her pocket under the table and shook her head. "I can't."

"Don't be stupid," Mrs Bolton said. "There are chores to do. You'd better move!"

Mrs. Bolton escorted her out the door and locked it behind her. "Now hurry home," Mrs. Bolton said. "I don't want your father blaming me for your lateness."

Jodi said nothing. Mrs. Bolton began to walk down the deserted street. The road had weeds growing up through its cracks. Mrs. Bolton stepped lightly, avoided the rough spots.

Jodi's house wasn't far away. But she wanted it to be. It should be in China, she thought. Daddy should be a little Chinaman with small hands.

She remembered when her brother James had spilled a full bucket of milk right after he'd gotten it from the cow. Daddy had grabbed him by the arm, his eyes blazing, and just stared at him for a moment. Jodi had seen it all from the "barn"—the house behind their house.

Then Daddy had bent James's body at the waist and pushed his face into the milky mud he'd just created. "Maybe you can drink enough for all of us," Daddy said. "Then it won't be a total waste."

James had jerked sobbing away, but Daddy reached out and grasped his neck. "Do you think we're rich? Sure, we've got things others haven't, but does that mean we can waste food?"

While Daddy was talking, James had gradually stiffened up, his eyes glazed over, and Jodi knew that he wasn't hearing. Daddy then pushed James away from him, and James fell like a stick to the ground. Daddy stomped away without looking back.

Two blocks to go. Jodi thought of Daddy as a Chinaman with small hands. The fingers would be slender and short. They'd be soft and easy.

If Daddy had been so mad about a bucket of milk, what would he do about the lost blue ribbon?

Jodi rounded the corner and saw their house in the middle of the block. It had once been a modern split-level, with bricks around the bottom half and nice brown siding on the top half. But now the siding's paint had all peeled off, leaving bleached and weather-beaten raw wood. The shingles on the roof were ragged, and some had blown off.

But still they had almost the whole block to themselves, and if the house they were in became too rundown, they could always find another that was adequate. When the Collapse had come lots of people had moved out into the country areas—and there were plenty of them surrounding Boise—in an effort to fend better for themselves off the land. The meek and hesitant inherited the town.

Daddy was standing on the porch. His face was dark. In his hand was the ribbon box, with the new dent in one corner. "You took the ribbons to school," he said.

Jodi nodded and tried to brush past him into the house. The screen door was hanging open, with all the screen material missing. Scavengers had cut it neatly away one night.

She was almost inside when Daddy's hand snaked in behind her and grabbed her hair. She stopped, shivering inside, but did not turn.

"Where are they?"

Her hand went to her dress pocket and pulled out the one she had, showing it over her shoulder.

"Did you wear them?"

Jodi nodded, mute.

"Why did you take them off?"

She gave a shrug and said, "Well, it got hot in the schoolroom today and I—"

Daddy interrupted. "Hey, where's the other?"

Jodi didn't answer.

"Where's its mate? You didn't lose its mate, did you, girl?"

Then Jodi spun around to face him and said in a tight voice, "No, I didn't lose it, Daddy. Reuben Schweitz took it from me." Her throat began to close like a hand was squeezing it, and she choked out, "He gave it to shy Betsy. She took it."

Daddy grabbed her by the shoulders and stared at her, his mouth working but no words coming out. His eyes were hot. Then he tossed her to the red-and-green couch they'd dragged in from the neighbors' after they'd left and began to unbuckle his belt. "We've kept our supplies hidden for years," he said. "And now you've shown the whole town." He pulled the belt from its loops in a firm rhythm. "And do you know how many ribbons are left in this entire city?" he asked. His teeth were clenched, as though he were trying to contain some awful monster that was trying to escape his mouh. He hulked over to Jodi, the belt becoming tiny in his hand. "There are exactly two ribbons left. They were a matching set. They were blue. And now the town knows! And now the set has been broken. Because you saw fit to give half of all the ribbons that exist in the world away to a girl who can't even say her name without biting her tongue!"

Jodi cowered back on the couch, refusing to

infuriate him more by "making excuses" or trying to run away. Daddy became this way every once in awhile. She'd drawn a crayon picture of him after one such occurrence: his hair stood straight up on his head; his eyes were large and red, filling two-thirds of his face; his hands were huge and hairy. The belt was a snake, slithering through the air to bite and sting.

After she was done with her portrait she'd hidden it in a box in her dresser. If Daddy saw it, he might leave and let the monster come get her.

Then she felt the first hard *thwack!* across her thighs. "Do you think we're rich?" Daddy asked. *Thwack!* "Do you think we can provide for the entire town?" *Thwack!* "I want my children to have nice things." *Thwack!* "I want my children to have the best I can offer." *Thwack!* "But there's not enough to go around to other children. They have to get by as best they can." *Thwack!* "Now do you think I can just send to New York for a replacement?" *Thwack!*

Then he was gone. Jodi didn't hear him leave; but his heavy breathing was gone, and the beating ceased. She sat up and wrapped her arms around herself, trying to pull away from that awful room into the secluded green meadows that sometimes waited in her mind. But all she could see inside was black.

Then Mommy was there, making Jodi lie on her tummy and stroking her thighs and buttocks with a cold, wet cloth. The cold against her hot skin shocked her, and Jodi suddenly opened her eyes, for the first time since she'd seen the snake coming through the air.

"You mustn't be angry at Daddy," Mommy said, stroking and stroking with the cold, wet cloth. "Daddy remembers when everybody had everything, when all you had to do was go into the store and give them money and you could have anything in the world. He feels bad he can't give you everything now."

Jodi pushed her face into the side of the couch, trying to shut out Mommy's soothing voice. She'd heard it all a thousand times before. She didn't want to hear it again.

"But Daddy was smart," Mommy said. "He was smart and he saw the Collapse coming. He tried to warn everybody but they all laughed." Mommy stopped stroking as she remembered. Jodi's legs began to burn again. "So he went out and bought everything he could. He bought canned foods and boxed foods and nice clothes and ribbons and jewels. When the money was gone, he began to charge it. I used to worry and say, 'Russell, don't charge so much, We'll never be able to pay.' And Daddy would laugh and say, 'Who cares, Norma? When the Collapse comes nobody will have anything and then nobody will be able to pay anything to anybody and we'll have all this stuff and not owe a cent.' Daddy used to laugh, back then, back when he thought the Collapse was going to come but it hadn't come yet and he was having fun preparing."

Mommy sighed and leaned back on the couch. Jodi wished she would start touching her with the cloth again, but Mommy just sat and stared at the wall—just as she always did.

Jodi had a dream once about that. She'd told James, but James only sneered and said that dreams were stupid. But Jodi knew her dream was true. In her dream Mommy had told *again* about the Collapse and how Daddy had prepared and how no one else had prepared so Daddy was the richest man in town when the economy fell out from under the world. And the world had tried to reconstruct what it had had, but no one would cooperate, so it only sank further and further from where it was. And then looters and scavengers began to try to get what Daddy had and he had hidden it and no one could prove he had anything. Then in the dream Mommy would get that look in her eyes and she would sit and stare at the wall with a half smile on her lips and then the looters would come in and carefully unbutton Mommy's dress and take it off her and they would unsnap her shoes and take them off and Mommy would be sitting there naked while the looters took her clothes away and she wouldn't even look, she only sat there and half smiled through it all.

James had laughed and said Jodi was stupid for having such dreams. But Jodi knew it was true.

And now Mommy was sitting there again, staring at the wall. The damp cloth sat in her lap, unnoticed, spreading a darker blue on a dark blue dress.

Jodi got up quietly, pulled her pants up gingerly, walked outside. She had done her chores and eaten and dressed for bed and crawled inside before she heard Daddy come back in. When he talked to Mommy then he sounded tired. His voice was small, and his words were small. "The blue ribbon," he said. "It could mean trouble."

"Yes," Mommy answered.

"You paid for it," James said.

Daddy sighed. "Yes, I paid for it." Then no one said anything. Jodi could hear them eating. Supper was soup, and Daddy liked to slurp.

Then Daddy said, "How's Jodi?" A spoon clinked quietly down on the table and a chair scraped back on the floor.

Mommy answered quietly; Jodi didn't hear the answer. But apparently Daddy didn't hear either, because then Mommy said more loudly, "She's very sad. She's sad."

The chair scraped back farther and then Jodi could hear Daddy coming up the stairs. He came into her room and sat on her bed. She had her eyes closed and didn't open them. Maybe he'd think she was asleep.

Daddy put his heavy hand down on her forehead and began to brush backward, stroking down across her hair, which lay spread across her pillow. "I'm sorry, baby," Daddy whispered. "I'm sorry."

Then he just sat and slowly brushed her hair. He didn't say anything. After awhile he took in his breath sharply, and let it out raggedly, and Jodi opened her eyes a crack. He was just sitting there looking out the window. His eyes were glistening in the moonlight. After a few minutes longer he stood, but he didn't walk out of the room. "I wish you had a pillow case," he whispered, almost to himself. "I remember starched pillow cases, and cool sheets that made your legs tingle when you crawled into bed, and Grandma's potted flowers that she kept by her living room window." Then he laughed quietly, and pulled Jodi's covers up to her neck, and smoothed her blankets, and walked out of the room. Then Jodi opened her eyes. He was whispering "Flowers!" as he passed through the door.

Late that night she was awakened by a pounding on the door. She heard Daddy swear; she heard the bedsprings in the next room creak; she heard Daddy's heavy steps down the hall and down the stairs. She heard Daddy open the door, then a louder curse.

Daddy growled, "What do you want?"

Then another man's voice. Jodi instantly knew it was the sheriff, because he was the only man in town who talked totally through his nose. Jodi wasn't sure how he did it, or why; she'd tried to imitate him unsuccessfully more than once. James, though, could do it quite well.

In fact, she could almost imagine that the caller in the night was James, who she very well knew slept in the next room; but the thought almost made her giggle, as she saw James's face and body with the voice coming up the stairs.

"Russell," the sheriff said, "you're in a heap of trouble, man."

Another quiet curse. Then: "This better be good, Bob. I don't hanker to getting up in the middle of the night. Life's unpleasant enough without losing vital sleep."

The sheriff coughed; he coughed a long time, as though he were trying to delay his errand; he coughed so long and hard that Jodi began to wonder if Daddy was choking him. But then the sheriff cleared his throat and spoke so loudly that James woke up: Jodi heard him grunt and sit up in his bed. "Russell," the sheriff said, "Betsy Parr came home from school today with a nice blue ribbon."

That's all he said.

It became so quiet downstairs that Jodi could hear their breathing.

Then Daddy said, "So? Is that all? I've got to get up early in the morning. A man can't just sit around and make a living anymore, you know."

"Your daughter Jodi had that ribbon. Reuben Schweitz took it from her. He gave it to Betsy Parr.

What I want to know, Russell, is this: where in the wide world did you get such a ribbon?"

Daddy didn't answer. Jodi could hear his breathing, heavy.

"Russell, there's a law against hoarding. I've heard tell that you've got all kinds of things hidden up: canned peaches, tuna fish, even dried bananas; dresses and skirts and belts and sashes and shoes and nice gloves and jewelry—even ribbons."

Daddy's voice was hard. "I know the law as well as you do. And I keep it. You know that."

The sheriff answered through his nose: "No, I don't know that. That's why I'm here. You know I like to give people the benefit of the doubt. I like to give them chances to show to me that they're law-abiding and honest. I've heard rumors about you before, Russell. You know they're around. But I didn't think it would be right to go on a rumor. Until Betsy Parr came home with that blue ribbon."

Daddy didn't answer.

Then the sheriff said, "Let's have a look." Then she heard Daddy grunt with effort and heard someone fall backward against the door, which had apparently been cracked open, because it slammed shut. It sounded to Jodi like the sheriff had tried to push his way into the house—and Daddy had shoved him back.

Then Daddy said, "All right." His voice was firm and calm. "You win, Bob." And he stomped up the stairs, stomped into his bedroom.

Jodi heard Mommy say, "What's happening down there? Is he going to arrest us?" and she heard Daddy say in a very sharp whisper, "Shut up!"

She heard him scrabble under his bed where he kept

his shotgun, but he dragged out a box instead of the gun. Then he stomped back down the hall, back down the stairs.

Jodi hadn't heard the sheriff move at all. She hadn't even heard him get up. But he apparently was standing at the bottom of the stairs, because Daddy didn't go all the way down. He stomped only partway down, then said in a whiney voice, "I'm very sorry, sheriff. I lost my head there. It's just so hard nowadays. Please forgive me." He paused a moment, then he said, "Here. This is the stuff. This box has all the things in it you thought I had—and more. I paid for them. They're mine. But I don't want to cause any more trouble here. Take them."

There seemed to be a laugh hiding back in the sheriff's throat when he answered, a laugh that he seemed to not want to let out. "Apology accepted," he said, "and no harm done. These are tense times for us all." Jodi heard him take the box. "So this is the entire collection?"

"Yes, sir. That's the whole thing."

"Well, we'll just consider the case closed then. Good night, Russell." The door closed behind him.

Daddy just stood there breathing for a moment; he was breathing heavily. He must have been standing there staring at the door, or maybe at the wall. Then he slowly climbed the stairs, went into his bedroom, and shut the door. Jodi could hear as Mommy began to whisper frantically, but she couldn't hear the words.

She decided to try to go to sleep. She rolled over and closed her eyes. But on her eyelids all she could see was James talking in the sheriff's voice, dancing by the doorway, holding Betsy's head by the hair. Tied midway down on her long, blonde hair was a smooth blue ribbon.

Then James was shaking her, and she awoke. She was sweating. He pushed his face close to hers, and she recoiled. "Hey, Sis," he said, "wake up. This is only me."

Then he went on, as though he were continuing a conversation that had never been interrupted. "So do you think the sheriff believed him?"

"What?" She rubbed her eyes and tried to clear her head. "What time is it?"

"I don't know. The sheriff was just here. Didn't you hear?" He pushed his face too close again.

So the sheriff had just left and she had fallen instantly asleep. She sat up and looked at James as though he had just come in. "I don't think the sheriff believed a word of it," she said. "He'll be back with searchers."

"Yeah, that's what I thought," he said. He turned to go back to bed, his business finished. But then he turned back and whispered, "Hey, you going to be okay at school tomorrow? I can come with you if you want, and we can take care of that Reuben character."

Jodi shook her head. James didn't go to school. He was thirteen, and was required to work in the fields all day. He had to work even harder than Daddy did. But she didn't want him to come with her. Then it would be even worse the following day. "Thanks, James," she said, and shook her head again.

By morning it had started to rain. A new leak started in the bathroom they never used, and one Daddy thought he had fixed started in the kitchen. Jodi toyed with the idea of not going to school, of staying home pretending to be sick—but then she'd have to be around Daddy all day, and she didn't want that.

Most of the children there acted as though nothing had happened. Betsy looked as she always had; she hadn't worn the blue ribbon. Reuben was normal too: rude and pesty. But no one seemed to notice that the world was slightly awry; no one seemed to notice that Jodi walked a little stiffly, that she's worn the oldest clothes possible, that her hair was uncombed. Jodi thought that the rain must be poison droplets from the gods, finally sent to cleanse the earth of all its scrambling madness but no one noticed. Jodi noticed; she was careful to protect herself from those droplets; she was careful to avoid the others, since they were all going to die today, and she didn't want to be with them.

At recess time, Jodi walked to a far corner of the yard, running quickly lest the drizzle destroy her. There she sat alone in an old wooden shed. Insight was coming to her so quickly that it was hard for her to arrange her thoughts, but she had to get it all in order before it was too late.

Then she had it: the collapse had been the end of the world; the gods had had to destroy civilization before they could destroy man. Now the rains were the final cleansing before the gods came down to finish their work.

Jodi sat there silently, smiling in her fantasy, when suddenly Shy Betsy stood in front of her. Jodi's smile fled, and she looked away. The gods were gone and soon the rain would stop. The gods were dead.

Betsy sat on the ground next to Jodi and stared at her. Neither spoke for a long while. Then Betsy said, stumbling, "Jodi, it's awful."

Jodi looked at her, eyes flashing, and said, "The gods are dead."

"It was your ribbon. I've never seen anyone else who had a ribbon. And I wanted one, just like you."

"Did you get rain on you?" Jodi smiled wisely. "There's rain in your hair and on your arms and all through your clothes." She pointed from place to place on Betsy's body, but did not touch.

"I put it in my hair last night. It was beautiful. It made my daddy cry and he said that I looked like an angel out of the past."

"Ribbons are good for strangling children," Jodi said, and stood to go. Then, feeling too cruel, she looked down at her backward friend. Her voice was soft. "If you'd asked I would have let you try them on."

Then she set herself to stride to sure suicide in the rain. But Betsy stopped her. She shoved her hand up at Jodi, holding it clenched. "Here," she said, slowly unwrapping fingers from around mangled blue ribbon. "It's yours."

Jodi looked at the ribbon, looked at Betsy. Jodi's eyes flared, and she said, "It's worthless. You've ruined it!"

Betsy stiffened, and Jodi feared for a moment that she was going to seize up and fall over the way James sometimes did. But Betsy simply blinked her eyes rapidly, choked and swallowed, swallowed again, stood, and looked at Jodi sideways, out of the sides of her eyes, as though she were afraid to face her directly. "My father," she said very slowly, "he took it from me. He was looking at it. Then my mother came and asked to see it. He held it up, dangling. He wouldn't let her touch. She grabbed it, and they pulled on both ends."

Betsy turned her face to Jodi and again extended her arm. "So they gave it back to me and told me it wasn't something I should keep."

Jodi didn't take it. She looked out of their shelter. The children were playing in the mud. Carl had taken another boy's old cap, and he and Reuben were playing Keep Away with it. Mrs. Bolton was standing at the door watching; Jodi knew she would soon call out her bell and they would all have to go in. The rain was still coming down, harder perhaps than before. But the fantasy was gone. The gods weren't coming. Betsy wasn't going to die of poisoning.

All that remained was a straggly blue ribbon.

"You keep it," Jodi said, not looking at Betsy. And she raced across the yard to the schoolroom, going inside before Mrs. Bolton called the bell.

Daddy came to school that afternoon. He came to the door and knocked, not entering before Mrs. Bolton called out in a high voice, "Come on in. But wipe your feet."

Then Daddy was standing in the doorway, his hair dripping wet onto his shoulders and onto the floor. He looked around the room until he spotted Jodi, then said, 'Excuse me, ma'am, but there's an emergency. I've got to take Jodi home early today." Then, not waiting for an answer, he strode over to Jodi's table and grasped her by the wrist. "Come on," he said.

They walked out into the rain. Puddles splashed under their feet as Daddy led her smoothly down the street. He didn't explain and Jodi didn't ask. But his grip tightened as they neared their house, and when they finally reached their block, Daddy exploded. "Blue ribbon," he said, spitting the words out like a curse.

He pulled her up into the house, where James and Mommy waited by a drip puddle coming from the ceiling.

"We're moving," he said angrily, pushing Jodi over by the others.

"He traded the cow for a pony," James said.

"Shut up," Daddy said.

James looked away, stared at the drip coming down near him.

"I want you to wear your blue ribbon when we leave," Daddy said. Then he went out into the backyard.

Mommy pulled Jodi close. "Daddy has a hunch the sheriff's coming with a search party," she said. "His knee is aching. Daddy and I couldn't give up all the nice things we've saved for all these years. He traded the cow for a pony so we would have something to haul everything on. But we've got to hurry." She turned to James, who still sat mesmerized by the drip. "James, go help Daddy. We've got to hurry."

James moved slowly out of the room, stepping in the puddle on the way.

Then Mommy took a hairbrush and the blue ribbon out of her pants pocket and began to brush Jodi's hair. She put it up in a ponytail. "There," she said. "Daddy wants you to look nice on our way out. He says people might see you and he wants them to know that you still have your blue ribbon."

When she was done she and Jodi went out the back door, where they waited. Finally James and Daddy came out of the barn with the pony. "We've only got a couple of hours to get the rest of our stuff," Daddy said.

"We've got to hurry." He stepped out into the rain, leading the half-loaded pony.

"We'll never make it, Daddy," Mommy said. "They'll catch us and take everything we own."

Daddy didn't answer, kept going. Jodi started to follow, then hung back. The heavy rain mashed and matted her hair. The blue ribbon pulled her scalp tight. Her head throbbed and felt like it was bleeding.

Daddy and James were hurrying along the block, making their way across empty backyards. Jodi noticed that the houses were watching them go, and suddenly she knew that before they reached the end of the block one of those houses was going to stretch out its gaping mouth and swallow them.

But they reached the end of the block, crossed the rough street, and continued down the next block, still staying in backyards.

Mommy then started out. "They're not going to wait for us," she said to Jodi. " Hurry." Then she shouted ahead in a shrill voice: "Daddy! Stop! We'll never make it! Let's hide!"

Daddy didn't slow, didn't answer.

Still Jodi waited. The dark clouds above were belching, and she knew they were going to fall and crush everything.

Mommy was running down the block. Daddy and James had reached a fence and had to cut into the front of the houses. The black clouds hadn't crushed them. Mommy was safe.

Jodi took a deep breath and began to run after them. Her ponytail flew up into the air and her scalp began to tingle. Soon she had caught up with Mommy. She passed her and ran on. She stumbled in the grass and fell and slid. Then she was up and ran on, her pants legs sopping in front. She turned at the fence and ran into the street. Daddy and James had stopped just ahead; Daddy had taken his shotgun out of the pony's pack and was loading it with two shells.

Jodi ran up and stopped, panting. The pony hung its head in the rain. "I'll blast them," Daddy said, sighting down the gun barrel from house to house.

Mommy came up. Her face was white; her eyes were red. "What?" she said.

Daddy shook his head. "Come on," he said. "The sheriff's coming."

"But it's too late," Mommy said.

"Shut up, Mommy," Daddy said. "We can make it. We'll get the rest of our stuff and they'll never know where we went." He patted the gun stock. "This is just in case we run into trouble."

Mommy closed her eyes and shook, wrapping her arms around herself. She started to cry, and the rain washed her tears down her face. "He wouldn't leave us unwatched, Daddy. He wouldn't. We'll be followed and killed."

Daddy's eyes suddenly flared. He looked at Mommy and said, "It's true, isn't it. They'll track us down and take our stuff."

Mommy nodded, wiping her eyes. Daddy hefted his gun. "We won't even try, then. They'll get us anyway, won't they, Mommy. But we can make them sorry." His face then relaxed and lost its hardness. "We'll make them sorry," he repeated in a soft voice. But his eyes looked sad.

He grabbed the pony by the halter and began to hurry down the road again.

Soon they were at Reuben's house. It was nearly time for school to be out, but only nearly, so Reuben and Carl weren't home. But their mother and father probably were. He worked the fields and she did odd jobs from house to house for trade; but not much would be going in a rain like this.

Daddy stopped again and aimed his shotgun at their big front window, going as close to the house as he dared. "I'll teach them," he said. He pulled the trigger on the gun. The glass shattered, roaring into the house, with wind and rain following it.

"Daddy!" Mommy shouted. "Their *windows*. You can't ruin their *windows!*"

Daddy smiled the way he did when he was mad and was getting ready to sting Jodi with his snake. "I know," he said. Then he handed the gun to James and took an iron bar out of the pack. "Go!" he yelled to them.

Mommy and James began to hurry down the street again. But Jodi stood and watched. Daddy moved up onto the porch and smashed in the door with three solid whacks of his bar. Then he quickly moved around the house, smashing in windows. Jodi had about decided that no one was home when Mr. Schweitz came out the doorway, his face red. "Hey," he yelled at her. "What is this?" He moved down the steps in a lunge, his fingers arching toward her.

Jodi ducked and dodged, but he grabbed her and threw her to the ground. She lay there, not getting up. Then he spotted her blue ribbon: "Hey, you're the Washington girl, aren't you! You trying to destroy what we've built?" He pushed his foot forward and gave her a heavy nudge in the ribs. "Eh?" He pulled his foot back and kicked her, hard. "Eh?"

A sharp fire erupted in Jodi's side, and she blacked out for a moment. But a second kick brought her back and she began to roll across the wet ground, trying to get away from the black boot.

"You Washingtons are better than everyone else because you have ribbons and frillys, aren't you!" He kicked after her like he would a rolling ball. But it unbalanced him, and he turned to another tactic: he grabbed for her with hairy arms, saying through clenched teeth, "We'll just root you folks out of here and we'll have no more blue ribbons!"

He finally got hold of her pony tail and pulled her up by the hair. Jodi felt like her scalp was going to come off. He held her there by the ends of her hair, using his other hand to pull the blue ribbon loose. "I'll have this," he whispered.

Then Daddy was there. He held his bar at one end, reared back, and swung the bar down on Mr. Schweitz's neck. Mr. Schweitz gasped, crumpled to the ground, lay still.

Daddy grinned. He reached over and pulled the ribbon from Jodi's tight fingers. Then he turned and began to stride away. Jodi looked down at Mr. Schweitz. An ugly purple and red and black was forming and spreading across his neck. He didn't move at all.

"Daddy!" she cried hoarsely.

But Daddy didn't turn.

Then, far down the street, Jodi heard shouting, and saw Reuben and Carl running toward them. She turned and ran after Daddy.

When they reached Mommy and James they were

breaking the windows in the sheriff's house. He wasn't home. Daddy nodded, then added a new feature to their destruction: he ran into the house and, using a flint lighter, lit afire the curtains. They curled up on themselves, a vivid orange on green through the window. Then Daddy came running out and they rushed on down the street, leading the pony behind them.

The houses on each side of them were dead, uninhabitable as long as there was a choice. Most of the windows were gone; on some the chimneys had crumpled down onto the roof. They hadn't been occupied for years. But Daddy went into a house at the end of the row and lit it afire too. When he came back out he curled his lips back over his teeth and said, pointing up at the sky, "The rain—but feel the wind!" Then he laughed. "We'll burn this whole *place* down!"

He went into the house across the street, knocking down the door with his big iron bar. When he came out Jodi could see the fire dance that was occurring indoors. He said nothing but went on down the street. Jodi, Mommy and James followed, none speaking.

"We'll go to Oregon," Daddy shouted over his shoulder. "We'll go to California. They'll not give us trouble there."

They stopped at another house, the Boltons'. Daddy took the gun and pointed it at the window. "No!" Jodi cried. "She was good to me!" But Daddy shook his head and fired smoothly, absorbing the kick with his shoulder rather than rolling with it.

"She let it start," Daddy said. "She let it happen." He turned to James and Mommy. "You go around opposite sides of the house and break in windows. I'm going in." Then he looked at Jodi. "Girl," he said, "you watch for trouble." Then they all were gone.

Jodi could hear the cracking as it proceeded around the house. She could hear Daddy ripping things down inside, cursing as he stomped around. And then she heard new sounds, and turned to see a crowd of people coming down the street toward them. A roar preceded them as they ran splashing through the rain. Some were carrying guns. Some had wooden cudgels or iron bars like Daddy's. They all looked angry.

"Daddy!" Jodi called, but her voice was tight with fear and her call came out a hoarse whisper. "Daddy!"

Then Mommy and James came back around the house. Then the mob was there and some of the men quietly took Jodi, and Mommy, and James, and held them tight, and held their mouths closed. James went stiff then, and his eyes became glassy and then he went limp in the arms of the two men who held him.

Then Daddy came out of the Boltons' house. One of the men immediately shot at him. Daddy jumped back into the house.

Jodi could see the flames swirling around the Boltons' living room. Daddy was in there with the flames. Some of the men ran up to the house and tried to look in the window. "He's burned," one of them said. "He's gone."

"No," another shouted, "maybe he's just gone through the back way."

"Check it out," the sheriff yelled. "Don't let him get away. Shoot if he won't stop."

The flames began to lick through the windows. Jodi looked down the street. The sky was becoming black with smoke. It looked as if the whole town was on fire.

Several men sloshed around the house. They were gone only a moment. Then they were back, two of them dragging Daddy by the arms. His hair was singed and his face blackened. He was coughing.

The two men let him go, and he fell onto the ground, face down. Then he got up on his hands and knees and reached a clenched hand toward Jodi. "Here," he croaked. Then one of the men shot him in the face. Daddy's smooth face went gaping and blood pitted. He didn't make a sound, fell again into the mud. His hand remained clenched, outstretched.

The man who'd shot went up to him. He grinned with a hole between his top center teeth. He unclenched Daddy's hand and pulled out the blue ribbon. He waved it in the air and said, "The flag of selfishness. Long may it wave." Then he dropped the blue ribbon onto the ground and smashed it into the mud with his heel.

The sheriff then yelled, "Fire!" and the people then noticed, apparently for the first time, how the fire was spreading. A great shout went up and they ran to the pony, madly fought over the pack's contents, then began to run back along the road, leaving Daddy dead in the mud, letting James slump down in his senselessness, and releasing and immediately forgetting Mommy and Jodi. One woman ran a few steps, then returned and took the pony with her.

Then they were gone. Suddenly it was very quiet, except for the hissing of the wind, the shouting of the fire, the gasping of rain against white heat, the *plink-plinking* of rain falling on fallen rain.

Jodi looked at James, who was crumpled in a wet heap. She looked at Mommy, who simply stared at the fire. She looked at where the man had smashed the blue ribbon into the ground. A thin, half-melted strand stuck up through the mud.

She didn't look at Daddy.

Then she looked up at the burning house. The east wall had become totally black with smoke. The flames were eating through the roof, and its center was beginning to sag. The wind was blowing through the broken windows, fanning the flames higher and higher.

Through the window Jodi could see a roaring dragon. Its tongue lolled, and it carelessly spread fire breath in every direction.

And then she knew that she did indeed understand. The gods were coming today. They'd sent the rain to cleanse before their presence, and now they were burning the earth; with a scorching they were removing its defilement.

She smiled to herself and went over to take Mommy's hand. It was nice to be right.